PUSHING DC

MARKED PULL

My Time in Yesterday's Police Force

Part I

Jim Graham

First published by James Graham [2022]
ISBN: 9798817878127
https://jimgraham579293579.wordpress.com

PREFACE

I am, or I was, Police Constable 776 and, later, Detective, James 'Jim' Graham. I served my community for over 32 years as a police officer. This is part one of my account of that wonderful journey in a now-forgotten era of policing, the 1970s and 1980s. These are true recollections of those early days, from leaving school to becoming a detective. The later books will detail my time investigating international drug traffickers and the world of undercover police work.

My police journey began in 1974 and the accounts could be from any police force in the country during that era. The characters are transferable. My story is of human tragedy, humour, and of course the many unsung heroes. The police force and names of individuals have been changed to protect identities and for the privacy of all. Excuse the emotive language but do enjoy the music.

—

CHAPTER ONE

THE END

Davey Peters was a big lad. Not in height, but stature. His reputation went before him. He'd obviously done the weights and with his labouring job, he cut a fine figure as he marched down the street. His fluorescent jacket, muddy work boots and barrel chest charged towards me.

'You C.I.D?' he barked.

I knew of Peters, a bouncer at local nightclubs. He was feared on the estate.

'Someone has screwed my house and nicked my telly and video, haven't they? It's the wife's jewellery and watches that hurts. I'm just telling you because someone is going to get killed.'

He wiped his sleeve across his mouth and approached a young couple on the other side of the street.

'Hey, you two, haven't heard anything about some gear being nicked from my house, have you?'

I carried on with my enquiries into other burglaries on the estate, watching Davey trudge up and down the street, stopping people in his quest to find the culprits. His technique was far more effective than any police method of investigation. When I returned to the police car, Davey was sitting on the bonnet. Fluorescent jacket, muddy boots, and all.

'Isaac Warren has had my gear. He's sold it to a bloke in Brough Ferry. Are you going to arrest him or am I going to kill him?'

It was an interesting dilemma and Davey was not one to be brushed aside with the conundrum of a lack of evidence. I suspected his weapon of choice would be his trusty baseball bat that all the local kids called 'Walter'. If there was any trouble on the estate, you knew that 'Walter' would get the call. As much as I tried to persuade Davey to let justice take its course, he was adamant there was only one kind of justice on this estate. Now, looking back after all these years and at our current criminal justice system, he was probably right.

'Hello Ronnie, it's Jim Graham here, ringing from the CID. Sorry to call you. Are you ok to speak at the moment?'

'Of course, young man. I know why you're ringing,' said Ronnie.

Ronnie was a bad-guy-turned-good. He was now in his early seventies. I had previously dealt with him and, more recently, his sons and grandsons. I had been through school with his family and knew them all. I had always tried to be fair and on the whole, Ronnie was only trying to provide for his family. However, I had a job to do and there appeared to be a mutual respect between us. When other officers in the CID office wanted to arrest a family member, but couldn't find them, I would give Ronnie a quick call and ask whoever was wanted to present themselves at the Police Station and ask for me. On the whole, the system worked.

'You've always been alright with me, son, so here you go,' said Ronnie. 'Kenny Bamford broke in Davey's house, with Mal Morrisey and another lad called Tony. I don't know this Tony, but they will all be at my house today at lunchtime. They've put the watches down the grid outside my house. They didn't know it was Davey's house. They're all shitting themselves.'

Later that day, two officers went to Ronnie's back door and two came to the front with me. I gave the usual police 'rat-a-tat-tat' on the door. Ronnie opened up. I acted as if I didn't know him.

'My name is Detective Constable Graham from Sandford CID. We are making enquiries about a burglary at the home of Davey Peters. You are under arrest. You do not have to say anything...'

Before I could go any further, three or four figures came hurtling towards the door from inside the house. Kenny Bamford was first. He was a likeable rogue, really. He was just stupid. Proper stupid and had a streak of deceptiveness intertwined with his stupidity. The result being, he always got caught. Previously, I arrested him for a burglary, which he vehemently denied. I explained that his fingerprints were found inside the house, and he claimed they couldn't have been, as he remembered he was wearing gloves on that particular job.

Kenny put his arm across Ronnie and pulled him back.

'You don't touch the old man right. He's fuck all to do with this,' Kenny shouted in my face.

By this time, the grid was up in front of Ronnie's house and the watches were being retrieved. Kenny, Malcolm, Tony and his older brother Andy were all arrested and walked past the piles of sludge and jewellery. Old Ronnie sat quietly, looking sorry for himself, handcuffed in the back of the police car. It was only a short drive down to the police station. A quick look in the mirror and the wink of an eye from Ronnie, was recognition of a job well done. Ronnie was released from custody shortly afterwards due to a lack of evidence. Three of those arrested admitted breaking into Davey Peters' house and exonerated Ronnie of any involvement. The watches were recovered but beyond repair and the TV, video recorder and jewellery, I was told, had been sold through the local estate Fagin, a man called Isaac Warren. A call from Davey Peters had been logged in the CID office journal that same afternoon.

'Tell DC Graham that I have got my telly back and I'm on my way to get my video recorder.' Like I said, Davey's techniques were far more effective.

Isaac Warren lived on the edge of the estate. He had two sons, Billy and Stephen. The whole family were wheeler dealers, and he traded in lawn mowers, stolen lawn mowers. That was his business. Warren came to the door, dishevelled and scruffy. He was a big man, baggy work pants with big black, braces. I identified myself, showed my police warrant card and introduced my partner, DC John Suthers. John followed as we both entered Isaac's front room. *Neighbours* was on the TV.

'Is this over that Peter's stuff?' he asked.

'It is, Isaac, and you are going to have to come to the police station. You are under arrest,' I replied.

'Can I finish my cup of tea?' and with that he stooped down to lift it off the settee.

'Of course,' I replied.

Isaac turned and faced me. His wife was sitting to my left, sipping out of a similar beaker.

'I'm going to finish my cup of tea before I go anywhere. In fact, I'm going to have a wash... In fact.'

The atmosphere changed. The beaker went down. Isaac came towards me,

'In fact, I'm not fucking coming. Get me the fucking knife, get the knife, get the fucking knife.'

I tried to hold on but couldn't. He was a big man and super strong. Something snapped inside him, and I knew I was in trouble. I held his left arm for as long as I could, but he brushed me off with ease and he dragged both John and me into the back kitchen. We were trying to hang on, but Isaac reached the sink area and turned to face us with a carving knife. He held it like a dagger above his head, *Psycho* style. Instinctively, I tried to grab his arm. We were face to face. I looked into his dark and empty eyes. I smelt his breath as both nostrils exhaled into my face. I looked up at the 10' blade coming down towards my head and tried to push back with all my might with both hands. It wasn't working. He was stronger, far stronger. I felt the sweat run down my face as the blade neared. He realised that I was just about holding him off, so he quickly swopped hands

4

and pulled the knife down towards me from the other side. I stuck out my hand and saw the blade come straight through my thumb and nail. I held on, pushing him back. The blood was now running down my right arm as Isaac withdrew the blade from my thumb and tried again. My sole focus was on the blade. I pushed and pushed as it got closer and closer to my face. This man was so strong, so agitated, and now, so intent on killing me. I took hold of the blade with my hand and tried to bend it away. I could feel the metal ripping into my palm, but there was no pain. The blood dripped onto my face. I could taste it. I could see the knife embedded in my right hand. His face, contorted with anger, was the last thing I was going to see. He was going to kill me. This is how I was going to die.

I hadn't said my goodbyes. I watched as the knife came down quickly towards my neck. This was the end.

CHAPTER TWO

THE BEGINNING

Well we sang shang-a-lang
and we ran with the gang
Doin' doo wop be dooby do ay

When and where did my police life begin? Why did I want to join Her Majesty's Constabulary? I was in the final year at Sandford High School, a place that had done me no favours whatsoever. Of course, I must take most of the blame for that, but from representing my town at previous school at sport and being academically minded, Sandford High school broke me. They gave up on me and me them. I was constantly reminded that I wasn't good enough. As the O Level exam period started at the end of my school days, my presence in the exam hall was futile. I had not revised. I had no inclination whatsoever to learn Latin, technically draw or learn that in the 18th century a pigsty, had a vote. I'm sure this is what the history teacher, Granny Grumpet, told me in a history lesson. I mentally opted out of the whole education process.

Miss Humphries, the Deputy Head and the local Careers Officer, held a 'Careers Day' to discuss our futures. I hadn't given much thought to the future, and I wasn't prepared for post school. I was too young, too immature.

We queued outside the careers room, in silence and single file. I was admiring the creases in my two-tone pants when, all of a sudden, the door burst open, and Miss Humphries stood there, holding 'Nipper' Smith by his right ear. Her very large Dame Edna style glasses did nothing to hide the anger in her twisted face. Nipper had nits. His head was infested, and everyone avoided sitting next to him in class. He was a nice lad, though, and was doing the best ballet impression I have ever seen from a lad off the estate. His shoes had worn down at the front and had been stuffed with newspaper to stop the wet coming in. It never did, as the paper went mushy and turned your toes black from all the ink. What it did provide, though, was a straight edge Nipper could balance on as Humphries attempted to separate his ear from his head.

'The next person who comes into this room unprepared and with no thought to their future career will follow this horrible boy to Mr. Simpson's office for the cane. Do you hear me?' screeched Humphries.

She let go of Nipper and he lost the six inches he had suddenly grown. He put his head down and began the trudge, passing the line of Humphries next victims.

'He's got nits, him,' someone shouted.

'Fuck off,' said Nipper as he turned to Anabelle Griffin, a doctor in the making.

'What did you just say to me, Smith?' shrieked Miss Humphries.

'I was speaking to Anabelle, Miss. Honest,' replied Nipper.

Before he could finish his words, he had been gripped in a vice like head lock by Humphries who was totally unaware of Nippers' parasitic companions. She was wearing a lovely tweed jacket, which I thought at the time could host one or two of the little critters, for a while at least. Poor Nipper and ear lobe were dragged past the shocked audience as Mr. Thompson, the Careers Officer, invited Kirk Dougan into the room. Those at the front peered through the small window in the door as news passed down the line that Thompson had Dougan in the room alone, and anything could happen. The rumour around school was that he liked *young boys*. It wasn't long before Humphries returned and blasted the line up a final time in a spittle induced frenzy.

'Come into this room without a career choice and you will be caned!' she blasted.

Now, we all know that 'caned' has many meanings, but the headmaster's cane was a fencing sword, and it hurt. He would strut up and down in assembly in the morning with his tinted glasses, vampire cloak, and fencing sword. It was extremely intimidating, even to a would-be bovver boy. Nonetheless, I now had a stark choice as I was fourth in line from an audience with Mr. Thompson, and she who must be obeyed.

I tried to be pleasant to Anabelle Griffin, who was with Elizabeth Sanders. Both were from rich families and were top of the class. Annabelle spoke fluent Latin and I must admit that becoming involved in the criminal justice system for nearly half a century, the Latin class in school held me in good stead not one bit! Never once did we learn about *actus reus* or *mens rea* or *inter alia* and what happened in that Latin class just passed me by. I had already worked out I may not have been intellectually or academically gifted. Teachers helped me reinforce that view as well. However, I had noticed that top swot and loner David Hargreaves always needed a chess partner. I couldn't play chess but obliged. The price? Full and unequivocal access to all David's homework for a year. Deal done and signed with the usual nod of the head. He understood. We had a symbiotic relationship and a mutual understanding. David was going to be a politician, although I think he may have been too honest. He needed 'protection' when the bullies came to class. I looked after David.

'What are you going to do when you leave school Anabelle?' I asked quietly in the poshest voice I could muster.

'I may go into the medical profession, but Father is trying to get me into university in America. I will be going in the sixth form, but not at this school. It's not good enough.'

I digested what she had said and quickly assessed what parts of it I could use to sway Humphries from inflicting pain on me. Sadly, none of it. Humphries would see through it as I was destined for a nil return on the exam results.

'Elizabeth, what are you going to do when you leave school?' I asked.

'I'm not leaving. I am staying on to do my A levels, then going to Business School as I am going into the family business.' I was nodding and giving the appearance of listening intently as she replied.

I was dismissed with a quick turn of their heads as Kirk came out of the room. Humphries stood in the doorway and shouted, 'Next,' and Ian Crowther went in. I was now number three and time was running out. I hadn't a clue what I was going to do when I left school in a few weeks' time. It was looking increasingly like a meeting with the fencing sword. I had a very low tolerance to pain, but I sure Humphries didn't care about that. I could, of course, just slip the queue and disappear, which was a skill I had acquired and perfected in this last year of my education. However, Humphries had given me the death stare too many times whilst in line. She knew I was there. The two ugly sisters, Griffin and Sanders, were in front, and then me. Ten minutes went by and then the door opened. Crowther walked out with a Cheshire cat grin. I practised my lines.

'Yes miss, I have given my future some real thought and just now I think my true vocation in life is either road sweeping, pushing trolleys at Tesco, working on the bins or going on the dole.'

It just didn't come across well, did it? Mum liked to tell everyone how good I was doing at school; How I was taking eleven O' levels and then A levels before going to university. I was going to be a doctor or barrister, apparently. I kept being pushed at school, but really needed to find my own level. I couldn't compete with those in my class. So, I mentally opted out. I just didn't know how I was going to resolve this matter with my parents, though.

'Can I push in Jim?' said a voice from behind me. 'I've got to get home quick tonight and the way this is going on I'll never get there.'

Kevin Hart was an 'alright' lad. I didn't knock around with him really, as he was in a different class. I knew he had an interesting taste in music, Pink Floyd, Led Zeppelin, Black Sabbath.

To me, that was weird stuff and a million miles away from Bay City Rollers and Slade. Harty was a trendsetter and had something about him. He was different and had an eye for fashion and the girls liked him. I noticed that he had a big folder with him. Anabelle walked out after a matter of minutes with a beaming 'look at how good I am' smile. Sanders went in and then it was me next.

'Harty, what's in the folder?' I asked.

'Oh, just some stuff I put together for today. Thought I'd better do something after what Humphries said about caning people.'

'What stuff? What are you going to do when you leave?' I asked.

At that point the door opened, and Humphries thanked Sanders as she skipped by smiling. Humphries looked at me, I looked at her, then Harty, then back at Humphries. I was now focused as pain inflicted with a fencing sword was imminent. I looked at Harty, and in slow motion I heard the low pitch tones come from his mouth,

'I've been to the cop-shop and got some joining leaflets. I'm going to join the police.'

Like a predator, I struck. One sharp back hand flick, into the testicles of Kevin Hart. His chin hit my shoulder as he doubled over in pain. The folder, yes, *the* folder, fell to the floor and with the agility of an orangutan, I scooped it up, walked into the classroom, placed it in front of Dame Edna Humphries, and retorted Kevin's lines.

'I've been to the cop-shop, Miss, and got some joining stuff. I've got half a mind to go in the police.'

Humphries looked directly at me, looked down at the folder and opened it.

'Sandford Police. You've got half a mind to go in the police, James?'

'Yes, Miss.'

'Well, to be frank with you, that's all you'll need.'

'What is, Miss?' I asked.

'Half a mind, that's all you will need to be a police officer, half a mind,' she giggled. 'Why do you think police officers walk around in pairs, John?'

'Oh, right Miss, I get you.' I didn't.

'Surely, you're not just thinking of being a constable on the beat, are you? You must be thinking of being a Detective Inspector or Chief Inspector at least?'

I was in unknown territory. This was a language I didn't understand. I thought about the reply, very briefly, before just nodding and saying,

'Indeed, Miss.' I just hoped that Mr. Thompson kept his mouth shut. He didn't.

'Where have you got the literature from Jim, the police station?' he asked.

Questioning technique is what I learnt later in my police career. Here's a tip to trainee investigators, don't ask a question and give someone the answer.

'The police station, Sir, yes, the police station,' I replied, nodding.

I knew was now going to ask me which police station and possibly who did I get the information from. I was quickly thinking on my feet.

'And who gave them to you? Was it the Charge Office Sergeant? I think he's called Marsh. Isn't half a character. Lovely man, ex Para,' said Thompson.

'I think it could well have been him Sir, yes, big man, a character.' I replied.

On a roll now, I thought.

'Yes, probably would have been him,' said Thompson smiling. 'He has tattoos, you know.'

'Oh yes, he did have tattoos,' I replied.

Just keep agreeing, just keep giving me the answers, please. This was getting easy.

'That's him. That's the man. And when do you join, Jim? Will it be in the August intake?' Another gift!

'Do you know Mr. Thompson, yes, I think it will be the August intake.'

'Well thank you young man. It's been good to reminisce about Marsh and don't forget, son, you will have to have your hair cut,' he laughed as he rearranged the documents in the folder.

'Thank you, Miss Humphries, and thank you, Mr. Thompson. I'm glad you like my career choice.'

'One last thing, son,' said Thompson, as I backed out of the room, 'there is quite a lot of literature in your folder regarding Robert Plant, Zeppelins, Supertramp and Frank Zappa. Who or what are they?'

CHAPTER THREE

THE EXAM

When will I see you again?
When will we share precious moments?

I opted out of the last year of my education. O level examinations were duly attended in body only, the mind elsewhere. Mum had continued telling everyone I was going to be a doctor or scientist, but sadly, I was to fail the lot, and I had to tell her at some point. Arguments soon began about my chosen career, and the police a very adamant 'No' from mum. War veteran, dad, on the other hand, saw a career in a disciplined organisation, which was something he could empathise with, something quite appealing. The application form to join Sandford Police Force was completed and delivered. The 'Black Sabbath' hairstyle would have to go.

'You will have to have your hair cut, son,' still echoed as I left Kev's barber shop. I looked at those black and white photos on display in the window. Adverts for Brylcreem reflected in the sunlight. I was trying to catch my image to see just how bad my hair now looked. From shoulder length 'Ozzie Osbourne' to short back and sides, in just under fifteen minutes. It was paranoid indeed. My head felt cold. I felt naked up top and became conscious of my ears. I knew I had a pair, but I hadn't seen them for a while.

The morning after the haircut, I caught the number 17 bus to Sandford for an interview and assessment to join the Police Cadets. I was not a city boy, so was quite disorientated with the long bus ride, the tall buildings, the cars and hustle and bustle of city life. I found the Police Headquarters in good time and was sent to the recruitment section. I joined several other spotty adolescents in the foyer and they looked as uncomfortable as I felt. Collars, ties, long dresses, and very short hair. My only real formal shirt was patterned with cartoon bull dogs playing American Football. It had a 'penny-round' collar and looked stupid. It was the only shirt I possessed and raised eyebrows in the waiting room. I wasn't wearing my dad's wedding suit though, as some were. I waited patiently for my name to be called as the audience began to thin out. The door opened and a tall Police Cadet walked in. He looked like a soldier. His boots gleaming like glass. The back of his head was shaved to the bone and the peak of his cap touched the top of his nose. I looked down at my face in his boots. He was immaculate.

'James Graham?' he called, 'James Graham?'

'Oh yeah, sorry,' as I took my eyes off his boots.

'Follow me, you are going for your medical.'

I marched behind, conscious of the staring eyes, as I negotiated the strewn legs. These were my best baggy pants and Noddy Holder shoes. The short hair, the new pair of ears, the cartoon shirt, the baggy trousers, and the Slade shoes, all created a spotlight for this shy, spotty, introverted sixteen-year-old.

I followed the Cadet, 'Mr. Military' passing offices and open doors, attracting the following comments:

'Employing circus acts, are we?'

'Looks like Charlie Cairoli, if you ask me.'

'Needs his fucking haircut.'

'Jobs fucked, if we are letting these in now.'

I walked into a large room with white and green tiles on the wall. I remember the white coat and stethoscope.

'Cough.'

'Excuse me,' I said.

'Cough.'

I stood naked with a mad professor style doctor holding a spoon under my testicles, with his face at my groin. This was all very new to me.

'Now turn around and bend over and touch your toes,' he said.

'Now wait a minute, Einstein,' I thought to myself, 'where's that spoon going?' I had been a bit savvy in avoiding the priest at Sunday School, so I knew what was going on, even in those early days.

'Come on, bend over,' the doctor said.

You know it's wrong, but you know you must do it. If this was the entrance procedure for one of the country's biggest police forces, then so be it, I thought. Was this the initiation? Ram the spoon right up and those that really want to join would stay. Sounded quite rational at the time, to a naked sixteen-year-old in the Police Headquarters. So, I bent over and braced myself.

'Spread your legs,' said Einstein.

Here goes, I thought, bite the lip, hope for a lubricated finger and not the spoon. For Queen and country.

With an okay here and a smile there, I pissed in the carton and was allowed to dress, noticing the spoon back on the trolley, ready for the next victim.

Mr. Military came in to collect me and I followed, close behind. After the stairs, I was shown into a doorway and a wall of thick blue smoke hit me. Noise, banging, shouting, laughter and loud police radios. It was a chaotic scene.

'Fried egg and chips, love,' shouted a rather large lady in a greasy apron, holding a plate aloft as she pushed through the bodies. The noise was deafening.

'Cup of tea please,' I whispered.

'Shout up love. Tea bags in the jar, water in the urn, milk, and sugar on the windowsill and, sausage, bacon, and egg anyone? Cups underneath the wash board, love. Ten pence please. Who's next? Come on, love, shift up.'

The ten pence piece changed hands, and I was bundled along the conveyor belt of bodies trying to recall what was where. The cups on the windowsill, the cups are over there, no they're not, the cups, the cups, where are the cups?

'Jim, Jim,' came a shout from the back of the room. I peered through the haze of smoke and who was sitting there, Robert Plant himself, aka Kevin Hart. I walked over relieved to see Harty and donated my ten pence cuppa to the dinner ladies' pension fund. It was far too stressful. I had forty pence left, which just about covered my bus fare home, with change, of course.

'So, you made it down here, then. Did your Mam bring you?' Harty laughed.

'Did she heck. I came on the bus. Did me Mam bring me? Oh yeah, as if I'd come with me Mam,' I replied.

I was a 'tough lad,' so I thought I would keep the anxiety hidden as best I could. I'd never really been out in the big city before and was way out of my depth.

About twenty of us young, spotty, would-be police cadets were then taken to a small gymnasium where tables were set out in rows. We were invited to sit at a table, but on no account must we turn over the sheet of paper. Those that did would fail the process and be asked to leave. We had 30 minutes in which to answer the questions, and when finished, had to sit quietly until the time was up. If successful, we would then be invited to an interview later that afternoon. Pretty clear to me, I thought.

'Any questions?' asked a Dickensian character at the front of the class. Waist coat and pocket watch included.

'Err, yeah,' came a voice from the far side, 'so what do we have to do?'

'When I tell you, turn over the paper in front of you and answer the questions. When you have finished, sit there quietly until everyone has completed the task or the thirty-minutes have elapsed,' said Mr Pickwick.

'What questions?' replied the voice.

'The questions that are on the desk in front of you. Answer those within the thirty-minute timeframe and then sit quietly.'

'There are no questions on my desk,' said the voice.

'There is a set of questions on the desk in front of you. I can see them. When I tell you to turn them over, answer them and sit quietly, No, no, no, I said do not turn them over until I told you to. Turn the paper back over,' said a now very irate Pickwick.

'I'm sorry mate, you just told me to turn them over, not being funny like.'

Mr. Pickwick was now getting flustered.

'Mate! Mate! What is your name?'

'Geoff.'

'No, your surname,' shouted Pickwick.

'Buckley, Geoff Buckley boss.'

'Well Buckley, you are off to a bad start. Turn the page back and wait until I tell you to turn it over and answer the questions. There is a pencil on the desk.'

'This one is broken,' said Buckley.

'I thought it would be,' said Pickwick as he rolled his eyes. He walked over to Buckley, who was on the far side, and then another angry outburst interrupted.

'MUFC and Buck Woz Ere,' shouted Pickwick as he held up the question sheet.

'Cadet Bamford, Cadet Bamford,' Pickwick squealed. Mr. Military walked in the room, boots clip clopping as he marched towards Pickwick and Buckley.

'Please take Mr. Buckley here and collect any of his belongings and show him the exit. He won't be taking the exam nor embarking on a career with Sandford Police.'

Harsh, but the message to the rest of us was clear.

Even though I was to fail my school exams, the police entrance 'test' was easy. I glanced around the room and noticed Harty at the back. I finished in about ten minutes and the only one I was troubled with was the division one. You know the question with the kid who has only so many chocolate bars and he shares them with his friends. How many has he left? That one!

At the end of the 'test', we all sat and waited, whilst Pickwick ticked away at the front. We watched and waited in silence.

'Crabtree.'

'Yeah,' came a voice behind me.

'You can leave. You have failed. Get your belongings,' said Pickwick.

Poor young Crabtree stood up, picked up his duffle bag and made the walk of shame to do the door. This continued until around twenty of us were left.

'Please wait here until we call your name out. You will be going for an interview soon,' added Pickwick.

I sat outside the interview room with some others, my hooped Slade socks on full view.

'So, you're the clever one then,' said the chair of the panel, '19 out of 20 in a police entrance exam and eleven O levels.'

This wasn't strictly true, as I wasn't going to pass the school exams. But I'd smashed it with the 19/20 if you asked me.

'Why do you want to join the police, then?' asked one of the commanding figures behind the large oak desk.

I had been expecting this question and had practised my responses. I delivered the line, 'I want to help society,' and sat back and waited for the smiles and nods. They never came. The three Victorian looking stooges all glared at me, and one said,

'If you wanted to help society, why didn't you become a social worker?'

Good point, I thought.

'If I wanted to be a social worker, I wouldn't have applied to join the police. I've always wanted to join the police, always.' I lied.

'Do you have family already in the police?' one asked.

'No.'

'Then why do you want to join the police?'

This was getting tough, and my thin veneer of honesty was being exposed. I could hardly say that I nicked Kevin Hart's folder, could I?

'It was to stop me from getting a fencing sword whipped across my buttocks, if you want me to be honest,' I thought to myself.

I knew that answer wouldn't work, so kept tight-lipped. I was really struggling when once again my interviewers became my rescuers.

'So, you want to help society by upholding the law and making Sandford a safer place?'

'Of course,' I stuttered, 'and that is what I was trying to say before.'

'Do you want to catch criminals?' asked another.

'Yes, of course, and these are the reasons I want to join.' I was on a roll.

'You are going to see some horrible things in your career,' Mr. Grey suit said.

'My mum is a district nurse, and I have been with her on her rounds, and I have seen some pretty nasty things already.' I was getting cocky now and had to be careful.

'Well young man, we will consider your application and we will let you know before you leave here today,' said the grey suit.

Cadet Military came into the room, clip clop, and I knew I had to follow. I turned and started to walk away when one of the panel members said,

'Don't forget, if you are successful today, you will have to get your hair cut.' My hair cut. I had no hair left!

I waited back in the gymnasium with those of us who were left. Mr. Pickwick walked in and stood at the front. He opened a clipboard and shouted,

'Cedar, Lloyd, Johnson, Lewis, Mills and Colclough, collect your belongings and leave the room. You have all failed. You can apply again for the next intake next year if you so wish.'

The silence was awful. The chairs screeched as the failures moved out and sauntered over to the side of the room to collect their belongings. I felt for them. There were now about ten of us left in the room.

'The rest of you are free to go and we will write to you about picking up your uniform before your intake begins on the 5th of August,' said Pickwick as he turned on his heels and walked out of the door.

I had passed. I couldn't believe it. Yes, I had passed. Apart from representing the town at sport, it was the first time I had really achieved something. I tingled with excitement as I was about to join Sandford City Police Force. I now had a job, and it didn't matter about the school exams and the impending bollocking from mum. It was a great feeling, and I looked over for Harty and gave him the thumbs up. He reciprocated. Maybe not a doctor, scientist or solicitor, as my mum would have liked, but a Police Officer! It was better than sweeping the streets.

Pickwick re-appeared in the room.

'Do we have James Graham here?' he asked.

Everyone turned and looked at me. Had they made a mistake? Had I failed?

'Err yeah, that's me,' I replied, cautiously.

'Your mum is here to pick you up, son.'

Harty burst into laughter. My 'street cred' shattered.

CHAPTER FOUR

POLICE CADET GRAHAM

Don't love me for fun, girl
Let me be the one, girl

Monday 5ᵗʰ August 1974. It was here. It came fast, very fast. The Osmonds pushed for the top spot as I stood with some familiar faces at the reception of Police Headquarters. The girl that wore her mam's dress to the interview was in the far corner. Another lad I saw recognised me and give me the nod and good old Harty was standing in the corner trying to impress the ladies. I felt awful. We were taken to a classroom and again sat behind the desks in the neat rows. At the back of the classroom were some police cadets in uniform who were enjoying watching this new fresh meat come into the room. Nervous, anxious, and not knowing what to expect.

'You will never be rich, you will never be poor,' bellowed the Chief Inspector as he introduced himself to the new audience.

'You will be part of a big family, like no other family. It will take care of you, if you take care of it. You will get out of the next two years what you put into it. Don't expect it to be easy.'

With an 'all stand', Chief Inspector Williams left the room, and we were introduced to other members of the training staff for the remainder of the morning. Lunch time was awful. I didn't know anyone. I was not hungry and there was small talk at every table.

'All male cadets have to be in reception at 1pm,' bellowed Mr. Military, 'you're all off to have your haircut.'

Never before or since have I had my hair cut with a blow torch whilst listening to a mynah bird making fun of me and swearing at everyone in the shop. It was a surreal moment as we all sat there in silence in a dimly lit barbers' shop in the inner-city. The mynah bird walking up and down, swearing and whistling as victim after victim, sat in the black chair of death. Dr. Frankenstein, or Monty, the barber, walked around with his metal comb and naked flame. We all sat in silence. Numb. The smell of burning human hair remains with me. I have never taken LSD, but I now have a gauge for it. We were bussed back to the headquarters with bristly cold heads. Like freshly plucked chickens, we were unrecognisable from the poor souls that left two hours earlier. The female cadets giggled, people smirked, egos were dented. A smell of burnt hair and clothing stores in the morning.

'They are surplus from the war, you know. Home Office boots, leather uppers and soles. Bloody good boots if you ask me,' said an older gent wearing the standard Home Office khaki coat.

They were indeed excellent boots I must say and lasted me well into my career. I had two pairs and, as advised, one pair for 'bulling up' for the inspections and the others for working. The skill of 'bulling boots' was yet to be learnt, but I had a good teacher in my war veteran father. The dark blue uniform was a good fit, although itchy, and the badges had to be sewn on before Friday of that first week. This was when my intake was to have its first 'training day.' We were given a white lanyard which went over the left shoulder and held the police whistle in the left tunic breast pocket. The training day, it was explained, was to be held twice a week, and our allotted days were Monday and Friday. We would be allocated PE kit on Thursday and had to present ourselves in full uniform at a local gymnasium at 0900 hrs. After a short run on the small running track around the gym, we would then do exercises and enjoy a nice swim before lunch.

After lunch, we had to parade at the local Army Depot and Drill Hall for inspection and then lessons in drill and marching. It sounded really good and interesting. I was playing amateur football at the time and was a fit sixteen-year-old. Or so I thought.

The next couple of days were classroom based and mainly theory about police work. We had guest speakers and one I shall never ever forget. It was a firearm's input and the instructor had brought a selection of firearms and ammunition for us all to look at. A pistol was passed around the class and the instructor was explaining what it was and how it was used. I cannot now recall the name of the gun, but what happened next will stay with me forever. The pistol duly arrived, being passed over my right shoulder by the lad behind me. I handled the gun and looked down the sights. The lad sat on the table next to me was called 'Fez' and I held him firmly in the sights. I squeezed the trigger slowly.

'BAAAAAAAAAAAANG,' with a very big B! The gun fired. The whole class was thrown into chaos. Blue smoke engulfed me. Fez and half the class on that side of the room hit the floor. I couldn't breathe. I couldn't hear. Everything was happening in slow motion. I dropped the gun and pushed my chair back. People were screaming, some crying. The instructor headed my way and calmly picked up the gun. The girl to my right was holding her head and sobbing. I was numb. I couldn't move.

'There is one in every village, ladies and gents. We do it on purpose as it happens on every course we do,' or at least that's what I think the instructor said.

It seemed there was a time delay from the words coming from his mouth to me digesting them.

'You won't do that again, son, will you? It was blank. Anyway, this next gun is…', and he carried on.

I think I wet my pants. I cannot recall the rest of the input. Fez was fine, and it was always the topic of conversation whenever we met over the years. I didn't sleep for three nights.

To get to Sandford city centre, I had to leave home at 6:30 a.m. and catch two buses. This would later become 05.45 and three buses with my first posting to the records office in the south of the city. I lived way up North, so the bus rides were not really appealing. I had to travel in full uniform, which made me extremely self-conscious as all the eyes were on me. I got the odd negative comment but on the whole people were ok. I was sixteen-years-old.

I arrived in the city centre on the first Friday morning, the training day, wearing my best uniform and highly polished parade boots. I had spent hours watching my dad clean them, iron my uniform and generally re-visit his army days. I walked into the male only gymnasium changing rooms. The ladies were being exercised elsewhere. It was very quiet. Very quiet. Lads were getting changed into their new PE kit in the corporate blue colours.

'Dum Dum Dum Dum Dum Dum Dum' was the overhead beat. The source of which no one had any idea. It was like a drum being beaten and all added to the tension in the changing rooms. I checked my bag, realising that I had forgotten the little white ankle socks and asked some of the other would-be victims if they had spares. They didn't. I then saw Mr. Military from the interview day walk in and nodded at him. He nodded back, and I asked him what he was doing. He explained that he was waiting to go to the National Police Training Centre and had a couple of weeks to wait to become a Police Constable. He was still too young. The management had suggested he may want to keep fit and volunteered him for extra fitness work.

'What's that noise?' I asked Cadet Military.

'Moss.'

'Moss?' I enquired.

'Yeah, your training Sergeant and drill pig. He comes in early and runs five miles. Then he runs another five miles with you lot. He's very fit and an absolute bastard.'

He runs five miles with us. I was about to run five miles. I played football and cricket, but I didn't run. I certainly didn't run five miles!

'I'm going to run five miles now? Is this really hard?' I asked as the tears started forming.

'Yeah, and if you don't finish within a certain time, they make you do it all again.'

It was no longer anxiety or tension. It was pure fear. I was standing to attention in a line with all the others in the gymnasium and Moss was pounding away above us on the track. It was mental torture. Names were called out, and we had to stand in alphabetical order. The names sounded like a shipping forecast.

'Graham.'

'Sir.'

'Bailey.'

'Sir.'

'Fisher.'

'Sir.'

'Lundy.'

'Sir.'

I waited and waited for 'German Bight' but to no avail. I had not seen the other two instructors before, and they began to walk down the line.

'What is this?' one asked.

'I've forgotten my socks.'

'I've forgotten my socks, sir,' came the reply.

'Sorry sir, it won't happen again.'

'I know. Upstairs everyone. Pair off, five laps each at the front, then move to the back. Off you go.'

Not a word was spoken from the gym floor, up the stairs to the small running track. 110 laps was five miles, and it had been well calculated, so each pair had five laps at the front. My running partner was a lad called Smith and the early pace was tortuous as the testosterone driven adolescents tried to jockey for position.

'I'm going to be sick,' said Smithy. I ignored him and concentrated on getting oxygen into my body. We were about forty laps in, and it was tough.

'Sir, sir, I'm going to be sick,' cried Smithy as he stopped in front of the instructors.

'Be sick then,' came the reply. So he was. Not only was it hard to get oxygen into the lungs, but we now had the stench of Smithy's stomach contents to contend with. We finished around the forty-minute mark and some lads had been or were still being sick. Smithy had first grab of the mop and bucket and had kept it out as others decided to empty their stomach contents. The smell of disinfectant took me back to my schooldays and the purple sawdust.

We were then paraded back on the gym floor, and it was explained that the instructors were being lenient as we were expected to finish within thirty-five minutes. That's what would be expected of us on Monday. Five miles in thirty-five minutes. We were still in our pairs. Smithy looked a whiter shade of pale. We were then split into different groups: the rope group, wall bars, sit-ups, bench press ups, step ups, etc. Off we went, five or so minutes on each. One kid was hanging on to the rope at the bottom, unable to move whilst others fell from wall bars holding their arms. It was like a scene from the film Kes. Lads were crying, holding their stomachs, or just walking around flapping their arms.

'Change,' and so it went on. When I look back, it was pure agony, but people pay £200 a month or so for less these days. It was a great way to keep fit. Very fit. If you didn't keep up. You were out. That was the message, loud and clear. Make or break you. After a quick skinny dip in an unheated saltwater pool, we were instructed to be at the Drill Hall on parade by 1:00 p.m. I was wet through with sweat, my uniform trousers felt like potato sacks. My new Van Heusen shirt was cutting into my neck and my nicely pressed uniform looked a bag of rags. My boots, my boots, what on earth had happened. We stood 'at ease' for an hour.

'Atten....shun,' came the cry. Shoulders back, chest, head, chin up, and legs together. The inspection party started making its way down the line. I could hear the click of the 'pace stick' and the clip clop of the boots.

Moss, Williams, and the top brass. I daren't look as they approached. I heard shouting. I saw the lad next to me move forward slowly, like he was drunk, and then collapse.

'Get him out of here,' came the bellow.

Moss then appeared in front of me, sharp features, square chin, low brim and immaculate.

'You have a cat?' he asked.

'I do sir.'

'A Police Uniform is something to respect, not something your cat sleeps on.' His voice steadily rising to a peak now,

'Have your boots ever seen polish, what on earth has happened to your lanyard, your creases son, your creases!'
The voice was now a shriek as I felt his spittle on my face.

'You are an absolute disgrace, a disgrace. I will be looking for you on Monday. Name?'
'Graham, sir, Cadet Graham.'

He then walked on to his next victim; the space next to me was vacant as the previous occupant sat at the side holding gauze to his deeply cut chin.

'By the left quick march. Left, right, left, right, left, right, leeeeeeeft. Hey bout turn.'
The marching lasted about two hours or so. It was hard.

The next morning, I awoke with my arms, legs and torso ringing with pain, unable to move. I pondered on what I had taken on. The words of Chief Inspector Williams echoed in my head.

'You will get out of the next two years what you put into it. Don't expect it to be easy'.

Unable to move, I smeared my arms, chest, and legs with copious amounts of Ralgex and Fiery Jack ointment. A mistake, a huge mistake. The skin irritant began burning instantly and did nothing to alleviate the muscle pain. It just increased it by burning my skin.

It was raining outside, pouring down in fact, so I decided to get a deck chair, strip off to my Asda undies and sit naked in the rain. I stayed outside in the rain for three hours to cool down. Every time I hear the song by Blue Pearl, *"Take Me Dancing Naked in the Rain,"* the psychological trauma returns.

CHAPTER FIVE

.

THE BAPTISM

Another Saturday night and I ain't got nobody
I've got some money cause I just got paid.

Cat Stevens wasn't the only one in an awful way. My body was being sharply reminded of just how underused those muscles had been. The five-mile runs, the push ups, sit ups, climb ups, drill, marching continued for the first few weeks and as was expected, the weak fell by the wayside. Not that I was strong, far from it, but I couldn't quit. Just couldn't. All my eggs were now in one basket. I didn't want to let mum or dad down. The police had to be my career. For me, there was no other choice. I was in for the long haul. No going back, I couldn't quit.

It was a lovely sunny day, August 1974, and I was in I was in full uniform, sixteen years of age, walking from the gymnasium to the drill centre in Sandford City centre. I was hot from all the running and exercising and concentrating on the marching that was to follow shortly. Then I had my first interaction with a member of the public.

'Excuse me, excuse me,' came a voice from behind, 'there's a bomb attached to the flyover there,' pointing toward the main Sandford flyover.

Several people had gathered and were now looking directly at me. A bomb? I had no idea what to do. Three weeks or so of running, marching, lectures, but nothing on how to deal with a bomb attached to a Sandford flyover.

I walked slowly towards the mini gathering, and the device was pointed out on a concrete pillar. I placed my kit bag down, told everyone to stand back, and began the slow walk towards the bomb. What was I doing! I could hear my heart making flushing sounds as the blood gushed through my body. My head pounded, the rim of my cap digging deep into the skin. The perspiration was now evident as I got closer and closer. 'If this goes off now, I'm dead,' I said to myself. What I didn't take into consideration was half of Sandford may suffer the same fate. I could now see wires, dials and batteries. This was real and as Sandford had already been a target for the IRA, it didn't look good.

I was now next to the device, which had a ticking arm going back and forth. I think we had explosives and bomb disposal in week six, so my inauguration with 'devices' was rather untimely. My head was banging as the blood pumped around. Like anyone in these circumstances would do, I bent down, looked at the device and picked it up. Of course, that's what you do with bombs, isn't it?
I closed my eyes, waited for the bang, but instead came a shout,

'Hey, what the hell are you doing?'

I opened my eyes to a beard, red-rimmed glasses and green corduroy trousers.

'It's a bomb,' I said, 'best if you walk over the roadside with the others. You will be safe there.'

'A bomb, a bomb. You idiot, it's not a bomb, it's a measuring device. We are checking air pollution. We are from the University,' said Professor Corduroy.

We would all have been killed instantly had the device not been a Sandford University air quality device. I handed it back to the Professor, who thanked me and walked back to the gathering of gossiping individuals, where I had left my bag. My heart was still thumping as I realised I was late and so had to run to the rest of the way to the Drill Hall. I expected the worst as I walked in where Moss was ready and waiting for me.

'A bomb, a bomb, don't be so stupid lad and fall into line. By the left, quick march,' he barked, as we marched and marched and marched.

A year later, the IRA bombed Sandford once again.

For the next four weeks I was seconded to the Force Operations Room, the centre, the hub, the place where it all happened. I was way, way out of my depth. The rabbit in the headlights and just a few weeks out of school.

'This is where they take the 999 calls, then they pass them onto the radio controllers who despatch patrols. You sit here next to Gary, answer the calls on this switchboard and if he needs your help, be ready,' explained the officer.

'What?', as my jaw dropped at the hive of activity. The room was alive.

'Get on the phone now to Brough Ferry. Tell them the lights are out at Manley Road and the Esplanade and there is a backlog of traffic and an RTA. I'm sending Alpha Papa 3 if they could deploy someone from the office or get someone from the south sub-division, ask their ETA, turn someone out from refs if they have to. Go on, go on, ring em,' shouted a very stressed Gary.

I froze. I just didn't know what to do. My time in the Operations room went very slowly. I hated it. Things came to a head when the Chief Superintendent invited me into his office and introduced me to the local MP. I wasn't old enough to vote, so wasn't interested in politics, nor did I know who the individual was.

'Make a pot of coffee for us, son. Don't use milk, I have my creamer,' said the Superintendent.

To be honest, I would have preferred to have dealt with the phone calls and Gary as I had never made a pot of coffee in my life. My Dad had always made a pot of tea in our house. We never drank coffee as it was too expensive, well, apart from that chicory stuff. Mum said it was coffee, but it wasn't.

I went to the staff room and searched for a teapot and cups and saucers. There was no one to ask how to do it, so I did the best I could with my limited knowledge. I carried the tray into the Superintendent's office and both gentlemen sat up in their chairs.

'Ah, here we are,' said the MP, 'a nice teapot of coffee.'

I poured the brown liquid into the two cups and when I had filled one; the Superintendent put his two teaspoons of powdered creamer into the liquid. Well, to be more precise, onto the liquid. It floated and congealed around his teaspoon as he vigorously stirred. He placed a hand on the cup.

'This is stone cold, you idiot. Have you made coffee with cold water?' he asked and held up the coagulated gunge on his spoon.

'Get out, get out and send the other cadet in. Hopefully he has some intelligence.'

Like I said, I was sixteen-years-old and didn't know how to make a pot of coffee. If he had wanted it hot, he should have said.

When I did eventually get to my thirty-two-year milestone and retirement, it was refreshing to read what that Chief Superintendent wrote in my personal file about my time in the Force Control Room;

'This officer is definitely not the brightest star in the sky. He will go through his police career pushing doors marked pull.'

He was indeed correct on some occasions.

My school exam results had now filtered through. When I say results, they were nil. Zero. Nothing. Not one. I failed the lot.

'But you took eleven O Levels, son. What on earth is this?' asked Williams as I stood to attention before him.

These terrible results were expected, only by me, of course, as everyone else had high expectations of me. The fact I couldn't compete with my academic peers was of no surprise to me. I had to tell my mum, which I knew would be met with anger and disappointment, but my plan was to offset that against my new chosen career.

I was to be given a second chance at education and was shipped off to Sandford College for a year to try again. I was to take five 'O'

Levels at the college and the expectation was to pass each one. No negotiation. It was pass or most definitely fail. No wiggle room this time. Fail any and I was out, explained Williams.

College was good. I enjoyed it and for me it was going back to school. Some lessons were good, others diabolically bad. Law seemed to be the worst subject, and the teacher didn't help. Nice guy but unable to really explain tort and why a snail should end up in a ginger beer bottle. For those who haven't studied law, the snail plays an integral part in interpreting our laws. Don't ask me why as the teacher wasn't very good. The physical aspect continued, but not on the same scale. Only in the college holidays did we have to go back for the running and drill bashing. Christmas fast approached and the college assessment reports were forwarded to the Police Training Branch, and of course Williams. Within minutes of them hitting the Chief Inspector's desk, I was summoned to headquarters, in full uniform, 'to be paraded.'

'Graham tends to be easily distracted and fools around in class.'

'He could try harder and is a bad influence on the others.'

'I find him immature and childish. I don't think he is taking this seriously.'

I stood to attention before Williams as he read the comments out.

'What do you know about boiled ham, son?' he asked

'Not much sir,' as I looked down at him under the peak of my cap.

'How much is it in Tesco? Do you know?' he shouted.

'I have no idea, sir. No idea how much boiled ham is in Tesco.'

'Well Graham, can I suggest on your way home son, you find out as you will be stacking it next week. Now sign here and get out, lad.'

I can honestly say that in those few seconds, I grew up. I was being sacked. I had to sign the pink form in front of me and agree to be sacked.

All kinds of things ran through my mind in those nano seconds. What else would or could I do? I will have to sweep the streets. What will I tell mum and dad? I refused to sign, my rationale being that facing Williams would be much easier than facing my mum.

It went down well with Williams. He didn't want wimps that buckled. He wanted young men who were strong and would prove people wrong. Which is what I obviously had to do. We struck a deal and if things hadn't improved by Easter; I was out. Simple as that.

A week later, the PE teacher at college was pushed, fully clothed, into the swimming pool as a prank. I was summoned to headquarters on Saturday morning to be asked again to sign the pink form. This time, no negotiation. I was out.

'But I wasn't at the baths, sir. I was at home sick. I had gastroenteritis.'

'Just sign the papers,' Williams said.

Again, I refused, and I had to produce my sick note as evidence and be interviewed by the complaints department, but quite simply, I wasn't there. Four cadets were sacked. If there was any doubt before about my career in policing, there wasn't now. One foot out of line and I was out.

I worked hard at college and managed to turn things around. I went the extra mile as I knew I had to and received good grades in all five O' levels. British Constitution, English Language, sociology, law and social economics. It was back to bulled boots, pressed uniforms, running and marching and being attached to different departments within the Police and also other emergency services. It was the summer of 1975. Unlike Typically Tropical, I wasn't going to Barbados, I was going to the streets of Sandford.

CHAPTER SIX

THE FIRST POSTING

So how can you tell me you're lonely
And say to you that the sun doesn't shine?

My first posting that summer was to South Sandford Hospital. Yes, a hospital, to work on the wards. As Ralph McTell led us through London streets, I walked through Sandford streets to catch three buses, leaving home at 5:45 a.m.to be on the ward by 8:00 a.m. I realised very quickly how lucky I was. I dealt with death for the very first time at the hospital and can still picture George very clearly. To the nursing staff, maybe it was just another day, another patient, another death. I was just sixteen when George passed away and I was asked to clean him before he was taken away.

I also spent some time on the children's ward and again, they didn't deserve to be there. My six months at the hospital finished with a spell in A&E. Broken bones, heart attacks, nails in skulls, stab wounds, headaches and the aftermath of RTAs or Road Traffic Accidents. The hospital attachment opened my eyes extremely wide, and it was good preparation for what was to come. Nurses, paramedics and hospital staff are the real heroes.

My next postings were to different departments around the force. CSI as it is called now, Records Office and an incident room investigating a murder that later transpired to be one of the greatest miscarriages of justice of our time. I was attached to the Intelligence Office, checking the criminal history of Sandford's residents and of course, making tea and now hot coffee, for everyone. I had been given some great advice, though. Always make a bad cup of tea. It was excellent advice, and when one senior officer told me that my brews were poor compared to Cadet Collins; I knew I had succeeded. Collins had to brew up every time.

Monday and Friday were still my running, gym and marching days. They did get less difficult, with the rest of the week spent on attachment to other departments. Eventually, as I neared the ripe old age of 18, I was allowed to go out on patrol in company with Police Constables. That is, of course, if they would take me. When I did accompany the officers, I learnt a trick or two that came in handy later in my career. My first experience was with 'Decker'. A stone faced, hard looking man. He had missing teeth and tattoos on his arms that he had to hide with his shirt. The self-inked ones on his hands and fingers were more difficult to hide. His hair was shaven up the back of his head and I knew he was ex-military or similar. He had that presence about him. He hardly said a word in the car. He answered the radio, then drove from one incident to the next. On some calls he told me to stay in the car, on others he told me to follow him. I obeyed his every word. His beat was the notorious Beacon Hill estate and again, for the first time, I saw poverty for what it was. I realised I had been a very lucky child. We were not rich as a family, but we were certainly not poor. Now I was seeing poor people. Very poor people.

One call was to an address on Beacon Hill and on this occasion, Decker said I should come and follow him. It was a 'domestic dispute' and Decker said *he* was a handy lad. We parked the police mini outside and, with his steel capped boots clicking away, Decker walked very rigidly and upright to the front door. There was a smell of alcohol and stale urine at the door. It slowly opened and a woman, well, I think it was a woman, stood there with her face bruised and covered in dried blood. Her hair was matted, and her blouse ripped and stained. She was in bare feet and stood in broken glass.

'He's fucked off, Decker. He came home pissed and wanted some more money, but I've got fuck all. I haven't got anything for the meter. He's smashed all the windows.' she said.

The house was freezing. It stunk. There was broken glass everywhere. Vomit, blood, dog mess and no doubt other body fluids and matter all over the place. The single light bulb swung in the wind from the ceiling. Decker looked at her face and advised her to go to hospital.

'How the fuck am I going to get there? Are you taking me?' she asked.

'Where is he now, love?' Decker asked and explained that he wanted to find 'Terry'.

We left, saying we would return shortly. We walked to the car in silence and drove slowly away. As I was thinking to myself what happens next, the car swerved to the right and Decker got out. I instinctively did the same and saw a man walking towards Decker. He was tall, thin, baggy jeans and a thin pencil moustache. He started shouting and raised his fists and came towards Decker. I could see the anger on his face. I panicked. One punch is all it took. Decker hardly moved. Right hand hook came from his side and hit, presumably, Terry, square on the chin. Like a Fred Dibnagh chimney, down went Terry and I remember him farting as he landed on the grass verge. It was awful; it smelt of pure sulphur. Disgusting. Decker moved one pace, put his snaps on Terry's wrist, and took out the PYE radio transmitter and spoke into it.

'4172 to Sandford. Junction of Beacon Hill Road and Lawn Crescent. Van, please, one to come in.'

'Sandford to 4172. Received,' came the reply. The police van was on its way to transport Terry to his awaiting cell.

Whilst we waited, any murmur from Terry instigated a turn of the 'snaps' and an immediate response. Snaps were an antiquated device, similar to one handcuff with a large handle. The smaller handcuff was 'snapped' around the wrist of the offender, or should I say non-compliant individual and the larger handle held by the officer. A slight twist of the larger handle resulted in a painful connection with the wrist bone and the handcuff. Immediate compliance.

Terry was too drunk to deal with at the police station, so luckily for me, Decker said we would take our refreshment break and both head back out afterwards. I warmed to Decker.

Not long after resuming patrol, we were back on Beacon Hill when in the middle of the road stood a young, tall, man, well-built, wearing a traffic cone on his head. Decker slowed the car down and wound down the window. In his very monotone way, with a total lack of any expression, he recommended that the young man put the cone down and behave.

'And what the fuck are you going to do if I don't?' came the reply.

The driver's door opened, the steel boots were out and despite my best efforts and facial expressions to this young man to go and go quickly. It was all too late. The kid took a swing first and that right hook just came up and again struck firmly on the chin. Down he went, and the snaps were out. The radio came out and you know the rest.

The next shift I ended up with Franky Fitzgerald, a rather large individual. He had asthma, I think, and certainly had trouble breathing. He had a polar approach to policing from Decker. He wouldn't have looked for Terry from the domestic assault, and he would have driven the other way when he saw the kid wearing the traffic cone. He was just downright lazy. There were plenty of Frankie's in my time with the Force. To add to his ineptitude, when he did deal with anything, it was usually so bad it drew complaints.

'If you're not being complained about, son, you're not doing your job,' he told me. I chose to ignore his advice.

Whilst on patrol with Frank, we were sent to a young lady who had inadvertently locked the car door with the keys still in the ignition. Bullshitter Frank said this was an easy call and he could sort it in minutes. Car door locks were nothing to him. I knew there was a large bucket of keys that had been handed in at the public enquiry counter. That is where I expected to go first. But no, Frank

Surprised me and drove directly to the Launderette from where the call had originated. As we arrived, I could see a small group of people and obviously a very upset young lady who walked towards the patrol car. She was extremely apologetic as Frank and I alighted from the car and approached her brand-new VW Beetle.

'Do you have spare keys or something? Do you have wires? How do you do it?' she enquired as Frank bumbled his way towards her, panting for breath.

'Easy, love, leave this to me,' said Frank as he withdrew his truncheon and smashed it straight through the driver's window of the Volkswagen. The glass shattered everywhere, and the truncheon was back in the pocket, and he was back in the car before I had moved. The small audience, mouths gaping, moved not one inch. Not a word was spoken. The young woman put her hands to her face. We were all in shock. I slowly retreated to the patrol car and sat in silence as Frank drove off.

'Sorted, eh, son,' he said when we got in the car. I sat in silence for the rest of the shift.

I kept my distance after that. I was interviewed by an Inspector about what had happened. I told the truth. Frank made his thirty years. He never moved from Sandford and spent most of his police life, I won't say career, answering telephones. Badly I may say.

When I wasn't playing sport for the cadet teams, I worked on the enquiry desk at Sandford Police Station, dealing with members of the public. It was a great balance. I used to stay out of the way of the older PCs and sergeants on the public enquiry counter, as the charge office behind it housed some of the grumpiest and ardent officers who dealt with those who had been arrested and charged.

PC Tommy Goodall hardly smiled. He always looked deadly serious, as though he had just lost £500 on the horses. Another hard man. He lived near my parents, so I sort of knew him. I think he had a soft spot for me as at least he acknowledged me but would ignore everyone else. I would get the nod of the head, but when he spoke, it was usually to chastise me. At best, he was just obstructive, at worst, rude, ignorant and unhelpful. He worked day shifts on the public enquiry desk, as I did. We were a good team, good cop, bad cop. He wasn't far off retirement and when working together, conversation wasn't at the top of his list.

One morning it was relatively quiet when a young man came into the enquiry desk saying that he had received a package in the post from Belfast. The sender was unknown, and he had no reason to receive a parcel from Northern Ireland. Of course, 1974 was a very poignant time in the history of Northern Ireland, so quite rightly, the young man believed it to be suspicious. Tommy never spoke. He took the package, nodded to me, and walked through the enquiry office into the charge office behind it. I took the nod to mean 'follow me'. It did. I followed him through the office and down to the cell corridor. Tommy stopped and opened the hatch in one of the big cell doors and with his head, beckoned me towards him. He held the package out for me to take.

'Now put your hands through the hatch and open the package inside the cell,' said Tommy.
What? How mad was this? Put my hands through the cell hatch with the package and then open 'the bomb'.

'But Tommy, what if…' he cut across me.

'I know what you're thinking,' he said. It didn't really take Einstein to work that one out, did it.

'Don't worry. If it explodes, the cell door will take most of the blast and all that you will lose are your hands and possibly arms. Don't stand too close to the hatch as it may get you in the chest and that could be nasty. Don't take all day.'

I could understand Tommy's logic here, but it was by anyone's imagination, deeply flawed or just mad. He left me and went back to the desk to deal with the next customer. I put my hands through the hatch but couldn't see the package. How was I supposed to do this? I felt for one corner and slowly tore it open. It was a
slow, slow process and I could feel the beads of sweat running down my temples. Slowly Jim, slowly, I thought to myself. Then
I'm sure I felt a wire. My worst nightmare. My mouth was dry and,

I started to panic. My knees were shaking. I peeped through the hatch and could see the metal wire now clearly protruding out from the envelope. I froze. I panicked and placed my forehead on the steel cell door. I wanted to cry. How on earth was I going to get out of this mess? I was on my own and the cell corridor was empty. Only me. One, two, three and rip. I closed my eyes. I held my breath and waited for my hands, arms, and chest to be blown through the hatch. My hands were shaking as Sergeant Conroy walked around the corner.

'What are you doing in my cell block, son?' he barked.

'Just opening a bomb, Sarge.'

Tommy was suitably advised for showing me the tricks of his trade, which didn't go down well for our relationship. However badly advised it was, I used Tommy's technique to open all kinds of bombs during my days on the enquiry desk. No one showed me another option.

The Sergeant on the front desk duties was Alex Conroy. An ex-Sergeant Major in the army. One did not speak in his presence. I fell foul of Sergeant Conroy after slipping in at 9:03 a.m. one morning. It was a freezing cold morning and my motorbike refused to start. I took off the jacket and went straight to work, dealing with more bombs and people's problems on the public desk. Phew, my tardiness had gone unnoticed. Or so it seemed until Conroy gave me the wiggly finger. After the sternest of lectures, for every minute I was late, I had to stay behind 15 minutes at the end of my shift. That meant working an extra 45 minutes for my misdemeanour. Conroy finished duty at 2:00 p.m. that day. I was due to finish at 5:00 p.m. He wouldn't be there at 5:00 p.m. to check on me, would he? Did I stay the extra 45 minutes? What do you think? He was brutal. So too was Marsh. Sergeant Marsh, who the careers teacher had waxed lyrical about in my High School days. Marsh went unchallenged and again, like many other officers of that time, was ex-military. Marsh used to disappear at lunchtime and get pissed. He wouldn't have paid for a drink as his reputation went before him. If Marsh was in the pub, it was guaranteed there would be no trouble. People respected him, totally. He dealt with things summarily and everyone knew him or knew of him. Cross him at your peril with the best policy being to stay well out of his way. I was nearly finished typing a report one day when he came into the office and asked me why I was using his typewriter. My report was jerked out of the machine, screwed up into a ball, and his hands turned blue from the carbon paper. I was told to leave. I did.

My days as a young police cadet were now coming to an end, and I had passed all my exams, played for all the sports teams, represented the force at football, swimming and cricket and was duly rewarded with more front desk duties, but this time at the main Force Headquarters in Sandford city centre. This was the place where all the 'Big Chiefs' lived. Assistant, Deputy and *the* Chief Constable of Sandford Police.

The Chief Inspector who advised me on selling boiled ham now wanted to look after my health. He thought as soon as I stopped the training days, my weight would balloon. So, he advised me to do a training day and run five miles every day for three months, interspersed with walking the police dogs and checking the consistency of their poo, followed by front desk duty in the city. That was my future for three months. When I say he advised me, it wasn't up for negotiation.

I had really taken up cricket and was fascinated by bowlers who could swing the ball. By shining one side of the cricket ball and roughing up the other, air travelled over the ball at different speeds, causing it to move in the air. To 'swing'. It fascinated me so much that I used to practice with a ping pong ball. Shine one half and sandpaper the other and then throw it to a colleague and watch as they held out their hands to catch it. The ball moved in the air, boomerang style, and they stood hands empty with the facial expression 'how on earth have you done that?'

Cadet Gary Dobson fell foul to my trick as I tried to alleviate the boredom one afternoon whilst on front desk duties. Dobson threw my ping pong ball into an empty public enquiry waiting area, expecting it to 'boomerang' back to him. Just at that moment, the doors swung open and Assistant Chief Constable Greyson, a fiery Scotsman, stood there and looked at Dobson. The ping pong ball struck him firmly on the forehead, before dropping to the floor and bouncing down all 25 steps to the front desk. I was within touching distance of becoming a police constable. I had three weeks left of dog poo analysis and I just knew that they were going to ask me to resign, again. As predicted, they did, but again I refused, as I didn't want to let my parents down. I blamed Dobson and asked why they hadn't asked him to resign. They had, and he had.

In the autumn of 1976, I packed my bags for the district training school and looked back on two wonderful years of pain, physical exhaustion, dog poo, death and an introduction to a vocation like no other. It was difficult to say farewell, but I knew other experiences and challenges lay ahead. In just over two years, I went from a schoolboy to a Police Constable, in fact, Police Constable 776 Graham.

CHAPTER SEVEN

FIRST 29 YEARS ARE A BASTARD

Oh, I don't know why she's leaving
Or where she's gonna go
I guess she's got her reasons
But I just don't want to know

My time at district training school passed quickly. Prior to being shipped off to live in dormitories for ten weeks, living next door to Alan, we had the induction course at Police HQ. It was a merger of highly trained, physically fit, obedient, and focused police cadets and those members of the public who had just been accepted and joined. The cadets had an air of arrogance but lacked the life skills the others possessed.

'You are now joining a disciplined organisation,' said the drill Sergeant, on that cold November morning. The former cadets nodded in acknowledgement. We knew what was coming. The former builders, plasterers and hairdressers were all new to this. Dormitories were segregated and many a prospective officer failed at the first hurdle when the effects of alcohol collided with temptation. Hospital visits, broken legs and smashed windows were some of the outcomes of when the strict segregation of the sexes was disobeyed. There was no second chance. Get caught in the female dorm and game over.

I remember being at an advantage when we had the visit to the mortuary, or when the blood and gore slide show came out. Several of the very new recruits couldn't cope with death and either fainted on the spot or had to be taken outside. At just over eighteen, I had already started to de-sensitise myself to the harsh realities of police life.

After the marching band refused to yield and the pomp of the passing out parade came to a close, I was posted to a small country hamlet just outside Sandford, called Littleton. It was away from the hustle, bustle and lights of downtown Sandford City, but I was happy and looked forward to my new start. Smokie was still living next door to Alice, and 'they' say one will never forget your first nor last day of service. 'They' are correct.

My first shift was 2:00 p.m.-10:00 p.m., in December 1976 and I arrived at Littleton Police Station in good time. Uniform, boots and haircut immaculate, I walked into the front enquiry office. There I met my first real adviser, John. He was a stereotypical old-fashioned barrel-chested cop. Twenty plus stone, big black leather belt, large smiling face, ruby cheeks and wispy greying hair. He was a gentleman and helped me many times in the turbulent years to follow. His advice on the three Ps stuck with me, as it did many others along the way. I lived by them.

'Policewomen, son, stay away. Things get very complicated if you don't,' he continued.

'Policemen's wives are a definite no, no.'

'Property will cause you problems if you don't book it into the system properly.'

There are different variations of the three Ps, but they were all mainly the same theme. As colleagues fell by the wayside, got divorced, disciplined, sacked, or even went to prison, a quick analysis of their misdemeanour always showed that one of the three Ps wasn't too far away. John's final piece of advice stuck with me, and he had a point,

'The first twenty-nine years of your thirty, son, are a bastard,' he said and smiled.

I was introduced to my new Sergeant, Dick Tibbs, my tutor constable Ricky Reynolds and other shift members. Five officers to cover a shift for Littleton, a very small piece of ruralshire. My tutor Ricky was a single lad and a thorough, enthusiastic worker. He always had my best interest at heart and upheld the law without fear or favour. He had a presence about him, and he wasn't much older than I was. He was a very good police officer, but he did have a weakness, as did most of the organisation, my upcoming best friend, alcohol.

My first day on patrol with Ricky was non-eventful and during the shift I was introduced to Eric the farmer and I just couldn't tell a word he was saying. An old time Westshire farmer who made a glorious cup of strong tea, garnished with milk straight from the cow's udder. It was a day of administration and reports for me, telling the police world I had arrived. New faces, new buildings, 'Hello I am…,' every five minutes and a noticeable few that didn't seem to care.

'Up here at Littleton, you're a name. Down in Sandford, you're a number and they don't give a shit about you.' Oh, ok, I thought. Good job I came to Littleton then.

'Just watch your back as some in this job will be out to get you,' the voices said. Why was that, I pondered? Why would people want to get me? I didn't understand.

I had to be in the sergeant's office at 6:00 p.m. to meet the Patrol Inspector. Every shift had an Inspector. In the chain of command, below the Inspector was the Sergeant. The Sergeants would supervise several constables that would patrol the beats. The Inspector was to be my new God. The one to answer to before it went higher to senior management. He was based at Sandford but was to drive out to Littleton to see me. He was very small in stature, didn't look like he'd been marching or on a drill square for a long time, and he needed a haircut.

He smoked roll up cigarettes and had his Inspector's cap pulled down to his ears. There was an aura about him though that said not to mess with him. He grunted at me, threw me my probationer's handbook, and told me to fill it in.

It was my logbook, my passport to get through the next two years. I was to be assessed at six-monthly intervals by my tutor constable, Ricky, my Sergeant Dick Tibbs, and then him.

I got the impression he didn't have much hope for me surviving the first two years. He left as uncontroversial as he arrived. I was to work for him again some twenty years later, when I became a detective.

Day two, Thursday, was the same shift: 2:00 p.m. until10:00 p.m., and I travelled to work on my beloved motorbike, making sure the boots stayed glass like. Ricky was there in the office with a cup of tea, waiting for me. Sergeant Tibbs came in shortly after, and very soon it was patrol time. As daylight faded, the temperature dropped and small flakes of snow landed on the windscreen. It was 6:00 p.m. and time for our refreshments break, or 'refs' as they are called. The snow was now falling quite heavily. An hour later, it was chaos. Buses stranded, cars crashing, people slipping, and the snow kept falling and falling.

The police radio crackled into life, 'Sierra One to all mobile patrols, all mobile patrols except the Land Rover to return to police stations. No driving of police vehicles in this weather is permitted.'

Sierra One was the call sign allocated to the force control room in Sandford. In the control room, two or three police officers answered the local telephone calls and allocated patrols to individual jobs via the police radios. It was all localised.

The evening's chaos had to be policed on foot, unless, of course, you had use of the Land Rover. We had one at Littleton, and it was now being used for every call. There were people sleeping in the police cells, hotels and guest houses were all full and roads gridlocked. I stayed on duty until way past midnight and was to return for the quick shift change over. The killer 6:00 a.m. shift. It was now 1:00 a.m., and I had to be back on duty in five hours

CHAPTER EIGHT

THE DOCTOR

Too many broken hearts have fallen in the river
Too many lonely souls have drifted out to sea
The things we do for love

The morning after the worst snowstorm for decades, roads were still closed, and utter chaos prevailed in Sandford. A 999 call had been made around 2:00 a.m. from the wife of Doctor Mitchell. The Mitchells lived way out in a secluded farmhouse on the tops on the border with Eastshire. The Doctor had abandoned his car in the snowstorm the previous night and had walked up the lanes to the farm, getting only so far before the white out. It took him four hours or so to walk the mile in blizzard conditions. He arrived home just before 2:00 a.m. and sadly collapsed in the bedroom. Calls to the police and ambulance service were futile as no-one could reach the farm. The Doctor wasn't breathing and there was no pulse.

The sun was now lighting the sky as Ricky attempted to drive the police Land Rover up the snow filled lane, tracing the doctor's steps. We found his abandoned car, and the journey became too much of a challenge, even for the Land Rover. We headed off on foot to try to reach the doctor's wife and, of course the Doctor.

The police and ambulance control rooms had been calling her through the night, but the worst was expected when we eventually arrived. Ricky was very courteous. I was impressed with his professionalism and empathy. He told me to go and check on the

Doctor, who was in the front, upstairs bedroom, whilst he completed the paperwork. I remember Mrs. Mitchell smoking a cigarette, which she held too close to her hair. It set on fire, but she didn't seem to notice, or care. I slowly walked up the carpeted stairs of the old farmhouse. It was cold as I neared the front bedroom door. I knew that behind this door, somewhere, was the body of the Doctor. There was a smell of alcohol and I breathed deeply as I reached out for the old-fashioned door latch. I squeezed on the latch and the clack startled me as the latch opened. I pushed the door gently ajar; the alcohol smell becoming stronger. I could see the windows and the large double bed to my right. I looked on the floor but no Doctor. I moved further into the room, stepping very gingerly as I neared the bottom of the bed. I was now level and peered around the corner. 'Aaaaaahhhhhhhhhh,' I screamed as I fell, losing my balance over the head. I landed full on the body and rolled to the side. My heart was thumping, and the crash had brought voices from downstairs.

'Be careful you don't trip over the rug. He wanted it in the bedroom,' came the shout from downstairs.

I was looking directly at the head of a brown grizzly bear, with prominent and ferocious looking incisors. The paws were at either side of its head and a body which flattened out into a rug at the bottom of the bed. I lay there for a while and gathered myself. I then rolled over on my side and took a peep down the far side of the bed. The Doctor, still in his thick overcoat, was in a peaceful praying position on the floor. There was no doubt he had left us. There was no need to check for a pulse as, even though I was still eighteen-years-old, I'd had enough experience of death to know.

The next challenge was to take the Doctor to a place of rest and although the snowstorm had abated, the lanes would not be passable for days or even weeks. I have never seen snow as high before or since. In the wind drifts, the wall of white was twenty feet high in places. Sandford Control Room, 'Sierra One', was continually asking for our estimated time of release from the farm, over the radio, but the challenge ahead was far from a simple one.

The on-call doctor and duty undertakers were now at the bottom of the lane, a mile away, unable to get any further. How were they going to get to the farm?

In the farmhouse barn was an old red tractor. It had a single bucket seat and over the years the foam had worn away, leaving the springs and cold hard metal to sit on. Ricky had an idea that if we could get the tractor started, then maybe we could get enough traction to get down the lane and maybe tow or escort the undertakers up the lane. With his experience on Eric's farm, Ricky soon had the tractor engine purring and off he set, along the snowy ridge, in the general direction of the lane. The tops of the hawthorn bushes that lined the lane, were just visible and provided a guide for the tractor. The snow was between 6 to 10 feet deep in parts. I watched as the tractor slid and chugged and slid again until it eventually went out of view, with the dark figure of Ricky and the black diesel fumes contrasting against the snow. The tractor, being driven by a police constable in full uniform, with helmet, on what was a cold, crisp, lovely morning, was a sight to see. I stayed and comforted the Doctor's wife, who, although upset, explained that his death had not been a surprise. He was overworked, didn't rest enough, and enjoyed a glass or three before he went to bed. He smoked big cigars, and his lifestyle was opposite to what he promoted to his patients.

We were interrupted by the noise of the tractor, and Ricky returned, driving through the deep snowdrifts. We stood in the hallway to discuss the plan. Ricky had collected a body bag from the undertakers and all we needed to do was get the Doctor on the tractor and take him down the hill. My knowledge of farming and tractors was nil. I was a boy off an estate, but not a country one. We eventually got the Doctor down the stairs and outside.

He was a heavy chap. There was, however, simply nowhere for him to go on the tractor unless he was to sit in the driver's seat, which was unlikely. Ricky disappeared and returned from the barn with a length of rope.

'We will tow him down. It's the only way I can see us getting him down,' said Ricky.

It sounded good to me. Firmly attached to the tow rope at the back of the tractor, the Doctor, Ricky and I set off on the mile journey down to the awaiting undertakers. I was in full uniform, stood on a small foot plate behind Ricky, capturing the diesel fumes as they left the exhaust pipe. As we climbed the small peak, our turning heads ensured the Doctor was still in place, sleigh style, as the tractor pulled him through the snow. Ricky turned right from the farmhouse into the lane and the front right wheel locked as it hit the first of many snow drifts. The tractor came to a sudden stop and projected me towards Ricky, to whom I clung like a falling rider from a horse. I held his head as my feet and shiny boots travelled up to the sky. The Doctor meanwhile was still travelling along the snow, bobsleigh style, and when the back end of the tractor slid out, it projected him catapult style towards the lane. The rope snapped clean from the body bag and like on the Cresta Run; the Doctor gained speed as he headed down the snow filled lane. The hawthorn trees kept him in check and on track as his speed increased, hurtling towards the decent. Ricky, now desperately trying to get the tractor out of the drift abandoned ship and ran through the snow along the pathway in pursuit of the speeding body bag. It disappeared over the ridge and down the lane.

'Shit, shit, shit. I think we're in trouble here, Jim,' said Ricky, as he lit his cigarette. It was only my second day, and it didn't look good.

We both got to the ridge and looked over the top and down the lane to see the undertakers waving up at us. The Doctor had come to rest just a metre away from the back of the hearse. Ricky and I just looked at each other.

We eventually got the tractor free and returned it to the barn. We spoke to Mrs. Mitchell who was totally unaware of the Doctor's rapid decent. Members of the family were now on their way to comfort her, and Ricky and I set off for the lane and eventually the mortuary, where the undertakers would be waiting.

'Genius lads, genius, eh Barry, these two, eh?' Both undertakers now stood at the side of the hearse on the hospital grounds. One of them pointing at us.

'Who thought of getting him down like that, lads? Genius,' one of them said to the other.

Ricky turned to me. 'Jim, that didn't happen, just didn't happen, okay?'

'Understood.'

CHAPTER NINE

DEATH AND DOMESTICS

Don't take away the music,
it's the only thing I've got
It's my piece of the rock

Despite the message from Tavares, in those early days, I just seemed to be dealing with death, domestic abuse, arguments, conflict, and more deaths. Littleton was a quiet place and young probationary constables, or 'sprogs' or 'proby's' as we were called, were under pressure to show our worth by the number of people we arrested or the number of motorists or members of the public we 'processed' for summons. The term 'process' became synonymous with booking people.

'How many 'process' have you done this week?' was a question repeatedly asked by the management.

We were told there were no league tables, but I was then told, if there were any, I was bottom. In downtown Sandford, my peers were kept busy with a very diverse mix of challenges and experiences. Work fell into their laps. For me, it was death and domestics in sleepy Littleton.

At the District Training Centre, delivering death messages was on the curriculum. We never applied the learning in practice or role play, just watched the overhead slides and made notes.

'Always get a neighbour to go with you,' was the instructor's message.

So, in this particular case, I did. My time with Ricky was now served, and I was now a fully-fledged nineteen-year-old police constable who was on unaccompanied patrol. I was about to deliver my first unexpected death message. It wasn't going to be nice for either of us, and I knew there would be tears. Poor old Bill was found collapsed after trying to push his car out of the garage on the local estate. The snow was still thick on the ground. Bill was in his late 70s but the death was unexpected, and his wife was waiting for his return with the car to go shopping.

As per my training, I knocked on the neighbour's door and explained the predicament. I kindly asked if she would accompany me, whilst I told Alice the devastating news. The neighbour agreed. I was thankful. As we walked up the garden path, I practised and practised in my head what to say. It never stopped swirling around. With the neighbour by my side, I rang the doorbell and anxiously waited. Through the frosted glass, I could see the figure of a lady approaching. Her greying hair and mauve cardigan were now visible as the door slowly opened. I removed my hat. Without warning, the neighbour pushed me aside, stood directly in front of me and stood face to face with poor Alice. She then shouted,

'They've found him dead in his car. You've got to go to the mortuary to identify the body.'

With that, the neighbour did an about turn, walked down the garden path and back to her house.

'Any time, love, not a problem. Happy to help,' the neighbour shouted as she rushed away.

Both Alice and I stood there with mouths wide open. What they didn't tell me at the Training Centre is that sometimes neighbours don't get along with each other. I learnt the hard way. It was my first official complaint.

I saw feet tied together, pennies placed on the deceased's eyes and, of course, the tragedy and trauma of suicide. The experiences were plentiful and not to dwell on doom, gloom and gore, but this was my introduction to police work. It was so sad to see, when so young the ease of ending life was greater than facing life itself. At that tender age, I was picking up body parts from railway embankments, cutting people down and witnessing the aftermath of the most tragic and traumatising events. It was sad, very sad. Very quickly, I became de-humanised and hardened to it all. I had to, to survive. There was no such word as stress, mental health, or well-being in those days. There were no counsellors, no listening ears, no support. A mere sign of weakness would mean resignation. So dark humour prevailed as a shield. Together with alcohol, humour became friend and my means of survival. I drank to forget.

CHAPTER TEN

.

ALBERT

I looked out this morning and the sun was gone
Turned on some music to start my day
I lost myself in a familiar song
I closed my eyes and I slipped away

It certainly was more than a feeling. Even though I had passed my police driving test and was authorised to drive police cars, my initiation was foot patrol. Walking everywhere was the ways things happened. Probationer constables, 'sprogs', did not drive. The beat I was allocated was Oscar Beat, which was three miles from the station. I had to walk three miles to the beat, patrol it, and then return to the station for my refreshment period. So, this meant leaving the station around 6.30 a.m., then walking three miles. I would arrive at the boundary of Oscar Beat around 7:45 a.m. only to touch a building, turn around, and walk back. I would call at the butchers on the way back for a breakfast wrap and arrive at the station around 9.00 a.m. Time spent on beat? Nil.

After my refreshment period, I would return to Oscar beat, three miles walking again, but this time would have the luxury of spending maybe an hour patrolling the beat, before heading off back to finish duty. For police car drivers to give a lift to a probationer constable, it was a disciplinary offence.

To raise the stupidity of what I was being asked to do by the supervisors, walk to my beat and come straight back was unthinkable. Just get on with it, I was told, and you are not paid to think.

In the hour I had patrolled Oscar beat, which incidentally was a poor area, I met a lovely and experienced character called Albert. He used to stand to attention in his doorway, breeches pulled up high to his armpits and overhanging the big black leather belt around his chest. His starched collarless white shirt was the type fastened with studs. His big black boots filled the doorstep as he stood and watched the day go by. He reminded me of my grandad, with his short grey hair and statue like figure. Albert was now in the winter of his life, late 70s, a former labourer who had given his all in the cotton mills of yesteryear. He looked tired. The cotton industry had taken its toll. His wife had sadly passed away years before and now Albert lived alone.

He stood at his door every day, watching me as I walked past. I would say, 'Good Morning,' but every day he ignored me with suspicion. Eventually we began talking and one day he invited me in to show me the latest creative invention. The tea bag. He had one pinned to his shirt to remind him to brew up. He told me his wife always pinned it to him, so he carried on the habit. Albert explained that someone had given a lot of thought to the exact amount of tea required for the perfect cuppa. He showed me the tea bag and then produced a pair of scissors. He cut off the top of the tea bag and emptied the tea leaves into a cup.

'The exact amount of tea, son. Exact amount, nothing wasted. Now that's clever thinking,' he said.

I didn't have the courage to tell him, and he produced a cup of tea, with plenty of floaters, obviously. The cup was the white and blue enamel type that he obviously had used in the mills. It was chipped along the rim and was well used. As I drank the liquid, the inside walls were stained deep orange with tannins.

One warm afternoon, I was sitting in Albert's front room. He was washing in the kitchen. He came through to where I was sitting and leaned over to reach a glass bowl near his chair. He held the bowl under his chin and spat what looked like a peanut into it. He took the nut out and dried it with his handkerchief.

'I love the chocolate son, but the nuts get under my teeth,' before placing it in my hand, 'Go on son, you have it.'

'I'm okay Albert thanks. Honestly I can't eat nuts,' I lied.
The nut went to the squirrel welfare fund on the walk back to Littleton nick.

One morning, I walked past Albert's door and noticed it was devoid of his presence. The door was open, so fearing the worst, I went inside.

'Albert, Albert,' I shouted. The footsteps above me reassured me.

'Get yourself a cup of tea son, the tea bag is pinned on my jacket and the scissors are on the top. Your cup is somewhere down there,' Albert shouted down.

The cup was on the windowsill, and it was occupied with Albert's dentures. I went and stood at the front door. Shortly after, I was joined by Albert, who said I had something on my chin. He produced a handkerchief from his pocket and with a deep nasal breath, gathered up enough sputum and spat in his hanky. It was moist. Well, soaked actually. He then cleaned my chin with his sputum and hanky.

'Can't have you going on patrol looking like that, son. Here's your tea.'

Yes, it was in the white cup and Albert dentures were now firmly glued to his gums. The tea had floaters again and the taste of Steradent was quite overpowering. I drank it. I had to. Albert then showed me photographs of his wife. His sideboard was full of them and also of his army days.

'Duke of Wellington Regiment, son. They took me out to India. Dimapur to keep them bloody Japs from taking the rail head. It was hell, oh and this one here is me in Singapore, and this one…'

He was a very proud man. He loved his photos, especially those of his wife Hilda, or Lil as he called her. He explained they didn't have children because of the war. It was too late in life, and they couldn't really afford it. They both worked in the cotton mills. Albert was a doffer and Lil worked in the carding room.

'She was lovely, Lil you know, son. I worshipped her. We met at the Pally, dancing. It was just after the war. We did everything together,' smiling as he told me. I could see the look of deep affection in his eyes as he held the frame up to his face.

The next shift came quickly. It was Monday morning and after the first cup of tea; I left the police station for the long trek to Oscar beat once again. I had some bad news for Albert as the new beats had been published and I was to patrol 'M' beat from the week after. I could still call and see Albert, of course, but I thought I'd better tell him. His front door was closed. It was a little early, about 8.30 a.m. but he was usually up by now. A neighbour saw me looking through the window and came outside.

'He died yesterday, love.'

CHAPTER ELEVEN

PROBATION

It's sad, so sad
Why can't we talk it over?
Oh, it seems to me
That sorry seems to be the hardest word

Life carried on at Littleton and slowly I started to get used to procedures, the foot beats and the staff. There were days when I hated it. Days I wanted to walk away. But I was now in for the long haul and didn't want to let anyone down by leaving, and that included myself. However, there were days when it was a joy to go to work and it soon became clear that this job was like no other. The comradery, the belonging, the being part of something. It was a nice feeling to belong. As other intakes joined, I got pushed up the pecking order for the butt of practical jokes and played tricks on more junior colleagues. It was dog eat dog and was another release from some of the trauma of day-to-day life of being a police officer.

I remember walking in the police station one morning for my breakfast and there stood in reception was the new probationer Constable, Geoff. He was holding a large black horse with a piece of rope around its neck. He was actually stood inside the reception area of the police station with other members of the public, with a horse on a piece of string. John, the station officer, and, Sergeant Bully, as I called him, were stood with him asking what the hell was going on. Sgt. Bully was the nickname I gave to this Sergeant for obvious reasons.

'I've just found it Sarge,' he told them both, 'found it wandering and I want to book it into lost property.' Heads were shaking.

Geoff turned up for work a couple of weeks later and had lost his police issue clip-on tie. We were issued clip on ties so that if you were in a tussle, the other party couldn't get hold of your tie and use it to their advantage. The tie just pulled off. Well, Geoff had lost his and full marks for ingenuity, but his dressing gown cord was a lot longer than he thought and did not have the same appearance as the standard police issue clip-on tie. He tucked the remainder of the cord down his trousers, which just didn't look good. A few weeks later, Geoff was arrested and sacked for fraud.

Harty was still working in Sandford and seemed to be doing well. He was a lot busier than I was. He had been posted to D shift down there, so we worked the same hours and I saw him from time to time. Comparing us to the latest intake of new officers, Harty and I weren't doing that badly.

My first arrest wasn't my really my arrest. Ricky, my tutor, had gone on his annual leave and my other comfort blanket, Sergeant Dick Tibbs, had moved on. The newly promoted Sergeant, Dave Tyson, started very soon after Dick left.

On my first 'independent' set of nights, I was called back to the station around 4:30 a.m. and told that there was a 'prisoner' for me. Prisoner was the name given to anyone that had been arrested and was in custody at the police station.

I had to walk back from Oscar beat, so it would take me a while. A man had walked up to the police station pleading to be arrested. I heard the radio calls from others requesting that the new Sergeant attend the police station to 'sort it out'.

It was explained to this young man that he simply couldn't be arrested, as he hadn't done anything wrong. So, he smashed the front door window of the police station as the Sergeant stood and watched and then asked to be arrested.

When I arrived at the station, it was nearly 5.45 a.m. and the end of shift was in fifteen minutes. I was introduced to the young man who

had been detained for causing 'criminal damage' and placed in a secure room by one of the others on the shift, with the Sergeant's supervision of course.

'He's yours,' said Tyson, 'you won't have an easier prisoner to deal with.'

I was shipped off, with this very agitated young man, in the back of a police van heading for Sandford Charge Office. Yes, the one where I worked as a Police Cadet, the bomb doors and all that. I approached the charge desk, and the infamous Sergeant Marsh was ready and waiting. I wasn't looking forward to this.

'Empty your pockets, take your belt off, shoelaces out,' he commanded.

'What did he say upon arrest?' looking directly at me.

'I don't know I wasn't there,' I replied, which I immediately recognised was not what Marsh was expecting nor wanted to hear. He looked at me with that inquisitive gnarl and said,

'I will ask you again, what did he say on arrest?'

As best I could, I tried to explain what had happened and by now my shift colleagues were probably tucked up fast asleep in their warm beds. I was feeling the wrath of Sergeant Marsh. Another lesson learnt in that you had to be strong and watch what your colleagues were doing. Don't get left holding the baby when the bath water had gone. If this was the easiest it was supposed to be, I didn't fancy my chances when it got difficult.

The detained man wanted to go to prison and remain in custody for his own reasons, but I strongly suspected it was because of his mental health. He was bailed to appear before Sandford Magistrate's Court on some future date.

It was now around 11.00 a.m. that morning and I battled with the fatigue as my lack of sleep kicked in. I needed to return to Littleton, but remember, probationer constables can't have a lift in a police car. I eventually got to bed around 2:00 p.m. that day and returned to work at 9.30 p.m. to go straight back on the night shift.

Dave Tyson, my new Sergeant, albeit newly promoted, was not a young man. He was nearer retirement than joining. He was not Dick Tibbs and although I had a confidante in my tutor constable; I started to lose my confidence, as I was left to sink or sink. Incidents in Littleton were few and far between, and as the saying goes, 'use it or lose it.' I was losing it. I was upsetting the locals as I was being hounded by management for 'process' (booking people). It was a tough time for a young lad, so I decided to put some fun in my days as a kind of release. By this time, I was progressing from my Oscar beat days to Mike, Romeo and Victor beats and recently I had been allocated Littleton Town Centre. When I say town centre, it was a big village. On nights you had to check all the premises on your beat and God help you should there be a break in on your patch during the night and you had not found it. You would be hoisted out of bed and instructed to parade before the Superintendent immediately in full uniform to explain why you hadn't done your job. It was basic bread and butter policing.

'Can you cover one beat tonight please? You are a police driver, aren't you?' asked Tyson.

I was being allowed to drive a patrol car for the first time. All on my own. Feeling quite excited, I drove out of the police station yard, and I hadn't got 250 yards away from the station when I had to pull in. There was something wrong with the car. It was making all sorts of noises. But only when moving. It was a whirring sound coming from the front end and reminded me of my younger days in the amusement arcade at the caravan park where we went for our annual holidays.

'Bastards,' said Ricky as he removed the metal hub caps off the police mini's front wheel. 'They've put marbles in your hub caps, so they keep spinning round even when the car stops.'

It was my introduction to the pranks, the banter, the glue that kept us all together. It had begun.

On the next night shift, I walked into the police station kitchen around 1:00 a.m. to eat my sandwiches or whatever I had made for my 'Refs' as they were called. Refs was usually a forty-five-minute break
midway through the eight-hour shift and there was a pecking order. Early refs, in the case of nights, was 1am or late refs, 2:00 a.m.. Late refs was better as you had less time to patrol afterwards. Here I was in the police station kitchen looking at Sergeant Tyson's tin of Irish stew. That's all he ever had, Irish stew on nights and no liquid after midnight. You know, pissing and all that as you get older. Every night, Irish Stew and Hovis bread. Without fail. As I reached into the cupboard to get the salt, I noticed on the top shelves the tins of Pedigree Chum dog food. Littleton housed the dog kennels for the whole of Sandford Police Division and when you were on desk duty, you had to feed the stray and injured dogs. They were collected every week by Sandford dog's home. What went through my mind at this point I have no explanation for, but it seemed like a very good idea at the time. As my career progressed, I had many supervisors and managers who I would have walked barefoot over broken glass to get the job done for them. Sergeant Tyson sadly wasn't one of them. I boiled the kettle and steamed off the Irish Stew label. It took a matter of seconds for the glue to melt, and I quickly swapped it with a label from the Pedigree Chum. I let the two cans stand there for a while for the glue to set and put Tyson's Irish stew way at the back of the Pedigree Chum tins. I left his newly sealed Pedigree Chum Stew next to his loaf of Hovis.

When I returned to the police station at 5:45 a.m. to finish the shift, the stench was apparent in the rear yard. I could see other shift members and staff pulling their faces and pointing at me. One was running his finger under his chin, cut-throat style, and then pointing at me. I walked in the door and there stood Tyson.

'My office, where's my stew?' he said and pointed to the door.

I gave the best bemused looking face I could give and denied everything. However, the price I paid was my card was now well and truly marked.

The next night, I had only just left the police station when the police radio crackled into life.

'Sierra One Control to any patrol to attend the Top House, large-scale fight in progress.'

The Top House was on my beat. It was on the edge of civilisation and miles from the police station or anywhere for that fact. I radioed that I was attending. I drove the five miles or so to the divisional boundary with Northshire and upon arrival, I saw the posse of fighters out in front of the pub. There were about a dozen fighting as I parked the police car in the pub car park. People were asking me to hurry and others saying, 'be careful lad,' as I walked towards the group. Jackie Lamb came up to meet me and blocked my path. He was big, very big. Open shirt, barrel chested and pissed. Jackie had been an amateur boxer in his earlier life and had helped kids off the estate by working with them in the gym. He wasn't all bad. I did, however, get the feeling that from now on in I was going to be dealing with the bad. Skirmishes started on the periphery of the group, and I remember someone being placed in a headlock and thrown to the floor. I was now in the centre of the group, with Jackie toe to toe. He was very agitated. He explained in a very irrational way what he was going to do to me and so I pressed the little yellow button on the Burndept police radio and asked for help, for 'assistance'. That word, assistance, should trigger a response from your colleagues, whereby they drop everything and come to your help. And I mean drop everything.

Jackie, now with hands around my throat, took hold of my tie to lift me up. It was a clip on, remember. The tie came off in Jackie's hand and once again, I pressed the radio button to call for assistance. There was silence. The radio was dead. In desperation, I asked someone on my left if they would ring the police.

'You are the police, dickhead,' came the reply.

The mobile phone had yet to be invented. It was no use, as I was now surrounded by the crowd who had their prey. They were bating Jackie to 'sort me out'. I suppose this is what they call fight-or-flight time and I couldn't really run off, but then I couldn't fight. Certainly not fight an amateur boxer who had me by the throat and with a reputation that went before him. I explained about my low threshold to pain and told Jackie I wasn't going to resist if he wanted to beat the living daylights out of me. I think he was intent on doing so. I remember him pushing me back and the commotion gaining energy and I really did think this was it. I was nineteen-years-old, alone, and the pack had me. I told him to get it over with quickly. I braced myself for the first punch and felt a thud as Jackie fell into my body. I was pushed backwards and lost my footing, falling over, hitting the ground hard. Jackie was now lying across my legs and was moaning. I was trying to make sense of things when I saw a large steel toe capped boot next to my face as it pressed hard into the car park surface. I then saw Jackie's wrist twisted in a 'snap' device and there was a noise like a squealing pig. In a very stern voice, I heard,

'Now if you don't fuck off, you will get what he got.'

I looked up to see Decker holding my tie. He had travelled all the way from Sandford. I slowly got to my feet, put my cap back on, and acted as if nothing had happened. I dusted myself down, thanked Decker, and it was re-assuring that none of my shift from Littleton turned up. Decker later explained that he had heard on the grapevine that Jackie Lamb was going to cause trouble in the Top House. Decker used to call in the Top House, Bottom House and every other ale house in Sandford when he could. Like Sergeant Marsh, he was well known about the town.

Now off nights and on a day shift, I was busy writing out my reports when I heard the front door open at the police station and a bellowing voice come inside. It was the Chief Inspector from Sandford.

He had travelled up to Littleton with the Patrol Inspector, the grumpy one, to see how we were coping and to probably ask me how many people I had booked. The senior officers were towering figures in those days, both physically and psychologically. Especially to a nineteen-year-old. I feared them.

'Who covers Downfield Park, young man,' the Chief Inspector bellowed at me.

'That's One, beat Sir,' I nervously replied standing to attention at the same time.

'One beat eh. Well young man, I want you to get a vehicle and travel to the road that runs to the Lake up there. We have just driven down and there are a number of chickens by the side of the road, pecking at grit in the gutter. Now, young man, find out who owns them and report them for animal cruelty. Poor things are so hungry they are eating grit out of the road.'

'But Sir, chickens actually do eat...' I was cut short.

'Go on young man, run along, go and report the owners and I expect to see a process report on my desk,' said the Chief Inspector as he walked off.

Even though still young and immature, I knew enough about the eating habits of chickens to really question this decision. These were our supervisors; our leaders and he wanted me to find out why chickens were pecking at grit? Don't forget, my role in the terms of Lord Tennyson was not to reason why, but to do and die. I never found the chickens. To be honest, I didn't even look and reported back to the Chief Inspector my findings, or lack of them.

It was about this time that I was sent to a call to a farm up near the Top House. They had been having their sheep attacked and Sergeant Tyson wanted to come with me. On the tops, in the open, the green fields and hills spread over to the horizon. It was a glorious view and the sun and warm weather were breaking through. The birds were starting to nest and there was a chorus of 'Peewit, Peewit,' as we walked towards the farm. Tyson looked up and pointed to some of the Lapwings and said,

'From Africa, you know. Come over here for the summer. Lovely bird the Swallow.'

'No,' I said, 'That's a Lapwing or Peewit.'

'I think not, Jim. I study birds and that is definitely a swallow. You need to swot up on your birds,' replied Tyson.

Me, swot up on my birds? Pride of possession in my library to this day is the book of birds that I got for Christmas in 1966. By Kirkman and Jourdain, British Birds, is a wonderful encyclopaedia of our domestic friends, with full descriptions, colour paintings, action photographs and an index of their eggs. I treasured that book as a child and still do. I studied it carefully and every Thursday I used to take it to my friend's house after school. Dad always worked late, and mum didn't get home sometimes until after 5:30 p.m. So, from 4:00 p.m. until I was ready for home, I went to Stephen's house. Stephen lived in the next street, and we all mucked in as kids and families in those days. Stephen was okay, and like most kids from the estate, later joined the army. The other route out of the estate was boxing, a la Jackie Lamb. Initially, Thursday nights at Stephens were good, and we used to share toys, books and stories. I always took my bird book, as at that time you gained street 'cred' off other kids from your bird's egg collection. However, I started to notice some peculiar behaviour creeping in from Stephen's Dad on Thursdays when I went over. Even for a child of tender years, I thought it very odd. Very odd indeed. Every Thursday, I noticed that his dad used to have a bath when I arrived. As Ste and I were in his front room playing, his dad used to come in and towel himself off in front of me. I therefore had a choice of concentrating on a naked, aroused, forty-five-year-old man with genitals swinging, or my beloved bird book. You probably can guess which one held my concentration. Sergeant Tyson, if you are still alive, it is with the greatest of respect, that when I say those birds, we saw that day were Peewits, also called Lapwings, Green Plover or even their Latin name of Vanellus Vanellus, I assure you, that's what they were. My eyes never left that bird book, I can assure you.

My probation period carried on unscathed really, and Littleton was certainly not the place to cut your teeth in policing. It was the place to end your career. I received notification, as all probationers did, of a two-week attachment to the Traffic Department and the CID. The Criminal Investigation Department. My time in Traffic, was good, and I experienced a few 999 calls and extremely fast responses and again re-visited my meetings with death at a nasty fatal road traffic collision. I suppose there isn't a fatal incident that isn't nasty really, is there?

My attachment to CID was an introduction to a department I served well for over three quarters of my service. The skill of investigation I still find addictive and fascinating. A very senior investigating officer told me once that if you find a matchstick at the murder scene, your job as an investigator is to find the tree it came from. My main duties on that initial attachment to the CID were to sit, listen and make pots of tea. If I answered the phone, I couldn't deal with the call as I didn't have a clue what to do. This was serious stuff now, Detectives and the CID!

'Do you play rugby, lad?' asked a Detective Sergeant one morning.

'I played rugby league at school. Played for the town and played a game or two for the cadets,' I replied as I stood to attention.

'Tommy,' the DS shouted down the corridor, 'cancel the last. This lad will play.'

Two hours later I was on a rugby field, wearing someone else's boots in a position that I had never played before. I was playing rugby union, a game I didn't understand nor know the rules. I remember very little about the game, only it was the semi-final of the Chief Constables Cup, and we were playing the Champions. I can picture now the ball coming along the line until eventually it hit me on the chest, and I wrapped my right arm around it. I turned to run for their line and I remember the fist coming, the flash of light, the pain and then a hot bath and a jug of beer. I thought it was a dream. I didn't remember much at all.

The morning after, I went in the CID office as usual but found myself unable to function. That is, put the kettle on and make tea. Voices were coming at me through cotton wool and my cognitive ability was nil. I felt intoxicated and quite unwell and was obviously displaying the same signs. I was taken to hospital and found to be suffering from a depressed cheekbone and concussion. I was kept in overnight and resumed back in the CID Office on Saturday morning. I was given a round of applause as I had apparently scored the match winning try. I put the kettle on.

Overnight, there had been what is called an 'aggravated burglary' at a local restaurant. The aggravation factor being that the hosts, a young couple and their parents, had been tied up and gagged whilst three armed men searched for the weekly takings. The majority of transactions were cash in those days. The restaurant was just over the border in the Northshire Policing area, so the Sandford division didn't police that area. What Sandford did police, though, was the area where the suspects lived. Something had happened during their escape and one of them was later found hiding on the moors. He was taken to the nearest police station, which was Sandford and Northshire Police had been contacted to come and collect him. He was well known about the town and had previous convictions for armed robbery, serious assaults, kidnap, and the like.

Peter 'Ned' Henderson was not one to mess with and I was instructed to sit with him in a small room whilst Northshire Police came to collect him. I was told to make a note of anything he said before being shown to the interview room. Ned was mid-thirties, muscular, tattooed, and looked evil. Robbing was his job. He was employed on a full-time basis.

'What kind of fucking shirt is that?' he asked as I walked into the room.

'What do you mean?' I said.

'Since when have CID been coming to work in fucking Mickey Mouse shirts?'

He was obviously referring to my American football cartoon shirt that had aged well from my cadet days. It was the only shirt I had. He tried to have a conversation with me and commented on how young I was, but to be honest, I felt like a mouse in the python's cage. I sat in silence throughout. Never said a word. Not one. I was too frightened. Soon after, Northshire Police arrived and took Ned away and I continued to make the tea for the office.

Nine months later, I received a Crown Court witness warning to attend Northshire Crown Court, in the case of Peter 'Ned' Henderson. I was being called as a witness by the defence, as Ned had alleged that when I had sat with him that morning, I had put pressure on him to admit the offence. As if the mouse had turned on the python. On the court day in question, I attended the CID Office, as other Detectives were travelling across to Northshire as they too were witnesses. In the car journey across, I was quiet and felt better when one of the detectives recognised me for scoring the try in the rugby semi-final. This was my first ever court appearance. I was to attend a Crown Court in front of a Judge: wigs, gowns, and juries. Way, way out of my league. What an intimidating place I found and always kept that in mind for witnesses in future court cases I had.

'Who is PC Graham?' asked a clerk.

'That's me,' I said.

'Mr Elias wants to speak with you,' said the clerk as he pulled on his cloak. 'He's over there speaking with the defence barrister.'

I looked over and could see two barristers sprawled on the seats, as they discussed the case with each other. I walked the short distance to the conferring duo and announced my arrival to who I presumed was Mr Elias, the prosecuting barrister, in the case against Ned. I stood there and waited. The conversation continued between the two. I stood and waited and waited until it became quite embarrassing and awkward. The two barristers chatted on and on and when they paused to take a breath, once again I announced myself to Mr. Elias.

'I know exactly who you are officer and when I have finished speaking, I will attend to you,' he replied. Consider myself spanked! Know your place Jim, I thought.

I didn't have any real evidence to give and when the defence barrister saw me, I am sure he felt it unwise to attempt to convince a jury that a spotty, weakling adolescent who wore a mickey mouse shirt had put pressure on an eighteen stone, muscle bound, armed robber to confess. I was relieved at not giving evidence and was allowed to sit in the court during the trial. I found it fascinating.

The adversarial justice system in this country is best described as a game with two teams, who go head-to-head, watched by an audience who don't have a clue about what is happening. One impatient judge is quoted as asking a barrister,

'Mr. Diamond, when am I going to hear the truth of the matter?'

'Your Honour, quite simply you are not, you are merely going to hear the evidence.'

The adversarial justice system that we have adopted in this country means,

'Who wins on the day'. It is not a search for the truth as in the inquisitorial judicial system is, which is mainly practised in Europe.

I listened to the trauma that family were put through that night of the burglary and hoped these evil men were locked away. Sadly, Sandford had its fair share of Neds.

'Would you identify yourself to the court, take the bible in your right hand and take the oath officer,' as a smart looking detective entered the witness box.

'Good afternoon Your Honour. Reginald Arbuthnot, Detective Sergeant, Northshire Constabulary, Serious Crime Division.'

I never forgot that name. Another one that reminded me of my grandad. Silver hair, brushed back, maroon tie, white shirt, silver jacket with a silk handkerchief in the top pocket. He was in his early 50s, immaculate and oozed experience.

He stood to attention and answered all the prosecutor's evidence with ease and clarity. I bet he wore Old Spice after shave as well, like Grandad. Arbuthnot had questioned Ned when he arrived at Northshire Police and Ned had allegedly made confessions to Detective Sergeant Arbuthnot. What the court nor I was expecting was what followed.

'When was the defendant arrested, Sergeant?' asked the defence counsel.

'He was arrested in the early hours of Saturday morning, Your Honour in Sandford.'

'When did you interview him, officer?'

'The first interview commenced at 2:00 p.m. on Sunday afternoon,' your Honour.

'On Sunday afternoon? You say on Sunday? So nearly 48 hours after his arrest, you decide to question him? Would you be so kind officer, to explain to this court why it took you so long to interview him? Why was there such a delay before the interview with the defendant? Why didn't you interview him on Saturday?'

'No problem, counsel,' Reginald replied as he turned to face the judge.

'Your Honour, for the last twenty-eight years I have opened bat for Northshire Police County Cricket team and neither Mr. Johnstone nor his client was going to deny me that opportunity on that day.'

The court fell silent. People looked at each other in amazement. Did he just say that? He went to play cricket rather than interview the suspect? There was a long silence eventually broken by the Judge.

'Very well, officer,' said the Judge, 'what was the outcome?'

'We won by five wickets, your Honour, if my memory serves me correctly. 84 not out and 2 for 34 off ten were my own figures.'

It was like someone had let a high-pitched fart out in a lift. Everyone in the place heard it but didn't know what to do or say. It was an uncomfortable silence. I did see, however, some with cheeks puffing in an effort to abate the giggles and laughter.

Others looked on in shock. It was a brilliant moment in time that I will never ever forget. The Judge rolled his eyes and leaned over to whisper to Reginald, I'm sure words to the effect,

'The outcome of the interview, you bumbling fucking idiot.'

I saw Ned a few weeks later in town. He nodded to me. He got off with it.

Crown Court is a fascinating place, and I devote a chapter to the theatre later in the book. I loved going, albeit always apprehensive. It was refreshing to see creative minds battle the interpretation of the law. It was also good to witness rewards for victims and witnesses in a system that is, at times, weighted against them.

Pomp, ceremony, history, class and privilege. The clip clop of the barrister's heels as they walked the marble floored corridors of power, holding their gowns, wigs aplomb arguing and interpreting the law in different ways.

CHAPTER TWELVE

THE PETROL CRISIS

I can tell by your eyes that you've probably been cryin' forever
And the stars in the sky don't mean nothin' to you,
they're a mirror
I don't want to talk about it, how you broke my heart

The Middle East was simmering, and although it was post petrol vouchers and power cuts, the cost of petrol kept on rising. Those in command at Headquarters or Sandford Towers, as we called it, duly responded by issuing a memo, restricting all police drivers to drive fewer miles per shift. Excessive mileage had to be accounted for. The author of the memo was the Superintendent at Sandford, the one just below the God of all Gods. The hierarchy of Sandford Police was 98% male, and they were ruthless. A constable couldn't ask an Inspector a question or submit a report to a Chief Inspector. The Constable had to report *only* to the Sergeant. There was a clear and obvious chain of command and try to usurp it at your peril. All reports, requests, memo's that went up the chain had to be signed by a Sergeant, Inspector, Chief Inspector and dependant on the report contents or request, Superintendent, Chief Superintendent and so on.

The Sandford Superintendent, I christened as 'Himmler'. I always tried to stay out of his way. This was a disciplined service, and we were to be disciplined. If Himmler caught you in the police station, you were in trouble.

As were your Sergeant and Inspector. He ruled by fear and the punishments ranged from bean counting during a shift, e.g., counting all the vehicles in the police pound or mind-numbing station guard duties. The vehicles in the pound were checked three times a day as the poor soul who was being punished on the previous shift had done exactly the same counting as you were about to do. Another punishment was stopping you from driving, or 'grounding you' for several weeks or months. That only punished the people of Sandford, as on some occasions, we had three patrol car officers 'grounded' for small, insignificant misdemeanours. Not wearing a cap when driving, being caught in a building, caught giving lifts in a police car, being late and so on. You didn't question things, you just did them. It was indeed Tennyson's world.

A directive came from Himmler;

'To reduce petrol costs, patrol car drivers must not exceed 22 miles per shift. Any digression from the authority will lead to disciplinary action. We need to bring down the amount of petrol we use.'

Maybe Himmler had the foresight of the carbon effect? Maybe not. What he had to ensure is that when they had the monthly meeting at Force Headquarters, he had answers for ACC Greyson. Remember the fiery Chief we hit with the ping pong ball?

There was a problem in Littleton. Unlike Sandford, the car beats were spread out, and we bordered on Northshire and Eastshire. They were wide open spaces that led onto the moors, with villages and farms miles away from Sandford. This was indeed ruralshire, heartbeat, Bronte land. Initially, I covered the car beat for one half of Littleton centre, whilst Ricky covered the other half and the surrounding areas. It was a huge geographical area.

If Himmler wanted to reduce petrol costs, I had a plan. It was radical and courageous, but worthy of exploration. At the end of every morning shift, we were supposed to fill the vehicle with petrol. The fuel, theoretically, would last until the next morning, so if the afternoon or night shift came in and had to answer an emergency call, they could drive straight out of the yard without the worry of having to fill up.

In each vehicle was a logbook in which you entered the miles driven, the amount of oil and petrol you had put in the vehicle, and any other observations for the next driver. If you did fuel up the vehicle, you also had to work out how much was left in the big fuel tank in the station yard. Why, you may ask? I have absolutely no idea, as the pump had a dial and the fuel companies would be summoned when the dial got to a certain number. The garage staff took care of all that, but we still had to calculate the amount of fuel in the big tank.

As you travelled away from Littleton towards Northshire Police area, you had to climb Littleton Edge. This was a well-known area for walkers and was bleak on the tops. My theory was to drive the mile or so to the top of Littleton Edge and await a call. When police services were requested, one could simply take off the handbrake and let the vehicle roll down the hill, building up sufficient speed to free wheel to anywhere in the beat area. Ingenious, I thought, less petrol used. So, as Ricky and I sat side by side in the police vehicles on Littleton Edge, the call came through from Sierra One Control Room,

'Any patrol at Littleton to attend….' and before they could say where, handbrakes were released and off we both went, freewheeling down Littleton Hill at speeds of up to 70mph. No engine sounds, no noise, no petrol use, just silence as the two police vehicles raced down the hill jockeying and slip streaming for position. People gasped as we both shot through Littleton Centre, unable to brake, to maintain maximum speed and ultimately our distances. On night shift, it was even better, as no one could hear the cars coming. The surprise on people's faces as the police car appeared from nowhere, no lights, no engines, no noise. Overtaking other cars as they travelled along at 30 mph, with just enough speed to get past them, if you were lucky. Petrol consumption went down by 50%.

When the local cricket club was broken into, the burglars had no chance. Like at Le Mans, we flew down the hill in total silence, lights off and arrived to see two startled local lads counting the money from the fruit machine.

'You were instructed, I repeat, instructed not to exceed 22 miles. Instructed Graham. Do you hear me? Instructed,' Himmler shouted as he looked at the vehicle report.

'I know, sir, but if you look for a moment at the petrol consumption you will find,' I was immediately cut off.

'I don't give a damn about your petrol consumption. You have disobeyed orders and will be on be on vehicle pound duty for four weeks,' spat Himmler as he adjusted his glasses. He was visibly upset. 'Now get out and send in the Sergeant,' he barked.

There were 57 vehicles in that pound. I knew all of them. How long they had been in, who brought them in, etc. Some had been there for years. There were some motorcycles, old and new, and I served my punishment on every shift for a month, under the window and gaze of Himmler's office.

Upon release, I was welcomed back on the shift at Littleton like Steve McQueen in the Great Escape. There had been some shift changes whilst I had been in the cooler with staff moving to different departments. I was allocated Whitfield car beat which was to the east of Littleton and the mileage embargo was still on. Word came through on the back channel of more constables being sent to the 'cooler' with baseball glove and ball for weeks or months in some cases.

Sergeant Tyson briefed me more than once not to exceed 22 miles, but I had a problem. To get to Whitfield, I had to drive 5 miles. To come back to the station for my 'Refs' period was another 5 miles. Going back to my entrance exam technique, I quickly adduced that if PC Graham was going to make four journeys at 5 miles each, that was twenty miles, leaving two, yes two miles for patrolling the area for 8 or 10 hours.

'You will just have to park up and walk,' exclaimed Sgt. Tyson.

'But what if a call comes in from up in the north of the beat? That's miles away?' I replied.

'You will just have to park up and walk,' repeated Tyson

Shortly after, I was paraded in front of the Patrol Inspector as to why it had taken so long to attend to a call regarding someone being assaulted.

'Because I had to walk, sir,' I flippantly replied.

'Why on earth did you have to walk all that way?' enquired the Inspector. 'I have spoken with Sgt Tyson and there is no way it should have taken you that long to attend an incident of such nature. I've had to go and explain to the lady and apologise on your behalf.'

Apologise on my behalf? On *my* behalf? Tyson should have been apologising and knocking on Himmler's door, asking him to see sense.

I made my own decision from then of not driving back for my refreshment period but was instructed to park the vehicle in Whitfield Council Offices yard. It was the old police station from yesteryear, which was semi-derelict. No one used it. The offices were smelly, dirty and dangerous, but a place where I took my break for the next few weeks. It was away from the gaze of the public, where I consumed the contents of my flask and my new delicacy, Irish stew.

One night, I was driving back to the station at Littleton in the early hours when I saw a shadow dart behind a wall. Sometimes on nights you did see things, like shadows or non-existent movements as the fatigue kicked in. But I'm sure it was a figure. I braked hard. I know you're probably asking about the mode of travel and yes; the engine was running as my freewheeling theory had been deemed as flawed. I quickly put the car in reverse, looked over my left shoulder, my left arm across the passenger seat, and set off after the shadow in reverse. The car screamed as it headed for the back alley and a quick glance back to the front, checking nothing was coming, revealed something remarkably interesting. The speedometer was not moving! The needle was not moving. It was on zero. I pressed on the accelerator and sped along backwards and turned back to look at the speed dial again and again. Zero. Not registering. I noted the mileage on the clock ended 289 and travelled the whole distance of the road, and it stayed on 289. I went up Littleton Edge in reverse. Still 289. I came down Littleton Hill, still 289, and I spent the last few minutes of the shift driving around Littleton, leaning across the passenger seat, looking out of the rear window as the police car screamed around, engine on high revs, going backwards. I couldn't wait for the next shift to start.

'Sierra One to any patrol,' announced the radio.

'776, yes, yes, I'm on my way,' I immediately responded. Then the next job,

'Sierra One to patrols, thieves on,'

'776, yes, yes, attending from Littleton,' and so it continued.

I would reverse all the way in my new, perfected driving position. Hours of shift completed, eight. Incidents attended, eighteen. Miles covered, four! The managers were scratching their heads.

The next night, Tyson gave a briefing on tampering with the speedometer, and anyone caught doing such a thing would be dismissed as it was an offence under the Road Traffic Act. It wasn't lost on me, and the message had been received, loud and clear. When I drove out of the station, I drove forward, in the 'normal' way. But once out of view, arm over the passenger seat, head looking over the left shoulder, gearbox in reverse and away I went.

Tyson asked to meet me on my beat, to which I had to agree. Words to the effect, 'put a chalk in for me,' from a Sergeant, meant that you had to enter in your notebook that an official meeting with the Sergeant had taken place. He could then show he was doing his job. Some Sergeants, without warning, would demand the notebook and sign and time it themselves, there and then. So, if it wasn't up to date, you were in trouble. I was on foot patrol when I met Tyson and he asked where the police car was. It was parked in the council yard where I had been told to park it. There was no doubt he had come to check the mileage on my police car. He left me shortly after and headed for the yard.

I waited and listened for the sound of his vehicle disappearing into the silence of the night. I returned to the yard, checked the area, and listened. Was Tyson hiding and waiting? Before long, I was in the car, the arm went across the seat, the gearbox in reverse and off I travelled, backwards of course, covering my beat.

At 5:30 a.m. I arrived back at the police station to finish the shift and the early shift officers were rolling in smelling of coffee, booze and aftershave. I was filling the logbook out when Tyson came out.

'Under twenty-two miles, I hope, Jim?' he asked.

'Indeed Sarge,' as I looked at the mileage, 'twenty miles exactly.'

Tyson looked curiously at me. He must have noted the mileage when he checked the car and had worked out how many calls I had answered afterwards. He never said anything, but the night after, he asked me to take out a different car, which I did. As per usual, I drove forwards and backwards during the shift and it was now more than a curiosity amongst all the shifts how I was attending calls, but still not exceeding the 22-mile embargo. It just didn't make sense to them. They were baffled. Tyson checked the vehicle again that night. He checked the speedometer, the mileage, and the logbook. He was confused, but none the wiser. The other consequence of travelling around in reverse gear is that petrol consumption goes down and down rapidly. Now they were bemused. How can he be doing less mileage and using more petrol?

My secret didn't last long. A rather intoxicated man, confused and upset with life, called at the front of Littleton Police station around 4.00 a.m. one morning. The station was locked as Sergeant Tyson was on patrol, trying to catch me out. There was an emergency phone at the front door, which the drunken man used. The police radio crackled into life.

'Sierra One Control to Sergeant Tyson receiving. Sarge, there is a gentleman at the front door of Littleton Police Station. He sounds very confused and drunk. He wants to give himself up as a drunk driver. He says he has just been overtaken three times by a police car going backwards. He has driven a little further and the police car has come past him again, going backwards. He's driven a little further and another police car has overtaken him, again going backwards. He's obviously drunk far too much Sarge, shall I show you State 2 and attending?'

The secret was out and the following shift, the majority of police cars flew around Littleton and Sandford in reverse, engines screaming and arms and heads looking out of the rear windscreen. Tyson didn't realise at first, but as everyone was now travelling in reverse, it wasn't long before he took notice. What exacerbated the issue that the next night, four out of the five car drivers at Sandford reported sick with stiff necks or bad backs. Ricky, my tutor constable, was also complaining of a stiff neck in front of Tyson and the finger to my lips made sure he kept his silence. The average mile per gallon for my vehicle went from 30mpg down to 11mpg, and I was asked to account for it. I couldn't and blamed it on my ignorance of vehicles. I was interviewed by the Patrol Inspector about the reverse theory, and of course, denied it. I had not been seen driving in reverse and if not for a drunken, middle of the road hugging dawdler, who knows how long it could have gone on for? Sadly, despite my denials, it was back to the cooler for me. I counted the cars in the pound for another four weeks.

It wasn't long before OPEC fell in love with the world again and petrol prices were reduced. Himmler retired, the Patrol Inspector moved on and Ricky, my tutor constable, joined the CID.

CHAPTER THIRTEEN

SANDFORD CALLING

I got chills
They're multiplyin'
And I'm losin' control

The next radio call I received; I was on night shift. I had to travel down to Sandford to meet the new Patrol Inspector. He had asked to see me as it was obvious to everyone I wasn't happy at work. Sergeant Tyson and Littleton were doing me no favours, and I only had weeks left before I became a fully-fledged Police Constable. I had nearly completed my two-year probationary period but was becoming extremely frustrated. For the first time, I really was thinking of leaving the job. I knew I would let my parents down, but by now it was becoming intolerable.

As I drove down to see the Inspector, I passed a side road and saw a shadow. I braked and looked over my left shoulder, arm across the passenger seat and assumed my old 'reverse' driving position. I was good at travelling in reverse by now. The car screamed backwards and in a squat position at the side of the road was a young lady, knickers around ankles. Was she urinating? I asked myself and could clearly see all and sundry down below. I looked away to the other side of the street to see another young lady. She too was in the squat position, knickers around ankles doing the same.

'We're just having a piss,' one of them exclaimed.

Even though still young, I had gathered enough experience in life and intelligence to work that one out.

'Been to Dreamers,' one of them said. That was another of Sandford's top night spots.

'Will you give us a lift home?' one of them asked as she pulled up her knickers and walked to the car. I thought for a minute, then considered my recent meetings with Himmler and my imminent meeting with the new patrol Inspector Jim Morley. Then the older of the two, about my age, slim and attractive, leaned in the car window and whispered,

'Aw go on, you can shag us both if you do.'

I know what you're thinking, but I wasn't late for the appointment, and Inspector Jim Morley was a lovely man. He was polar opposite to the outgoing Inspector, and I immediately warmed to him. He asked me how life was in Littleton, and I was honest and explained the challenges I faced. He intimated that life may be better for me at Sandford and that he would monitor the situation. He thanked me, yes thanked me for the hard work I had already done, and looked forward to working with me in the future, down at Sandford. It was the first time in two years that I felt appreciated.

I drove back to Littleton as the faint signs of dawn appeared, like cracks in the sky, for a final trip up Littleton Hill and a quick freewheel down before finishing. On the ascent, a small Bedford box van came hurtling towards me on the wrong side of the road. No lights and it was that time of day, at dawn or dusk, when it's neither light nor dark and extremely difficult to see.

'Is this your vehicle, sir?' I asked, always polite.

'It is, yeah, I'm on my way to work at the slaughterhouse. I'm late. Was I speeding?' the young driver replied.

'It wasn't your speed, but do you think you should have your lights on?' I said.

'Lights on? No, I can see. I don't need em,' he replied.

'We are high on Littleton Hill, sir, what would you do if mist or fog came down?' I asked.

He looked at me, puzzled.

'I would first put on Mister Sidelights, then put on Mister Headlights,' he replied.

There comes a time when people take it just that little bit too far. This was just over the line, I thought.

'Are you taking the piss out of me?' I enquired, 'Mr Sidelights and Mr Headlights.'

'Well,' he said, 'you started it.'

I paused and said, 'Listen carefully and watch my lips. I will say it slowly. What would you do if mist *OR* fog came down, not Mister fog?'

'I'm sorry,' he said, as we both burst out laughing.

'You're being reported for speeding now,' I said.

'Oh, you're joking, aren't you?' he asked.

'Yes, I am, but you started it. Now get your lights on Mister Fog and be gone with you.'

We had a good laugh, and it was good banter between us in the village whenever I saw him.

The next night, Mrs. Collinson called the police station to report some suspicious activity at the rear of her house. She lived in a row of terraced houses that backed on to the beginning of the moors and Littleton Hill. It was a horrible night, cold, dark and raining hard. There was a lady in the street as I parked and as I got out of the police car, I asked if she was Mrs. Collinson. She held a newspaper over her head and explained she wasn't but had just seen a ginger cat get run over. The car had driven off, but under the Road Traffic Law, had no lawful need to stop. The cat was in the gutter. Deceased.

'I think it belongs here,' she said as she pointed to the white door.

Yes, it was the Collinson's door. I opened the boot of the police car and amongst the debris, including of all things a dead rabbit, sour milk, overcoat and empty beer bottles, was a police exhibits bag. With the rain now falling hard, I stood at the white door and waited to deliver yet another death message.

Tommy (I know you're thinking: 'how original for a cat's name') was ten years old. They loved that cat. Treasured it. It was a kitten from the farm, and I remained silent as the elderly couple sat in front of me crying like babies. Mr. Collinson tried to speak at one point but was too emotional, and when he opened his mouth, his top set of dentures fell out of his mouth. With quick fire reactions, the left hand scooped them out of the air and back into the oral cavity before Mrs. Collinson realised. It was awful to see them so upset.

'We could never get another Tommy,' she cried as she held the handkerchief to her face.

'No, never, never,' added Mr. Collinson with his left hand ready for the flying dentures. They had never had children, they explained, but to them, Tommy was their child.

'I suppose we will have to bury him now,' he added.

In the torrential rain, I shovelled away in the small back garden as the hills looked down upon us. It was dark and cold and just like a set from a Stephen King novel. When I reached the required depth, I asked for the body and gracefully Mr. Collinson picked up the exhibits bag, placed the side of his face on the bag, and whispered his final goodbye to his beloved Tommy. He passed the bag to Mrs. Collinson, who was inconsolable. She muttered some words and then passed the bag to me for Tommy to be lowered into his final resting place.

'Officer,' asked Mrs. Collinson, 'could we please say the Lord's prayer?'

All three of us stood holding hands in the falling rain, the dark hills looking down in this moment of grief. I began to emotionally utter the words,

'Our father, which heart in heaven, hallowed be thy name.'

Mrs. Collinson threw down some soil. It was mud to be honest, then looked at me to do the same. I was soaking wet and despite looking after me for two years, the police gaberdine had started to leak.

Mr. Collinson then started to sing Abide with Me, but soon ran out of the words and started to hum the rest. His left hand was ready for the flying dentures. When he finished and the handkerchiefs were back in the pockets, I smoothed over the soil, before joining the Collinson's back in the lounge. The suspicious activity was immaterial by now and as I was so wet, I thought it best I leave them to grieve in peace. It is interesting how we all react differently to death, and I felt for the Collinson's. I really did. I said my goodbyes and if they ever needed anything, they only had to call. I opened the front door and a like a flash, a ginger tom cat dashed in and jumped up on the back of the sofa.

'Tommy,' shrieked Mrs. Collinson.

There was still time for one or two Littleton classics before I left and staying with animals, Littleton Moors had sadly claimed another life, that of local farmer Bert Craggs. Craggsy had been out on the tops looking for his sheep and had not returned. He'd been missing for a couple of days when the alarm was raised and so we set off in our various search parties, over the vast space that led to Northshire. On the second day of searching, someone spotted in the distance, Laddie, Craggs's sheep dog, on a hillside. It was continually dipping down out of sight and then coming back up. We all headed that way and uncovered the inevitable. The post-mortem revealed that Craggsy had suffered a massive heart attack and at the age of eighty-two, in the middle of nowhere, his chance of survival was nil. Enter Chief Inspector Chicken Grit. Remember him, the one that said the owner was cruel because his chickens were hungry and pecking at grit?

He put Laddie forward for the Animal Hero Rescue Award for the fact the dog stayed with his beloved owner, night, and day until he was found.

'Despite the bad weather, Laddie displayed the utmost loyalty and devotion by remaining with farmer Albert Craggs until help arrived. Staying out for two days and two nights,

Laddie alerted the rescuers to Albert's position by running up and down the hillside and despite their best efforts, the emergency teams could not revive him. Laddie is to be rewarded with the Animal Hero Rescue Award for 1978.'

Not a good idea, I thought, when I saw it. The presentation night, amongst other rescue and bravery awards, had been scheduled in a few weeks' time and the Mayor of Sandford, Alderman Gregory, was to present the dog with an award. The local press became interested, and the Chief Inspector Chicken Grit was revelling in the attention. He was photographed with the dog on his lap, and it was all over the front pages. Laddie even wore the Chief's police hat on some photos. I couldn't speak to a Chief Inspector, remember, I had to speak to the Sergeant, who then spoke to the Inspector, who then, and so on. So, I spoke to Sgt. Tyson, who wasn't interested, and I again I told him it wasn't a good idea to give the dog an award. It was too late, however, and not my decision.

I was told, the Awards night went down really well, but was spoilt by a very uncomfortable moment when, during Laddie's moment of glory, a member of the Council presentation team asked, over the microphone, how many days and nights the dog stayed up on the tops with Bert.

'Laddie was up there for over 72 hours?' came the reply.

'What, with no food or water? What did the poor dog eat?' enquired a member of the press.

Boom, and there you have it. I said it wasn't a good idea. They wouldn't listen and I guess you would call it a mic drop these days. The audience, the stage, the presentation team fell silent as it suddenly sank in what or who the dog had eaten to stay alive. Bert's brother did comment on how light the coffin was when he carried his 'large' brother to his resting place. Laddie wagged his tail, licked his lips, proud of his new blue ribbon and medal.

Inspector Jim Morley had made it clear that he wanted me down at Sandford as soon as possible. He could see that Littleton was not the place for someone cutting his teeth in the job. Morley, however, was ruled by the same chicken grit managers, and so it took a little longer. One of those senior managers had cause to ring the Force control room one Sunday afternoon regarding a large-scale fight and disturbance at Littleton Workingmen's Club. It was a serious public order incident happening now. Assistant Chief Constable King was witnessing the disturbance on television at home and demanded that *his* patrols got to the club as soon as possible to quell the riot. The police radio came alive.

'Control room to 776. When you arrive, can you give me a situation report? ACC King is monitoring the channel,' said the radio operator.

The Police Chief was at home watching television on that Sunday afternoon when the presenter said,

'And now we go to Sandford for the latest action from the National Darts Knockout.'

Yes, fame for Sandford at last when the local darts hero, Cheeky Chalky White, took on one of the greatest dart players of all time, the Crafty Cockney. The Chief was watching but was not happy with events. Cheeky pulled the stunt of all stunts when the Crafty Cockney was way ahead in the game. Cheeky said that the dart board was damaged and was not the correct dimensions stipulated in the competition rules. The crowd was incensed. Beer was being thrown, there was jostling, pushing and then fighting. The police radio crackled into life once again.

'776 we have the Tactical Unit from Sandcome on its way. The dog man (and it was a man in those days) is en route from Sandford, Traffic Department are also making their way. ACC King estimates between two-three hundred involved in a public disorder incident. Sierra One Control to Inspector Morley, did you receive the last?'

World War III had officially been declared on Littleton Workingmen's Club and ACC King was Commander-in-Chief, nowadays called the Gold Commander. It was around 4:00 p.m. and I had stopped to write some reports in the police vehicle. Apart from the imminent beginning of World War III at Littleton Workingmen's

Club, it was relatively quiet on the streets that Sunday. Sierra One control room was now upping the ante and telling me neighbouring Divisions were being asked to provide reinforcements. This was large scale, as in, very large. However, I was troubled by it all and very curious. I was sitting in the police vehicle writing my reports, wait for it, in the car park of Littleton Workingmen's Club. I was there at the club where the riot was taking place. I knew the steward, Phil Rutter, we both went to the same barbers, Kev's, and I went to school with his girlfriend.

'776, do we have a sit rep please for ACC King? Should I show you at the scene?' asked the panicking radio operator.

It was only a matter of time before riot shields, crash helmets, batons and stormtroopers would be marching through the front doors to do battle with the revellers. But it was extremely quiet in the car park, a couple of cars maybe. A quick peek through the club windows revealed the bar and concert room in darkness. How odd, I thought as the sirens in the distance became louder and louder. I knew that Phil and his girlfriend, Janet, had the apartment above the club. It was accessible via a rear door and up some stairs. I knocked at the door and could see two figures sat on the settee through the frosted glass. As one of them moved to answer the door, I saw the TV screen and adduced they were both watching the telly.

'Jimmy,' Phil said as he opened the door, 'I'm just watching telly, Chalkie White stuffing it up that cockney wanker. You should have come down last week. It was a brilliant atmosphere. Great darts match.'

Oh dear, last week. Did he say last week?

'Last week Phil?' I asked.

'Yeah, last week why?' he replied

I confirmed with Phil that the club was closed and empty. I walked back to the front car park to see police personnel carriers, twenty officers, crash helmets, riot shields, traffic vehicles, blue flashing lights, a police dog and a few heads pressed against the club windows looking curiously inside.

'Sierra One to 776. ACC King wants an immediate update. He also wants the steward reporting for holding a disorderly house as well,' the operator blasted out.

Like a comedian with his audience before him, I stood and waited. Timing was of the essence. All the police radios were now on 'talk through' or, to put it simply, everyone could now hear what I was about to say, including Assistant Chief Constable King. Inspector Morley tried to push past me. I held out my arm to stop him. I stood there, the focus of attention, everyone looking at me. I pressed the yellow transmit button on the radio, allowing me to speak to my ever-growing audience.

'776 to Sierra One Control. All quiet on arrival, the club is empty and closed. The TV programme that ACC King is watching *at home* at this moment in time is recorded. The darts game was last Sunday. Can everyone stand down please? There is no disorder whatsoever at Littleton Workingmens Club,' and I let go of the yellow talk button.

There was complete silence in the car park. Even the police dogs sensed something was amiss. Mouths opened in front of me, shoulders shrugged. The audience was not amused, eyebrows raised that high that even Dick Fosbury would have struggled to get over them. The radio fell silent as no doubt the operators were evaluating what I had just said. The crowd in front of me broke the silence.

'He's watching a recording of last week's match on TV, fucking joke.'

'Are you joking?'

'We've just come all the way from...'

'You are winding me up now.'

'Which clown has called this in?'

'776 to Sierra One Control. Did you receive? Can you make sure Assistant Chief Constable King is made aware, please? The darts match was played last Sunday. The Chief is watching a recording.'

CHAPTER FOURTEEN

DOWNTOWN

By the rivers of Babylon
Where we sat down

My first shift at Sandford was from 2:00 p.m. until 10:00 p.m. More commonly known as 'afternoons'. I was allocated the mobile patrol beat of the Dudkirk estate. It was next door to Beacon Hill's estate and another deprived area of the city. In places it was bad, in other places very bad. Inspector Jim Morley was as good as his word, and my transfer eventually went through. What expedited matters were during my last night shift at Littleton, a local fishing tackle shop was broken into and although this was pre-DNA era, the offender(s) had left quite a sizeable chunk of their hand in the window of the shop. There was a trail of blood which I followed down the street to a nursery and from the elevated building looked out over Littleton and to the bright lights of Sandford in the distance. In between was the Beacon Hill estate. It was like Moses was standing before me and parted the seas to show a direct pathway from the fishing tackle shop to the estate.

'Go now my son, your passage will be safe,' said Moses, 'go and catch the bad guys.'

I knew the road where the pathway came out; it was near Kev's barbers. It was back to the police mini and this time travelling forwards; I headed towards Beacon Hill estate. Once again, timing, was impeccable, as Robert Parkinson and his mate were just crossing the main dual carriageway to enter the estate. I could see them in the distance and a police patrol car was heading their way. I radioed for the police driver to stop the two lads. Inspector Morley did just that and when I saw that Robert was missing half his hand, the pair were arrested. All the fishing tackle, air guns and as much as the two lads could carry were recovered from some allotments on the path Moses created for me. Morley was impressed again and the day after, it was done. I was transferred.

Sgt Tyson was now, thankfully, history and my new Sergeants, Darcy and Richards, welcomed me into the new parade room. I was apprehensive and sat around for the formal parade. 'Stand please,' said a voice as the inspector and sergeants walked in. Handcuffs, truncheon, pocket notebook and torch had to be displayed, and Inspector Morley walked up and down the line, inspecting the shift. All fifteen of us. Morley sat in the middle of Darcy and Richards as they allocated the beats and refreshment times. It was all new to me and I was given three incidents to attend on Dudkirk estate before I had even left the station. That was unheard of in sleepy Littleton. I checked the police vehicle before driving out. You know, for ball bearings, marbles, dead rabbits, smelly fish, ginger tom cats and the like, but was told nothing like that happened at Sandford.

As I approached the end council house on the Dudkirk estate for the first job in the list, I could clearly see there was no garden gate or fence like all the other houses and, worryingly, no front door. Passing through the doorway diagonally was a very long wooden telegraph pole. It protruded from the front door and went over next door's garden and nearly onto the roadway. Inside the front door area of the house, I could see the eaves and a drop down to the foundations and waste rubble under the house. The floorboards had all gone, and the telegraph pole went through the front door space and into the area that one would call the front room. It was merely a shell. I looked upstairs and saw a ladder. There was no staircase. There was a crackling sound coming from the corner of the room and I tip toed across the eaves to try to find the victim of a burglary at the address. Sat over a metal dustbin with the end of the telegraph pole burning away, smoking a roll up cigarette, was a thin, scraggily dressed man in his 60s. He had long untidy grey, matted hair and a wispy catweazle type beard.

'Bastards have screwed me, haven't they? Took the lot,' he mumbled.

As I got near, he told me to watch the corner as it was over the toilet. I looked up to the ceiling to find a plank of wood across the eaves up above, which I presumed he used as a toilet. He was obviously climbing the ladder and going to the toilet as if there was one present, which there wasn't. It was a long way down but in the corner of the back room, well back shell not room, is where the human waste dropped and was congregating. It stank.

'Got the meters, haven't they? Took everything.' He said as I looked around. Everything! I questioned myself.

'Where are the floorboards, the doors, the fence?' I asked.

'Burnt em. How am I supposed to keep warm? Anyway, can I have a crime number for the social so I can get some money?'
He was 38 years of age.

The Craddocks was my next call, a notorious family with five young brothers carrying out the family's tradition of crime, or 'grafting', as they called it. They saw it as a vocation and were good at it. The father, Bill Craddock, was a crafty old fox and when a council electrician found plastic bags full of jewellery, watches and cash in the loft, he called the police. I met the electrician at the call box on the estate and when he told me the address it meant nothing, but when he mentioned the name Craddock, it meant everything. I knew that father Bill would not let me in unless I had a search warrant, issued by a Magistrate of course. This would have taken time, and it was more a matter for the CID Department in those days. I decided to go to the Craddocks and chance my luck.
Unlike my colleagues, I had never really had any dealings with the family, being based in Littleton. I didn't know what to expect,

I was naive. Well, in some respects, I did know what to expect, abuse, and I got it. Bill in his string vest and sons blocked the front door.

'You're not going anywhere, pal. Not unless you've got a warrant,' shouted Bill as his spittle showered my face. The three sons behind him goading and laughing at me. I tried to explain, as best I could, about obtaining a warrant and that I would get one if he didn't let me look in the loft. Bill was having none of it. One of my new sergeants arrived and before long, three police vehicles were parked outside the Craddocks.

'One look in that loft, Bill, and then we are on our way,' said one of my colleagues. He had dealt with the family before and knew Bill. There seemed to be a small chance now.

'You'll need some ladders and you're not borrowing mine,' said Bill as he pulled the door open.

'Fuck em Dad, don't let em in, fuck em,' came the chorus from the sons.

Sergeant Richards, Steve Spencer and yours truly stood at the top of Bill Craddock's stairs, looking up at the loft hatch. The plan was to lift 'Spenny', who was the smallest of the three, up to the hatch for him to take a quick peek. All went according to plan. We held Spencer up long enough for him to unlatch the hook and eye lock on the loft door and climb in.

'You'll find fuck all up there,' said the gathering at the bottom of the stairs.

As Spenny shone his torch, came the inevitable announcement,

'No, no bags at all up here Sarge,' and as he edged himself to drop back down to our outstretched arms, his tunic belt caught on the hook on the loft hatch. Like a scene from a pantomime, PC Steven Spencer swung backwards and forwards, suspended from the ceiling by the loft hook. The bellows of laughter from family Craddock was deafening and two of the lads ran into the street, shouting for people to come in and see the swinging cop.

'Get me down, get me down,' cried Spencer.

Sergeant Richards and I joined the remaining members of the family as we fell about, laughing hysterically at Spencer. He was attempting to reach back into the loft and kicked the bedroom door. Immediately, the laughter stopped. Bill Craddock came running up the stairs.

'Don't you fucking dare kick that door or go into the bedroom, do you hear me? Don't you dare.'

'Is that where the stolen goods are, Bill?' shouted Spencer.

'No. There are no stolen goods. None, never have been. The donkey is in the bedroom. It's got a cholic, don't disturb it,' replied Bill as he tried to protect the door with open arms.

The laughter stopped immediately. Did he just say there was a donkey in the bedroom with cholic?

Sergeant Richards opened the bedroom door to indeed reveal a donkey in the middle of the room. It appeared that the animal was unwell due to the state of the bedroom floor and the stench. Picture the scene, a donkey looking at me curiously whilst stood in pools of shit, the stench disgusting and my colleague PC Spencer, swinging from the roof in full uniform in between us, shouting 'Help, Help, get me down.' The Craddock family are on the stairs, not sure whether to physically assault us or laugh. I was a little unsure of what to do next. This was my first day on my new shift. Sgt. Richards leant forward and whispered in my ear, 'Welcome to Sandford Division, son.'

Inspector Morley seemed happy I was now at Sandford, and I soon learned the ropes, getting used to new colleagues and staff. Unlike Littleton, once you had been allocated your beat at parade time, you left the station and didn't come back until your refreshment period or end of shift. Himmler had long gone, and I met his replacement, not by appointment, but by chance. Superintendent Brown lived on Sandford Police Division. He had come back to Sandford to retire. He didn't have long left in the job and was looking forward to his pension.

On the afternoon shift one Saturday, I was sent to an address in the north of the city after a call about a grandson, a skateboard, and a robbery. When the front door opened, there stood Superintendent Brown in his dressing gown and slippers. He explained that his grandson had been playing down on the estate with some other friends when the local thugs descended upon them and relieved the youngsters of their skateboards, with threats and the odd slap here and there. The grandson told me the story and gave me the descriptions of the four suspects and skateboards. The name 'Chirpy' had been mentioned, which was the nickname for the Finch family. Young Gary Finch was a tearaway, and I went to school with his dad, Malcolm. I left the Superintendent's house, and he asked to be kept updated. I went straight to the Finch address and Dad, Malcolm, gave me a hard time, even though I knew him well. Police always picking on his lad for no reason. At that moment, Gary and three others came around the corner on said stolen skateboards. Dad couldn't run, but his bellows were enough for Gary and family to later attend Sandford Police Station where the youngster apologised but said the other three lads had made him do it. At the request of Dad, I took young Gary down to the cells, where only a couple of years before I had been opening bombs. I left him behind the locked door of a cell, as his dad asked me to. It had a minimal effect on the young tearaway who later became a guest at many of Her Majesty's hotels.

I returned the skateboards to Superintendent Brown and updated him about the four suspects and that they had all been put forward for a police caution. He was very impressed, and now I had a get out of jail card in my back pocket. Gary was refused a police caution and ended up in the courts. I could now walk the corridors of Sandford nick, chest out without the fear of being an 'unknown'. *I* was the one who got the Superintendents grandsons skateboard back and arrested the suspects. *I* was in the very best of good books with the Superintendent and it lasted well just over a week.

Inspector Lee Fearon had a desk job somewhere. That is, until he upset someone, probably Himmler, and was returned to 'patrol duties' as the Station Inspector. He was now a very angry and irritable man and took great delight in telling me that detecting the Superintendents' crime meant absolutely nothing to him. Nothing. His shouts and threats could be heard everyday up and down the corridors. It was best to get out and stay out. It wasn't long before Superintendent Brown retired, and the final days of my jail card had been played. The next incumbent to the top post was out of the Inspector Fearon school of fear and communication.

I was in trouble almost immediately as very early one morning a sports car pulled into the police station car park and headed my way. It was the new superintendent who wound down his car window. He was in his disco gear and reminded me of the older mid-life, 'Mr. Medallion Man' I had seen propped at many a night club bar. His red Hawaiian shirt was open to his waist and his hairy chest and medallion fully exposed.

'Do you know who I am, son?' he enquired.

'I do Sir. You're the new Superintendent, Mr. Ahern,' I replied.

'Well, why are you not stood to attention and saluting me?' he barked.

The notion of emotional intelligence or EQ was a long way off but even then, as a very young naive constable, I knew that if I told him the reason why I was not saluting him was because he was dressed like a twat, I wouldn't be able to handle the repercussions. I tried to explain that he was not able to return the salute, but it was futile. His sports car set off, wheels spinning, as he headed for his parking space in the garage. It was pointless going anywhere as I knew I would be hauled back in to face the Superintendent, or worst still, Inspector Fearon. As predicted, the police radio soon crackled into life,

'PC 776 receiving. Can you make your way to Sandford Police Office and see Inspector Morley?'

Phew! A least my own shift Inspector, who I knew would look at this from my perspective. I had always been taught, when marching the many thousands of miles, I stamped out in that drill hall, that you salute the uniform, not the person. And the person must be in a position to salute you back. No uniform, no salute. Ahern wasn't the US president.

'I know that,' said Morley, 'but he's not happy and he says you came across as arrogant.'

I was 'grounded' for four weeks, which meant I couldn't drive police vehicles and had to perform Station Security every day for a month. I was like Steve McQueen being locked in the cooler again. Word quickly got around the station about Ahern and my punishment and I was approached by a Police Federation (Police Union) representative who said Ahern was totally in the wrong and to complain about him. It was still futile. It was his train set; he did what he wanted with it.

When my sentence was completed, I returned the cooler baseball and glove to the office and continued to carry out both foot and mobile patrol duties in Sandford. It was a busy place and crime was rising. I was still cutting my teeth. I was asked if I was interested in performing the role of a 'tutor constable'. This was a role whereby you took a recruit under your wing, as PC Ricky Reynolds had done with me, to show them the ropes, so to speak. I suppose it would give me some credibility, so I volunteered my services. I was then introduced to the new recruit I was to mentor, Police Constable Willy Townsend. I knew from the start that I had made a terrible mistake.

'Just a minor point, Jim,' he said to me on our first meeting, 'but your shoes are a little dirty tonight, and I wouldn't have dealt with that last incident like you did. What I would have done was…'
Willy had only just joined, and he was becoming instantly irritating.

I tried my best to advise Willy without stating the obvious. He was a mature recruit and more experienced in life than I was.
I chatted through with my grandad one day over a cup of tea and he told me that when he was foreman on the building sites,

they had employed a brew boy called a Willy Townsend. It couldn't obviously be the same person, as my grandad said that 'his' Willy Townsend was really stupid. There was no way he would get in the police.

'We couldn't trust him with the dinner list,' my grandad said. 'He was good for brewing up and mixing cement, but he even got that wrong, sometimes.'

Yes, you've guessed already, it was indeed the same Willy Townsend and when I told my grandad, he nearly swallowed his false teeth.

The police radio burst into life,

'Any patrol to attend a large-scale fight at the junction of Moor Road and Brown Street.'

It was around 1:30 a.m. as we drove to the fight. On arrival, there seemed to be a dozen or so young lads in the middle of the road. Arms down by their side, fists clenched and just waiting for the spark. They looked angry. Two against twelve were not the odds I liked. Willy was quiet and stood behind me. It was tense and my very diplomatic approach was getting me nowhere. The lads were moving closer and closer, and I sensed the inevitable.

'You a goalkeeper?' asked a big lad at the front. I nodded.

'We played you a couple of weeks ago and you saved a penalty.' He turned to the others and said, 'cracking goalkeeper.' The tension lifted and we chatted about football, and I explained that young families lived on the street and could the lads keep the noise down a little.

'No problem, mate, no problem. All the best now and hope you get a good draw in the cup. What time is it, pal?' We started to shake hands. As I turned my wrist to look at my new Casio watch, one of the others in the group said,

'Nearly quarter to two, Baz.'

PC Willy Townsend, please enter the stage.

'When Mickey Mouse's hand reaches two and the other hand reaches eight. Who's a clever boy then? Who can tell the time then?' the clown spurted out. Twelve heads spun around on their shoulders and looked directly at us. The anger etched deep.

'What did you just fucking say?' one of them asked Willy.

The first punch is always the worst to take as the adrenalin hasn't kicked in by then. You still see the stars and feel something in the second and third punches but just hope your colleagues come quickly. They weren't too far away and two or three of the lads were eventually arrested for assault and affray. My relationship with Willy ended there. It was over. He tried to explain, but I told him to keep quiet. Every incident we attended, keep quiet, just keep quiet, Willy.

'Willy, Willy, just shut the fuck up!' I blurted out on one occasion.

The next weekend was the afternoon shift, 2:00 p.m.-10:00 p.m. and often the night shift sergeants would come in and ask for volunteers to stay on until 2:00 a.m. When I say volunteer, it is with tongue in cheek. They always dropped it on you at the last minute as you had the regular 'Friday night Franks,' who would go sick every weekend when on night shift. It was nearing 10:00 p.m., and I was heading back to the police station, no doubt to be volunteered to stay on until 2:00 a.m.. I got a call to attend the Happy Trees estate. This was a concrete monstrosity, built in the late 1960s to avert the housing crisis and give the cash strapped council some more grants from the Government of the day. It was called Happy Trees because the road that the estate replaced was called Happy Oak Road. Some of the blocks of flats were named after trees.

'Miss Ashworth, 153 Chestnut reporting suspicious circumstances, 776.' Crackled the police radio.

When the door opened, Miss Ashworth, I presumed, presented herself in a totally see-through negligee, revealing everything underneath. No, not the usual cardigan, tracksuit bottoms and

Slippers, but everything else. Or should I say, lack of everything else. She was dressed in white and left nothing to the imagination. It was all out on the kitchen table for all to see. Willy didn't have to be told to be quiet. He remained motionless as he couldn't take his eyes off Miss Ashworth.

The young lady was surprised there were two of us and asked if I knew PC Decker. He was lovely; she told me, and she liked him as he looked out for her. I bet he did. But I wasn't going to make an issue with it. Best to keep on the right side of Decker. As I took details of this would be 'suspicious character', I could see Willy was mesmerised. He couldn't take his eyes off her long legs, naked thighs and white lacy bra.

'Could one of you not stay to make sure this man doesn't come back?' she asked. 'In fact, you both could stay as it may be fun with two of you.'

Now that wasn't difficult to translate, was it? Willy, on the other hand, was a little slow on the uptake and engaged Miss Ashworth on the resource and financial issues affecting Sandford Police and why it wouldn't be justified to the rate payers of the city for us to stay. When we got back into the police car and headed for the Police Station to finish, the conversation was obviously on Miss Ashworth's lack of clothing and the way she presented herself.

'What do you mean?' asked Willy.

I explained that the probability of there being a suspicious character was nil and she had rung because it was Saturday night, 9:40 p.m. and the wine had probably kicked in. She perhaps wanted Decker to call to 'comfort' her as she lived alone.

'Know what I mean Willy?' as I winked at him. 'Stay well away, well away.'

'Do you mean there wasn't a suspicious man she was really interested in?'

'Yes Willy, yes, did you not read the signals? Don't ever get tempted.'

'Oh wow,' said Willy, 'I never thought she wanted male company, fancy that.'

I walked up into the briefing room to finish duty and go and meet my good friend, alcohol.

'776 you have to stay on until 2:00 a.m. as Frank has gone sick from the night shift,' said the Sergeant. 'We only need one of you so PC Townsend can go home.'

Friday night, Frank always went sick on nights. I was allocated a beat I hadn't worked before, Mountford car beat. It was out east of the town and neighboured on Eastshire Police area. It was a usual Saturday night with calls to fights, domestic disputes, road traffic accidents and then, around 1:00 a.m. a radio call that caught my attention.

'Any patrol please, fight in progress, 153, Chestnut, Happy Trees Estate. Ambulance en route.'

I made my way but coming from out east, other patrols were arriving a lot earlier than I was. I parked near the other police vehicles and ambulance and could see officers grappling with a young lad on the floor. The ambulance to my right had its doors open and someone was being attended to. He or she looked a mess.

'Fucking get off me, he was shagging my missus. Get off, get off,' said the lad on the floor. Stood at the door of 153 was Miss Ashworth with a policewoman. There were lots of tears, tissues and sniffles. I walked towards the ambulance and with a head that resembled a beetroot, he turned towards me. I recognised the voice before the face.

'Hiya Jim. I suppose you think I've been stupid, don't you?' said the patient.

'Willy?'

Grandad was right. That was the end of Willy.

Throughout my career, I was a tutor for numerous of my colleagues. Some later became Police Chiefs. The majority stayed midstream, but some fell by the wayside, some became alcoholics, some were arrested, some ended up on the front pages and the odd one went to prison. Some never made it, such is the rich tapestry of life.

CHAPTER FIFTEEN

POLICE HUMOUR

The silicon chip inside her head
Gets switched to overload
Tell me why I don't like Mondays

'Sierra One Control to PC 776. Can you attend suspicious circumstances on York Street, near Wimpey's. Report of a man lying in a shop doorway,' announced the call taker on the radio.

It was around 1:00 a.m. as I made my way on foot. What awaited me? A drunk, a dead body? I arrived in quick time and sure enough, there was a figure of a man, face down in the doorway. The area was a good spot for the foot patrols as it was a long way back from the street and there was a small wall near the door and a protruding drainpipe. So, in the darkness, you could walk up the pathway, sit on the wall and slide behind the drainpipe. You could still see the main shopping street, York St., but no one could see you. Many an officer had previously watched a passionate couple or two get down to their thing after meeting in Dreamers' night club.

The body was indeed there, face down. It looked disfigured. I moved closer and could see blood trickling, but couldn't see where from. I pressed the radio button,

'776 to Sierra Control. I am at the scene now. There is one injured party, face down and bleeding,' I reported.

'Sierra Control, is the person breathing?' the Control Room asked.

'Wait one, Sierra Control, I will turn him over.'

I leant down and took hold of the right shoulder. It was closest to me. I pulled on it and asked as I did so,

'Alright mate? Hello, can you hear me, mate?'

I pulled hard on the shoulder and turned over the torso. There appeared to be some kind of thin line attached to the man's shirt and it was wrapped around the drainpipe. I pulled hard on it.

'776, 776, 776, 776...' I stuttered out into the radio as I fell backwards, 'can you, can you, there's a dead, dead, dead body, ambulance, please, ambulance quickly,' I screamed into the radio.

The body seemed to empty itself all over my shiny boots. It was disgusting, and I looked down and tip toed around what looked like large body organs. There was now lots of blood and I immediately jumped backwards as this flood of internal offal came gushing out, following me into York Street.

The laughter came first, followed by the applause. I looked across York Street to see some of the shift, and the afternoon shift, the ones that got ordered to stay on, laughing and clapping away at me. I looked again at the body and back at the officers. They were falling about laughing. As the blood and guts trickled away, I could now see under torchlight the mannequin's head and a very deflated body. The Police Control Room was transmitting,

'Sierra One to PC 776 do you need... 'laughter'... Do you need an... 'laughter'... ambulance?'

Bastards! I forgave, but I never forgot!

And so it went on. That was the way things happened back then.

Some weeks later, the radio crackled into life once more,

'Sierra One Control to PC 1464 receiving.'

'1464 go ahead.'

'Can you make your way to the cricket ground please? The spare land adjacent to the car park. There's a suspicious package.'

Not quite a Willy Townsend, but not far off. PC 1461 Jordan Barclay was not well liked. Someone described his character as akin to

eating salt and vinegar crisps with cuts on your fingers. That aggravating stinging sensation when he was around you. He wasn't on my shift and once again I had been ordered to stay on until 2:00 a.m.. Barclay arrived in the police car at the spare ground to find a white polystyrene box sat in the middle of the empty space.

'1464 to Sierra One. I've arrived at the car park and yes, there is a white box in the middle of the car park,' radioed Barclay.

'Sierra One to 1464, can you describe the box?' asked the radio operator.

'Yeah, white, polystyrene with a yellow sticker on it saying Biohazard.'

'Sierra One Control to 1464, can you come back to the police office please? You will need to be suited and booted up for this.'

A gap of fifteen minutes passed before PC Barclay returned and parked his police vehicle on the spare land. Without prompting, the police radio crackled back into life,

'Sierra One to 1464, don't park too close to the package if it's Biohazard.'

Barclay duly got back in the police vehicle and drove it to the edge of the spare land, and once again got out. He went to the rear of the police vehicle and the gathered audience now began to giggle very quietly as he removed a white forensic suit and start to put it on.

'Sierra One Control to 1464, please ensure that there is tape over the extremities of the suit and your wellington boots and gloves,' the control room instructed.

For the next twenty minutes Barclay put on the white suit, wellingtons and gloves and taped over them to ensure the biohazard would not get on his skin. He then took out of the back of the police car what can only be described as a very large plastic cock pit. It transpires that someone on his shift had made it from his daughter's paddling pool, plastic camping poles and duct tape. It was huge, and he placed it over his head and shoulders. He looked like a rectangular version of

Mr. Blobby or a giant Buzz Lightyear as he started the long walk back to the white box. The front of the kiddy pool helmet was see-through but started to steam up.

'1464 to Sierra One receiving. I'm struggling with this clothing, to be honest,' Barclay said into his radio.

'Keep going 1464,' the control room replied, 'we have been on to the isolation hospital, and it seems it's one of their boxes. Can you take it to the police vehicle please and they will collect it when they arrive later?'

Barclay walked slowly, sometimes tripping, as he balanced the polythene frame on his head and shoulders. He was holding it with one hand and then bent down to pick up the box. The box balanced with one hand and the polythene helmet held with the other. Then, the unthinkable happened.

'1464 to Sierra One, come in quickly. 1464, come in Sierra One. 1464 come in please. Someone's pinching my police car,' Barclay screamed into his police radio.

A dark figure had slipped into the driver's seat, started the engine, and drove away. PC Jordan Barclay was now watching his police vehicle drive off whilst holding the white biohazard box and his Mr. Blobby helmet. He set off running, tripping over the oversized wellington boots. The bio box went up in the air, landing with a crash.

'Sierra One Control received that, thanks,' said the radio operator who was obviously in on the prank, 'can you ensure that the contents of the box don't get spilled please? Any patrol available to attend the Cricket Club, 1464 reporting his police car being stolen.'

The audience, now hysterical, slipped away as the white suited Mr. Blobby sat in the middle of the cricket club car park. The biohazard was a coffee jar full of water, which was now smashed. The walk back to the police station wasn't too far for Barclay, but it must have seemed a lifetime away.

As the other patrol cars drove by, they sounded their horns and waved at Barclay. I am told that the reception committee, his shift, had a guard of honour and just applauded him all the way into the police station. His police car was parked in a bay in the car park.

To his credit, that time, Barclay saw the funny side of things and no doubt joined in the many japes and pranks that followed. Barclay joined the CID later in his short career and I could see why his shift played the prank they did. They were happy to see the back of him, by all accounts. I worked with him for a very short period of time, and he made the new recruit Willy 'the negligee' Townsend, look a saint. We fell out many times, but when he arrested some witnesses from one of my investigations, he crossed the line. Barclay eventually resigned, saying that Sandford Police was full of idiots. He had a university education and found it difficult to work with lemmings. I think the best word to describe him is sanctimonious. He took up a post with Hong Kong Police and I haven't heard of him since, thankfully.

I was still learning the new procedures at Sandford Police station. I had now worked some of the beats and had been subject to the car pound duties from time to time. Another punishment duty was standing guard at the front gates of the police station checking vehicles and occupants etc. as they drove in. My misfortune was to be allocated the 'station duty' shift, for a four-hour period, one particular night shift. My time stood to attention was from 2.00am until 6.00am. It certainly wasn't a busy period!

Around 4:00 a.m. the police radio crackled into life once again.

'Sierra One to 776 receiving. Can you collect the keys and open the mortuary please? One coming in,' said the radio operator.

It was customary for the station duty officer to open the mortuary for any incoming deceased. This saved the undertakers from calling at the police station with the body in their vehicle. Undertakers were also on a call out rota and so it was always seen that the police should manage the mortuary.

As a child, I was always scared of the dark and bogey men, because we were all taught, 'they will come to get you'. The thought of collecting the keys, opening the back door of the mortuary, walking inside in the dark, didn't really enthral me, but I was a grown man now and so I did it. Frightened of bogey men, me?

The mortuary was on the other side of the town centre, so the walk from the police station, across the deserted market square, was a distance and lonely. It was exactly 4:00 a.m.. The market clock chimed as I walked past. I arrived at the old Victorian building and looked up at the gargoyles on each corner looking out over the square. They were devil like figures with teeth and angry looking faces. A breeze was blowing, and I became aware of a rustling sound coming from behind the building. I paused and opened the old iron gates. The hinges creaked as I did so. The rustling became louder when a group of dried leaves blew towards me in a wind funnel. The square was quiet. Not a soul around. Not a sound. It was eerily quiet. Vincent Price and Peter Cushing wouldn't be out of place. I clicked my police issue torch into action and walked slowly down the path at the side of the mortuary. The front door was obviously in public view, so only the living ever walked in and out that way. My job was to ensure the doors were open at the back for the inbound deceased. I could hear my leather soles crunch on the gravel floor as I fumbled the old key into the lock. It was very dark, and it took a few attempts with the key, as I nervously looked around. I turned the key slowly, pulled on the latch, and the clunk startled me. I had never done this before and was hoping my first time would be in daylight. I pushed on door and watched it move slowly backwards. The leaves blew around my feet and all that was missing was the sound of Michael Jackson's 'Thriller'.

The smell hit me immediately. A mix of lavender, stale alcohol, and disinfectant. Each mortuary smelled the same, it was distinctive. I stood there and watched some the leaves go before me onto the tiled mortuary floor. The torch light illuminated the two big plastic doors in front of me, which I presumed were the entrance to the main examination area. I fumbled for the light switches but couldn't find them. The click of my boots on the floor loudly echoed as I slowly made my way inside. It was very dark and I remember looking upwards and the ceiling being very high. There was a big wooden beam overhead. I slowly pushed open one of the big plastic doors. The wind gushed in and 'bang'. A loud noise from behind me.

The leaves fell to the floor. The wind stopped. It was now even quieter and darker. I turned around quickly and shone the torch at the back of the now closed door. It had slammed shut. This was becoming quite unpleasant, and I could hear my heart thumping away. I kept talking to myself as I ventured further into the building. I let the plastic door close slowly behind me and now entered the main examination room. I froze. I was immediately conscious of the two examination tables to my right and noticed that they were both occupied. Both had the customary white sheets pulled over the corpses. I shone the torch around the walls in desperation to find the light switches. I kept telling myself that dead bodies are dead bodies, they won't move. None the less, I kept looking. I kept telling myself dead people wouldn't harm me and to keep going. I stood in silence with the two dead bodies to my right, with the small torchlight illuminating their bodies, unable to find the light switch.

On the far wall, I saw the switch and slowly edged my way past the two corpses. There was a noise. Was there? Did I hear something? I definitely heard it. This was now scary. I'm sure the noise came from one of the two examination tables. It sounded like a faint groan. It is not uncommon for gases to escape sometimes, but this rationale didn't seem to calm me at 4:00 a.m. in the darkness. I stood motionless and listened again. There was a deafening silence. My heart was pumping as fast as ever. I quickly looked behind me, but there was nothing there. Then I remembered the key. Oh no, the key was still in the door! I shone my torch towards the door and the first body start to rise. I froze. The second followed soon after, both groaning as they rose.

I hit the plastic doors with such force they both burst open and slapped hard into the walls as I reached for the back door and the latch, but it wouldn't open. I tried and tried, but the thing was stuck. I glanced over my shoulder to see the sheeted white figures coming through the plastic doors, groaning as they came towards me. I started to panic as the latch eventually flew open. The wind blew into my face and the branches of the trees swayed over head as I ran and ran and ran. I could hear the gargoyles laughing at me as I hit the market square. I really don't know what happened after that. I think I broke the 100-metre world record as I ran and ran, not looking over my shoulder. I didn't stop. Like Forest Gump, I kept on running and running into the night.

When I thought I was at a safe distance, and under the street lighting, I slowed and turned to face whatever it was that was chasing. I heard some clapping and whistling, which somehow didn't fit in with the scenario. Then I saw them, the whole shift were applauding, with some on their knees, laughing hysterically. The two sheeted bodies now clapping loudly and beckoning me back over towards them. It was all part and parcel of the job. Welcome to Sandford!

Unfortunately, all didn't end well. I survived the jape and so did my two stooges, who had probably had the prank played on them. A few months later, another young in service 'victim' but ex para smashed the first 'corpse' across the face with his truncheon and held the second in a headlock until they passed out. Both were hospitalised. Other tales of empty coffins in the church yards ended badly. Maybe jape or prank is the wrong word, but at the time it was all part of the job. The culture. The release. It's how we forgot.

CHAPTER SIXTEEN

HAPPY TREES

Just a castaway, an island lost at sea, oh
Another lonely day, with no one here but me, oh
I'll send an S.O.S to the world

As previously mentioned, the monstrosity, Happy Trees estate, was built in the late 1960s, to avert a housing crisis and to bring much needed income into the area. Sadly, the promised funding didn't fully materialise, which resulted in cheap and plentiful. There were some good people on the estate and nice flats, but you had to look for them. Headlines in the national press proclaimed that Happy Trees Estate was *the* benefits capital of the UK. Over 90% of the inhabitants claimed some form of state aid.

When I was first allocated the Happy Trees car beat, I was totally unprepared. I was lucky that the car was 'doubled up', due to the nature of previous incidents and some of the residents. I can't remember who my colleague was on that first day on that beat, but when we attended a call to one of the 16 tower blocks, I was told to back the car away from the allotted car parking spaces.

'Don't park in there, whatever you do,' he said as I manoeuvred the police car.

Before I could ask why, the windscreen was covered in what I first thought was rain but we either had extremely large seagulls or it was something much worse.

'See what I mean? It will wash off. Last week Decker parked on here and a fridge freezer came through the roof.'

It always intrigued me when politicians and so-called leaders went on TV saying, 'we will make the parents more accountable. Children will be made to do this and that.' Not on Happy Trees estate they wouldn't. Kids didn't know where mum or dad were half the time. They stole to eat and survive. There were literally thousands of instances of domestic and violent disturbances, children left abandoned, feral youths roaming. The child abuse scandals were to land a couple of decades later.

A radio call, one night, to a 'domestic dispute' was nothing out of the ordinary on Happy Trees. I didn't know the family and when the front door opened a young woman, dressed in pyjamas, presented herself. She sported two black eyes and had long black uncombed hair, matted with what looked like peas and blood. In a strong Irish accent but in a sympathetic whisper, she said,

'He's gone now sir, it's ok now. He's gone.'

She was a pitiful sight, and with some persuasion, I entered the flat. It was a mess. I could sense she just wanted me to go. I explained that no one should tolerate what she had obviously been through and he couldn't get away with it. Head bowed, now showing the physical evidence, she whispered,

'It's ok Sir. I'm ok, it will be fine.'

She didn't want to pursue a complaint. Her partner had come home for the benefits money to gamble away and when she resisted, she got the pan of peas about her head and face. The only positive being that the pan and peas were cold. Back then, the police approach was basic and dismal. If she didn't want to pursue the complaint all the way through to court, then that was it. No further action. Sign the pocketbook and away to the next job. She didn't want to go to hospital, one reason being it was too far, and he had taken all the money. Another was the sad state of her acceptance. This is how it is. I hate you approach, but please don't leave me.

I eventually traced her partner to a local pub, The Brown Cow. He was busy playing cards and gambling the money away. I took great delight in embarrassing him in front of his fellow gamblers, and I am not a fighter by any stretch of the imagination, not at all. But this guy wasn't either. Robert Horrocks was a total wimp and a poor excuse for a human being. But I was a professional. My job wasn't to judge, mine was to collect all the information and present it to the courts, who would judge and decide. He denied everything in the interview and although there was clear evidence of what I had seen and the medical evidence; it came down to her word against his. He was kept in police custody overnight and appeared at Sandford Magistrates in the morning. He pleaded not guilty, and when the question of bail arose, there was an obvious problem. They both lived at the same address. His solicitor addressed the court.

'Your worships, the defendant has a brother who, I am told, has agreed to let him stay at his house until the matter goes to trial,' said his solicitor, opening his application for bail. In reality, this meant he would stay one night with his brother and then go back to the flat on Happy Trees and kick the shit out of her once again. Eventually, he was bailed and yes, two nights later he went back to the flat and did what I predicted. I was off duty at the time but once again, the same procedure applied and he was presented to the magistrate's court in custody to apply for his bail, once again.

'We have to be crystal clear, Mr. Horrocks. If you appear before this bench again, you will not be granted bail. Do you hear me?' said the angry-looking magistrate.

Two nights later, he was back in custody again and this time his bail was refused. He was remanded in custody to HMP Sandford to await his trial for more assaults on his partner.

His legal team made a further application for bail to the crown court and once again Horrocks was successful in obtaining his liberty. However, the court stated he must now stay away from his partner and the flat on Happy Trees, which he did. However, he did arrange to meet her one Saturday night in the Brown Cow and take her out to Dreamers nightclub for a treat. On the way to the nightclub, he decided to call into the public toilets around the corner and, for whatever reason, his good lady followed. What resulted was a phone call to the police from Albert Crabtree, a council employee and the custodian of the toilets, stating that a man was in a cubicle with a woman, and it sounded like he was using her as a punch bag. Once again Horrocks was arrested and this time he stayed in custody. He was charged with numerous counts of causing actual and grievous bodily harm. The trial was set for the crown court as the Magistrates deemed they had insufficient powers to deal with the man before them.

Fast forward six months to my first appearance at Sandford Crown Court, to give evidence, of course, and not a defendant. The marbled floor, the clicks of the barrister's heels as they walked and talked, still echo in my mind. Holding their robes at the shoulders, discussing and debating the finer points of law as they walked the corridors, their robes trailing behind them.

Albert Crabtree, the toilet janitor, was sitting outside court number two and I went over to join him. I gave him a copy of his written statement, which told the story of the events of that night, the night he called the police. Albert was a lovely man. In his early seventies, he was smartly dressed, tie and jacket and a lovely pair of brand-new plastic shoes that he probably got from an offer in the Daily Mail newspaper. He wore his best Farah slacks, pulled up to his chin.

'What it is, son, them toilets are my pride and joy. Since my wife passed away, it has taken over my life looking after them. I clean all the brass pipes with brasso, I mop three and four times a day and did you know I came runner up in the Toilet of the Year Awards?' he explained. I could smell mints on his breath, and I nodded as he explained his achievements and continued.

'I keep open at weekends until 11:00 p.m. and do you know son, people come into my toilets now for sex, they come in to inject bloody drugs, they come in for this for that. Do you know, when someone comes in for a shit, it really is like a breath of fresh air.'

Mary Horrocks walked past us, dressed immaculately, with her hair pulled back, displaying her natural beauty. Her scars and bruises were long gone. The peas and blood a distant memory as she was now to give evidence in *support* of her partner and his liberty. She was to admit provoking him and thus burdening the blame. The prosecution and defence barristers clip clopped along the marble floor discussing the case and then Mr. Diamond, the prosecuting counsel, approached me to say that it wasn't in the public interest to carry on with a trial and that the Crown would accept a 'binding over order' for Horrocks. This meant he had to be of good behaviour for a set period. If he didn't behave, then he would face all the charges again. I was only very young in service and didn't really know what to say to a Crown Counsel, so I muttered words to the effect,

'Well, it's up to you. You do what you want.'

'I know and I will,' Diamond curtly responded.

The Horrocks's left the court hand in hand and the cycle of violence continued until some years later, I received a call from a detective working in the major incident room at Sandford. He was enquiring about the Horrocks case I had dealt with. He wanted to know the finer details of the case, as he had to prepare a case summary for court in relation to the murder of Mary Horrocks. A classic case of, *'I hate you, don't leave me.'*

Nora Perch was a large woman, both physically and character wise. She was always walking and talking, more talking actually, on the Happy Trees estate. When I say walking, what I mean is walking to the shop at the bottom of Cedar block and back to her top floor flat. She rarely went anywhere else and wasn't really gifted with intelligence. She really was a difficult person to ignore, but do you know, sometimes I really do think it was worth the effort. Conversations with Nora were hardly stimulating, but she was a nice lady who always spoke to officers when patrolling. She could talk, usually, about the most mundane things and make them less interesting. People used to say,

'I've just given Nora a bloody good listening to for half an hour, which is thirty minutes of my life I will never get back.'

She had a heart of gold and would help anyone, but always one for the melodrama was our Nora. She was always ringing the police, complaining about the kids on the estate, and to be fair, they were harsh on her. She was at least twenty-five stone, so when she threatened them and said,

'Just wait until I catch you,' the replies were along the lines of,

'Come on then, you fat bastard,' before some object would be thrown at her.

The kids taunted her and put all kinds of things through her letterbox. I would see her in the late afternoon waddling along the fifth floor landing in slippers and night dress.

'Ready for bed already, Nora?' I asked.

'No love, what it is, right, I was that busy this morning, so I couldn't be arsed getting dressed.'

The next week I was on the estate dealing with an incident when I heard someone shouting, 'Jim, Jim! Here yar love. Jim, Jim, here yar.'

I looked across and saw Nora, arm in arm with a wisp of a man.

'Off shopping Nora?' I asked and but knew the answer.

'Yeah, I'm just calling for some bits. This is Tom, officer. My new fella.'

Nora was wearing her usual beige Macintosh, which was heavily grease stained round the collar, and nightdress with her best track suit bottoms underneath.

Tom was a lot older, a lot thinner, and the partnership just didn't seem right. He was scrawny and, although local, he attempted to sound 'clever' when he spoke. He was obviously a man of many previous convictions, just by the look of him. They were not a match. Something was amiss, but who was I to interfere in Nora's love life?

The weeks went by, and I ended up on Happy Trees estate several times. Domestic disputes, assaults, sexual abuse and, of course, the numerous burglaries.

The police radio blasted out,

'Any patrol to 556 Cedar, Happy Trees, ambulance attending a stabbing.'

'776, on my way,' I answered.

Cedar block was where Nora lived. Flat 556 was on the top and fifth floor, but I wasn't sure if that was Nora's. When I arrived, the ambulance was parked away from the parking bays to avoid the excrement. I walked up the staircase as the lift, as usual, wasn't working. Never was. The permanent stench from the stairs was a mixture of urine and disinfectant. When I got to the fifth floor, I recognised the door of 556 and it was indeed Nora's flat. The door was open, and I immediately noticed the blood on door handles, carpet, and door frames. I walked in and down the stairs to the living area. The flats were a concrete monstrosity, with living upstairs and downstairs in alternative flats.

'Hiya, love,' Nora shouted to me, 'put kettle on if you want a brew love.'

There was blood everywhere. Paramedics were working on Nora in the front room. She still had the same nightdress on, and her huge overweight arms hung down by her side. I could see a huge wound in her arm and the opening exposed all her body fat.

'Gone and stabbed me, hasn't he. Bastard. Tried to electrocute me as well, you know, threw the electric fire in the bath. Then he tried to strangle me, love, the bastard, eh.'

New boyfriend Tom, for whatever reason, had set about Nora whilst she was taking a bath. I walked into the bathroom and the bath was still full of crimson-coloured water. On the floor I saw a black handled carving knife, the blade bent at 90 degrees to the handle. It was full of Nora's body fat. There was also an electric fire in the bath water, still plugged into the wall socket. I looked back outside and into the front room and one of the paramedics had gone to the ambulance.

'He tried to strangle me as well, cock,' she said as she pointed to the red marks around her neck. I could see the blood dripping onto the floor from underneath her nightie. Her legs were red. I looked down and saw a length of wire flex on the bathroom floor in amongst the congealed blood and snot. It wasn't a pleasant sight.

Nora had been subjected to a frenzied and horrific attack whilst taking a bath. New boyfriend Tom had obviously lost control and when the stabbing didn't have the desired effect, he brought the electric fire into the bathroom and throw it in the bath with her. When that didn't kill her, he wrapped the wire flex around her neck and tried to strangle her. Luckily, neighbours heard Nora's screams and when they came to investigate, boyfriend Tom made a quick exit.

The paramedic returned, and we began discussing the main problem, which was how to get Nora down to the ambulance. The lift for the block was not working and they couldn't take a 25 stone woman down the piss drenched staircases on a chair or stretcher. The nearest working lift was on the other side of the estate, which meant a walk further than to the ambulance.

'I'll walk, love, don't worry,' such was Nora's character. 'I'll be fine, what's all the fuss about?'

Poor Nora walked down the staircase in her greasy Macintosh and slippers. A trail of deep crimson blood marking her route. Neighbours came to their doors to wish her well, and of course, she stopped and chatted. The paramedics trying to hurry her along to the ambulance. Nora wasn't having any of that. This was her moment. Her fifteen minutes of fame. Other patrols had started to arrive by then, and I had locked the flat door. It was sealed off, and I had the key.

As I knew Nora and had some rapport with her, the paramedics requested that I travel in the ambulance with her to the hospital.

'Hold my hand, love, come on I'll be fine,' she said, 'Ronnie, Ronnie... oh there's Ronnie, love. Bastard stabbed me Ronnie, Ronnie.'

A diminutive figure of a man, smoking a roll up, walked behind the ambulance and into the stairwell. He either didn't hear or chose to ignore Nora. I held her hand and agreed somewhat with the request to go with her to hospital but decided to drive up to Kings

Cross in the police car. As Nora waved her final goodbyes to the small crowd, the rear doors of the ambulance finally closed. On came the blue lights, and we began the two-mile journey to Kings Cross Hospital. I informed the Control Room, 'Sierra One', of the situation and requested that CID be informed. Nora's flat was now locked and secure. Scene preserved and contained. I handed the flat keys to one of the Sergeants, who had just arrived.

The journey to the hospital didn't take long and I was greeted by a serious looking Doctor Rhodes. I knew him as the police surgeon and had seen him around the custody office from time to time.

'Do we know who next of kin is?' he barked. He looked agitated.

'I don't know, let me...'

'She is going to die,' he added.

I stopped. I froze and felt the punch in my stomach.

'She's what? But she walked to the...'

'Arterial bleed. It looks like she's not going to make it,' the Doctor confirmed.

I was speechless, and my mind started racing. Should I have got a dying declaration? Could I have done any more? Should I? Things then got extremely frantic with phone calls, radio calls and a search for a next of kin. Nora was on the operating table.

Two CID officers arrived at the hospital, and I briefed them as to what had happened. They went seeking the nursing staff to be told again what I had just told them. Nora's blood pressure had crashed.

'Did you get a written statement off her?' asked one CID officer. He was a Detective Sergeant, and both officers were on ECP (Evening Crime Patrol). I didn't know either of them.

'I didn't get the chance to, she was being treated.'

'Did you get her to sign your pocketbook?' he asked.

'There wasn't time to do any of that, she was being treated and...' He cut across me.

'You should have got a written statement naming him. If she croaks it, we've got fuck all.'

The two officers spoke into their radios, and without speaking to me further, they left. Shortly afterwards, one of my shift sergeants

Arrived, and I was summoned back to the police station. Inspector Morley was waiting for me and told me that one of the CID bosses wanted to see me upstairs in the CID office.

'Did you preserve the scene?' asked the Inspector.

'Yes, of course, the door was locked,' I replied.

'What did she say to you?' Morley looked quite serious, which wasn't the norm.

'She told me that her new boyfriend had stabbed, electrocuted, and strangled her. He'd really tried to kill her,' I said.

'You better go and tell him that,' and with that Morley pointed upstairs.

At that time, I had no intention of joining the CID. I was only twenty-one-years old and very inexperienced. Detectives were older, wiser, experienced, and far more knowledgeable, or so I thought. So far, I had stayed away from the CID offices on the third floor, but now had to walk the full length of the corridor to where DCI McAvoy was waiting in his office. The corridor was quiet, dimly lit as it was now into the evening. McAvoy's office was at the far end of the corridor and as usual, my leather soles gave my arrival away. McAvoy wasn't the top boss, but that didn't matter.

'Hello Sir, PC Graham. You wanted to see me?' I said as I stood in his lit doorway.

'Where did you do your training, son? Because whoever trained you needs sacking,' he growled.

I never got a chance to speak. Not one word.

'Why didn't you inform the CID of this? Why didn't you tell your sergeants what had really happened? You abandoned the scene; you didn't preserve it. What the hell were you doing up there?'

'But Sir, I did…'

'You did what? Did you get a statement off her? No, you didn't. A total dereliction of your duty. Now get off my CID floor'.

It was a very lonely walk back down the corridor. My time in the police cadets had stood me in good stead for being bawled and shouted at, but I wasn't in a good place after this mauling. I ran it through my head time and time again what I could have done differently. I couldn't think of anything. The paramedics were trying to save Nora's life. I couldn't get a written statement, could I? I preserved the scene, I informed my sergeants and so it went on, over and over in my head.

Inspector Morley was waiting for me on the first floor. He called me into his office and put the virtual arm around my shoulders. I wanted to resign there and then but again immediately thought of mum and dad. I was young and naive, and I didn't understand the game or the politics. All I knew was that I took the 'hit' but no one ever told me what for. I had done everything that could be expected. Later that night, I walked in the report writing room to finish duty at 10:00 p.m. where my shift were gathered. All went quiet when I walked into the room and the whispering began. It didn't feel nice. I then made an appointment to meet my new best friend at the time, alcohol. For four hours or so at least, he helped me along.

The next shift, I paraded for duty and one or two colleagues were asking me about the previous evening's events. They sided with me and asked themselves what McAvoy was expecting of me. I went to the murder incident room to see if Nora had passed away, but it was empty. That was a relief and the control room told me that Nora had survived but was still in intensive care but was on the mend. There was a manhunt, however, for Thomas Fredericks, who was now wanted for her attempted murder. Nora's excess weight and body fat had saved her. She had been stabbed more than forty times, with some wounds cutting through arteries and veins. When boyfriend Tom threw the electric fire in the bath, the whole electric system fused. Nora had been very lucky.

Months later, I saw Nora waddling along on another estate, Beacon Hill. By this time Fredericks had been arrested and was awaiting trial. Nora was still as bubbly and as daft as ever.

'What they said, love, right, was that my fat had stopped him killing me. So, there you are, love, more cream cakes and custard pies all round,' she laughed.

The greasy Macintosh had gone and was replaced by a parka jacket with a big fur hood. I remember the food stains down the front. She never returned to Happy Trees and now lived in a 'nice house' on Beacon Hill. Thomas Fredericks elected trial at the Crown Court, his defence being diminished responsibilities caused by the numerous drugs and tranquilisers he was taking at the time of the attack. He was found guilty and sentenced to spend 11 years at Her Majesty's pleasure. He served around half his sentence and when released, he went to live near the docks. I lost track of him for a while but then and saw his name sometime later on the local BBC news with the headline, *'Woman's body found buried in cellar.'*

When the council placed a CPO order on the house he lived in, the demolition teams made the grim discovery. Fredericks went undetected for a decade and again pleaded guilty to murdering his next girlfriend and burying her in the cellar. He lived in the house all the time she was there. Once again, he elected Crown Court trial, claiming his medication made him kill her. He was convicted and was sentenced to life in prison. Nora was very lucky.

Shortly after Nora's demise, I was sent to a sudden death on Happy Trees. It was Sunday afternoon and a middle-aged couple had enjoyed a liquid lunch before returning home to make the chips. They both fell asleep with the chip pan on the cooker. When they woke, in the smoke and ensuing panic, the lady of the house had fallen down the stairs and was now deceased. The paramedics were there and packing up. The doctor was on his way to certify death and the rota undertakers were en route.

'We woke up to the smoke, and she went upstairs. Then I heard a crash, and she fell down the stairs,' said the man I presumed to be her husband.

I made a note of his exact words in my pocket notebook. The deceased was face up on the settee and had a black eye. I asked everyone to leave and secured the scene. There were lots of unanswered questions, so I picked up the police radio,

'776 to Sierra One. Can you ask Sgt. Darcy or Sgt. Richards to attend this sudden death please?'

'Is there any reason why they should attend, 776?' asked the control room operator.

'Yes, because I want them here,' was my very curt reply.

At 8:00 a.m. the next morning, I was at home, in bed, when the phone rang. It was DCI McAvoy and my dad answered the phone. I was off duty, but that didn't matter to McAvoy. The Coroners Officer had inspected the body at the mortuary, yes that mortuary where the ghosts chase you out. He wasn't happy with the circumstances of the death and the deceased had injuries that were inconsistent with the husband's account.

McAvoy started his tirade,

'Why didn't you....'

'I did.'

'You should have…'

'I did.'

'Why didn't you…'

'I did.'

'You should have...'

'I did Sir. I noted everything and requested supervision to attend due to my concerns,' I replied before replacing the receiver.

I had to be careful not to come across as flippant, but it was my early introduction to accountability and the 'Shudder Squad' as we called them. Those who, with the beauty of hindsight and time, picked away at any early actions or decisions you made to then create a blame culture. You 'shudder' done this, you 'shudder' done that. The 'Shudder Squad' I am told is still alive and well today. The husband was arrested on suspicion of murder but later released due to lack of evidence. Sergeant Darcy took the hit this time. I was learning.

Happy Trees estate was full of different characters. Hard-working people to the downright lazy and those who saw crime as a vocation.

It was a very interesting place to work and to give you a snapshot of the residents. Early one morning, I was on duty when a car pulled away from Harry's shop on the estate. I could see a small child in the back who was climbing over the seats and onto the parcel shelf. As the car approached the give way sign, mum in the driver's seat braked suddenly and the child came over the seats into the front. I could see the flaying arms and the ensuing battle between mum and child. The kid must have only been six or seven and was having none of it. I stopped the vehicle and tried to explain to mum that the child should be strapped in, but I could see she looked defeated.

'You try and explain that to the little brat,' she shouted at me.

She explained that she had tried and tried to get young Kyle to sit in the child's seat but had now given up. She looked desperate. I had a plan. I took mum out of the driver's seat and walked her to the police vehicle, and sat her in the back. As I walked back to her car, young Kyle was now lying across the back shelf kicking his legs at the rear windscreen. I opened the back door and asked his name. He didn't reply.

'Kyle, can I just explain to you that because you're not being a good boy and you're not sitting in your seat with your seat belt on, I have had to arrest your poor mummy. What do you think about your poor mummy being arrested for you being a naughty boy?'

'Fuck her,' came the reply.

Yes, this was Happy Trees estate.

Just on the on the outskirts of the estate were some nice houses. It was rare we got a call to them, but when we did, they would have been the victims of the Happy Trees 'grafters'. As I stood with a householder one night in his kitchen, we scratched our heads at the dilemma before us.

'I'm telling you', said the bemused house owner, 'the video recorder has gone, the microwave and some food from the fridge.'

'Where did they break in?' I asked.

'That's the problem, officer, I don't know. Both doors are locked, no windows are broken. Someone must have a key, but I know we don't have spare keys.'

I filled in the crime report, but it was returned from DCI McAvoy as 'No Crime'. McAvoy's logic being, how could this be a burglary if there is no break in? Probably the owners claiming on the insurance, McAvoy's comments insinuated.

The next day, I went to another similar occurrence. No sign of a break=in, but the TV had gone. And so, it continued for weeks. A complete mystery until I attended another call where the offenders had been disturbed. Around 2:00 a.m. the occupant of the house had come downstairs for a cup of tea and heard scuffling at the back door. Upon investigation, the external door handle mechanism, screws etc. were on the floor outside, leaving the internal lock and keyhole exposed.

'Did you leave your keys in the back door when you went to bed?' I asked.

'Always do. It's a bit of a bugger when you can't leave things in your own home now, isn't it?' he replied. How times have changed.

There it was. The culprits were removing the door handle mechanism to get at the key from the other side of the lock. But how were they turning the key? They must have an implement to grab the key to turn it. Once inside, they would steal the items and then replace the mechanisms and screws, leaving the house occupants none the wiser of their illegal entry.

For the next couple of weeks, extra patrols, CID and plain clothes officers mounted a nightly operation on the estates around Happy Trees. There was no doubt it was Happy Tree's finest that were up to this new trick, but nobody knew who or really how. The observations went on for weeks without success, and the canal towpath seemed a good route for the criminals to travel.

Plain clothes officers would be wrapped up in blankets on cold winter nights, hidden in bushes, watching and waiting. The crimes continued. Every night there was at least one or two burglaries in different areas and at one address the victim made a cup of tea around 4:00 a.m. as they couldn't sleep. Things were fine but at 6.30 a.m. they came down to then find the kettle, TV, video, microwave all missing. At the last count, a total of 138 dwelling house burglaries had been recorded by using the door handle modus operandi. Whoever these were, they were good.

One of a police officer's best friends is supposedly the weather and 'PC rain'. For me it was 'PC snow'. On a blizzard like night, the snow was falling heavily when a doctor returned home from work in the early hours. He lived about a mile from Happy Trees estate. As the cars headlights lit up his driveway, two figures scattered away into the darkness, like hares across a field. Upon investigation, the doctor found his rear door handle mechanism and screws on the floor. His house keys were in the back door lock on the inside of the house. He was lucky.

Phil Young, an older lad off the shift, joined me at the house. Phil was a nice lad. He worked with my dad at Taylors factory, so we had something in common. We set off, following the two sets of footprints from the rear of the doctor's house. It was 2:00 a.m. and virgin snow. The tracks were plain to see and went through gardens, over fences, under barbed wire, down back alleys and eventually onto the hills. The night was very still and eerily quiet. It was now 2.30 a.m. and not a soul was about. The footprints carried on over the hills and started to drop down near to the canal. By this time, both Phil and I were running, and it seemed from the footprints that our intended prey were as well.

The control room wanted both of us to stop the search and attend other calls, but this was now the hunters versus the hunted. I was out of breath and my chest was burning. Phil was a big smoker, and he was lagging behind. We continued towards Happy Trees estate and still, no sign of anyone. Not only were these two good, but they were also fit and fast as well. I decided to come off the canal and get back to the street that ran parallel. That way I could see if they came out from the canal towpath to get on the estate. I waited for Phil and as we came out onto the street, there they were. Two small black dots about a quarter of a mile ahead, throwing snowballs at each other. One good thing about police uniforms, there weren't many by the way, was you could step back into the shadows and not be seen in the dark. That was, of course, if it wasn't snowing. Both Phil and I stood out in the white background in our dark uniforms. They would spot us easily. Phil wanted to radio for back up, but due to the weather, a vehicle would do well to navigate the roads. Also, the noise from a vehicle would alert them. We followed on, jogging, puffing and panting in the hope that the two wouldn't turn around. I was now carrying my helmet and trying to do the best impression of a snowman as I could. What did help was to stand full into the wind as the snow covered the police issue gaberdine. Happy Trees estate was nearing. I could see the tower blocks and the floodlit gangways, or 'rat runs', as we called them. It looked like a prison, from my vantage point, and I'm sure some occupants often felt the same way.

The two figures weren't getting any closer. Then STOP! They both turned around. Phil was gasping for breath and fell into a doorway.

'Let's pack in. We don't even know it's them,' he said as he slid down the wall. I could see the steam rising from underneath his uniform. I stood perfectly still as the snowflakes landed on my face. Both figures, like startled deers, looked back at us. I'm sure they had seen us. I didn't move. Phil curled up in a ball. Both figures were now looking directly at us. The snowflakes started tickling my nose as I remained motionless. It seemed like an eternity and then they both started walking back towards us. What were they doing? They were now directly opposite one of the entrances to the estate. The road we were on was elevated as part of the estate was in a valley. These two could walk through that entrance and directly onto the walkways on the third or fourth floor. Once on there, they would disappear across the many walkways, landings, and 'rat runs'. Had they seen us? Were they taunting us? Do I make my move now? One of them bent down. I slowly knelt and then lay flat on my stomach, inching myself towards them. I could hear laughing and swearing, and then they started rolling snowballs. As the snowballs grew bigger, I moved forward, and could see their intention; to block the access route to the estate with giant snowballs.

I continued to crawl and gestured to Phil to stay on the road. He was on his hands and knees and steam was coming out of the back of his collar. I wanted to get on the other side of them, in like a scissor movement. I crawled slowly along, watching them as I did so. They were both young, about the same age as me, with dark hair, scruffy clothing. They were laughing as their two snowballs grew bigger. They stopped. A light came on in a house on the street. One of them put his fingers to his lips and the other looked directly at me. I was flat on my stomach, covered in snow, but unable to hide the dark police uniform. This was it; they were going to run. I held my breath.

'I'm telling you there.' one said.

'Where?' the other replied.

They both stood together and looked up the street. They had spotted Phil.

'I'm telling you, that's a bloke.'

I got to my knees slowly. They continued to look down the street at Phil.

'Is it fuck a bloke? You're seeing things, you dick.'

'Hiya lads, you ok?' I said as I got to my feet.

They both looked startled and turned to face me. One of the snowballs was in position at the entrance to the walkway and both of them were on my side of it. It wasn't too big, and they could have jumped over it, but the only way onto the walkway was now past me. Phil approached them from the street. They looked at me, then Phil, then me. They realised we had cut them off. It was decision time. Were they going to bolt? I was close enough to them now, and they realised that. We were now an hour and a couple of miles from the burglary at the Doctor's house, so hopefully they wouldn't connect our presence here with that burglary.

'Yeah fine, we're just dicking about in the snow,' the smaller one said. I remember he had a lazy eye.

'Where have you been?' I inquired.

'Nowhere, we live on the estate and just couldn't sleep, so thought we'd come out and mess about in the snow,' the taller one replied.

They were going to try and bluff it out. I said to lazy eye,

'What's in your pockets?'

'Nothing,' as he began to pat down his pockets on his army style jacket. 'No, nothing. Honest, we are just dicking about in the snow.'

The cold night air was tense. I could sense they were going to run. I walked in between them, so now I had the snowball at my back and the entrance to the estate. Phil was on the other side of them. There was a sense of realisation.

'Honestly, we've only just come out as it was snowing,' said lazy eye.

I felt the outside of his pocket and it wasn't empty. He had some tools in there. They felt like screwdrivers.

'What's these in your pocket then?' I asked.

'Oh yeah, sorry them. There just some tools I have for my bike to put the chain back on. Sorry forgot they were there,' he said.

He then took out of his jacket pocket two screwdrivers, one a Philips, the other straight. Phil shone his torch. There was also a pair of pliers, but like I had never seen before. Long thin jaws that had been ground down. They looked like the beak of a platypus.

'And these?' I asked, as I took hold of them.

There was a pause with everyone. Both lads looked at each other. They knew that we knew. I looked at Phil. The 'long-nosed plier' burglars stood before us. Lazy eye broke first and jumped at the snowball. I grabbed the collar of his jacket as he tried to wriggle free. The other one bolted and tried to get past Phil. I concentrated on lazy eye as he tried to get over his own snowball. Memories of that rugby match came flooding back as my shoulder crunched into his thighs. I wrapped my arms around his legs and he let out a squeal as we both hit the floor. I looked back to see Phil holding the other in a headlock. We both lay on the floor, panting.

'You are under arrest. You are not obliged to say anything...'

'Alright, alright fucking get off me'

Steven Dack and his stepbrother Glynn admitted their part in just short of 200 dwelling house burglaries, using the long-nosed plier technique. Most stolen items were stashed in previously identified locations and the two stepbrothers returned the next day to sell the goods on the estate and to local taxi drivers for pennies. I worked with Steven's stepbrother in my part-time job at school at the local supermarket. I knew their dad, Barry, who was a regular in my local. We were indeed a close knit family in Sandford.

Steven & Glynn were sent to the 'big house', the Crown Court, for sentencing after admitting all the burglaries. Little, if any of the property was recovered. They each received three years' imprisonment.

For the first time in my short career, I was to receive a commendation from the Area Commander. Both Phil and I had been put forward by Inspector Morley for a commendation, for what was seen as the arrest of the year. Both of us presented ourselves on the fifth floor where we had to wait outside the Chief's office until the red light on the door turned green and his secretary invited us to enter. Inside this palatial suite, with its egotistical wall of photographs, medals and busts, we were faced with the Area Commander and our very own, Superintendent 'medallion man' Ahern. I could see the rage behind Ahern's eyes as there was no doubt he had tried everything within his power to stop me receiving this commendation. I shook Ahern's hand and smiled. He knew that I knew.

CHAPTER SEVENTEEN

THE CRADDOCKS

We don't need no education
We don't need no thought control
Hey! Teachers! Leave them kids alone!

Happy Trees produced some of the finest criminals in the area. Some later went into the 'semi legitimate' business world and still live in the area today in their farmhouses with land, horses and stables. After a few months of working Happy Trees beat, the Craddock family, remember donkey with the colic in the bedroom, were continually coming down onto the estate. In particular, Colin Craddock and the new kid on the block, Happy Trees finest, Patrick Davidson, seemed to be joining forces. Patrick was a small-time thief who seemed to be moving up the ladder quickly. Colin had been attracted to that, and both of them would be seen driving around in a new Ford XR2i. It was a smart car and one which neither of them could afford nor should possess. But they did. The car and occupants were checked many times by police patrols during the small hours. But every time they were allowed to drive away as nothing was ever found. To me, this didn't seem right. They would drive about into the early hours, being stopped, messing around and just being nuisances. We should have ignored them when they were out and about and being nuisances. It was when they were quiet, when we didn't see them, we should have been proactive and gone looking for them. If we didn't see them racing around, they were either scheming, plotting, or pillaging. We should have been looking when we didn't see.

'Sierra One Control from 1219. Can I have a PNC check please for a vehicle?' came over the radio waves. PNC being the police national computer which houses a vast amount of data, including vehicle numbers and registered keepers.

'1219 go ahead to the PNC,' replied the radio operator.

'Yeah, Sierra One, it's a red hatchback, Victor Romeo Foxtrot 216 Victor.'

'1219 from Sierra One Control, that's an Audi Quattro in red, current keeper is Brendan Marland of Sandford.'

'1219 to Sierra One, I'm behind this vehicle now on London Road, it's travelling extremely slowly. Appears to be four on board. I'm just… 1219 Sierra One, chasing, chasing, four masked men in the vehicle, lights are off and the vehicle is now travelling at excessive speed towards the town centre.'

'Sierra One, exact location please, 1219,' asked the Control room as things became heated.

'1219 to Sierra One, vehicle lost Dalebarn Road. Travelling too fast.'

A new era!

At the time, the Audi Quattro was best described as a four-wheel-drive vehicle that could travel in excess of 180mph, on three wheels if necessary. I know, maybe a slight exaggeration, but compared to the police 850cc mini, we were a little outclassed. The Traffic Department did have 2.8 Litre Ford Capris, but the Quattro was Premier League. It had been stolen that night from the drive of a local solicitor, and the thieves had used a crowbar to open the sunroof and gain access to the car. Word on the street was that it was the Craddocks and the new boy Davidson who stole it and was still in possession of it.

Just before 10pm and on shift changeover time, the police radio crackled into life once again.

'Sierra One Control to any patrol, please, to attend Tesco petrol station. Miss Crowther reporting that her boyfriend's car has just been stolen when she went to pay the cashier. A masked man jumped into the Ford Sierra Cosworth and drove off towards Brough Ferry. A red Audi Quattro travelling behind the stolen car. Any patrol please.' There was a stunned silence.

The next night the Quattro was seen cruising along Queensway, a dual carriageway, in tandem with, yes, you've guessed, the Ford Cosworth. It was futile. These vehicles could do 0-60mph in less than 4 seconds. The police panda car 0-60mph could be plotted on a calendar.

'Sierra One Control to any patrol please. Vehicle reversed into Bargain Booze. Four masked men loading up a van and two cars.'

I was some distance away but answered on the radio that I would attend. I was driving the standard 850cc police mini and my foot was down on the floor on the accelerator. The steering wheel was wobbling as I turned left into Queen Elizabeth Way. There in front of me in the nearside lane was the red Audi Quattro slowly cruising along. No lights. I pressed the radio button,

'776 to Sierra One. I'm currently on QE Way and behind the Audi Quattro. Do we have any traffic patrols to assist, please?'

The police 2.8 litre Ford Capri was fast but not fast enough. The Capri was also a poor handler and the Quattro could go around corners on three wheels. The police mini was screaming away as it neared 70mph along the dual carriageway. I was catching the Quattro, which began to slow.

'776 to Sierra One Control, direction of travel is towards the Shottick area. Vehicle slowing, masked man now climbing out through the sunroof and sitting on the roof looking at me. Objects being passed to him by the other occupants. Are you receiving this transmission, Sierra One?'

'Sierra One to 776, yes receiving, keep the commentary coming please,' the operator replied.

It was silly, as the Audi could have left at any time. I followed and was about 50 yards behind. I looked at the speedo and I was travelling at 50mph. I looked at the figure sat on top of the Audi. The white skin around the ski mask eye holes prominent in the dark of the night. He was laughing at me and looking down into the car at the others. The back seat passengers were looking at me and they, too, were laughing. Black ski masks and the whites of their eyes.

'Boosh!'. The first beer can hit the windscreen full on. The alcohol splattered everywhere, and the smell of beer enveloped the car. Then another and another and another. The windscreen wipers were now damaged, and the windscreen was cracked. I had to slow down; the Audi slowed to. I could hear the radio crackling as other patrols made their way. The roof top assailant was laughing and clapping. Then he climbed back down into the vehicle. The two ski masks in the back seats were laughing and one waved as if to say goodbye. The rear of the Audi 'sat down', as two huge plumes of exhaust smoke indicated their intentions. The car sped off, a quick left, quick right and into the darkness.

Over the coming weeks, electrical stores, supermarkets, off licenses and the like were all targeted by the gang. The Audi and Ford Cosworth were never far away from each other, and the gang was growing in numbers. The Police Ford Capris were no match. Word on the street was that the Craddocks and associates had teamed up with the Happy Trees lads, led by Davidson. The talk on the estate was that the police were beaten, but the best was yet to come.

The most precious item in the house at that time was the VCR (Video Cassette Recorder). VHS or Betamax? We know who won that race. Stopping or starting the tape was, by the way of a new conception, the remote control. This was technology at its finest and people were amazed that a little black box on the end of a wire could stop and start this giant machine that sat underneath the television. People couldn't really afford to buy the VCR, so one rented it and the same rental store let you hire all the current VHS films for a day or two. It was a breakthrough in home entertainment despite the fact the remote-control wire was only short and didn't reach the sofa.

Norton's Electrical store was subjected to a 'ram raid', when masked raiders reversed a stolen Ford transit van through the store's shutters, and display windows. The Audi and Ford Cosworth drove around town at warp speeds, distracting the police, whilst the intruders helped themselves to the electrical goods at Norton's and the video club ledger. This held the names and addresses of all customers that either hired video recorders from the store or rented films. This was a game changer.

Police shifts in those days were three patterns of earlies, afternoons, and nights. Occasionally they would throw a day shift in here and there of 8/4 or 10/6. All the shifts were jumbled around except nights. You worked seven continuous nights of 10:00 p.m.-6:00 a.m., finishing at 6:00 a.m. on the Monday morning and were expected to be back at work at 2:00 p.m. on Wednesday. It was brutal and a reason that at one time the life expectancy of a retired police officer was between ninety-five days and seven years. Obviously, diet and alcohol had a massive influence in that as well.

On the very last night shift, in the very last few minutes, around 5.50 a.m. on that last Monday morning, the radios crackled into life once again,

'Sierra One, any patrol please to attend the Sandcome Road Service Station. Armed robbery in progress, men with guns.'

Everyone was ready to go home for a well-earned rest. Despite guns being mentioned, all the shift headed off towards the danger once again. I nearly put my boot through the floor in the police mini, but as it screamed along, it went through my mind that Sandcome Road Service Station was not an all-night garage. It was way out from Sandford Centre and on the border with Eastshire Police. It was one road there and one road back. The offenders could only come back towards the armada of police vehicles heading their way or slip over into Eastshire. It took me about ten minutes to get there and nothing had passed me travelling in the opposite direction.
I was first at the scene. The robbers were ether still at the service station, or slipped over into Eastshire. I parked a couple of streets away and jogged up to the perimeter fence. The garage was in darkness. It was locked. There was no robbery in progress.

'776 to Sierra One Control. Garage in darkness. No persons here. I will just check the building,' I whispered into the microphone.

I tiptoed around the back of the garage and could hear the other patrol cars screaming their way along Sandcome Road.

'Sierra One Control Room to any patrol. Masked men just thrown a dustbin through the front window of a house on Maxwell Way and stolen the video.'

'Sierra One to patrols, masked men also thrown something through the front window on Castletown Drive.'

'Sierra One… Another one patrols, masked men thrown the dustbin through the front window of a house in Marsh Lane.'

'Yet another one patrols, front window smashed 347 Market Street, masked men climbing out of the house with the VCR.'

It went on until, in total, six houses were raided at the same time. The only item stolen was the VHS video recorder which had been hired from, yes, you've guessed it, Norton's electrical store. Some of you may be thinking about the size of wheelie bins these days, but way back then, dustbins were small, metal and emptied every week.

The attacks continued and usually happened at shift change over times. Not only were people leaving the lights and radio on when they went out, in case of burglars, but were now covering the flashing VCR's display panel with cushions.

I was in the process of hiring my VCR from Radio Rentals in Sandford and when they asked for my home address, I refused and gave them the police station address. They wouldn't accept it stating that no one would break into their store just to steal the VCR ledger. They did, a week later.

Operations were now being set up to catch those responsible. Word on the street was that the Audi was being garaged in the Happy Trees estate somewhere. There were hundreds of empty garages, as most residents couldn't afford a car.

The house attacks seemed to slow down, and I was tasked with checking all lock-up garages on my beat, Happy Trees. Behind Willow block, on the estate, were rows and rows of brick garages, some with doors off their hinges, some with no doors. One garage stood out.

It had a brand-new lock on it where all the others didn't have any.

Unfortunately, there were no windows, but through the gaps I could see the outline of a red car inside. It had to be the Audi. Together with the foot beat officer for Happy Trees, we visited every garage on the estate. Out of hundreds, only twelve were locked. The red Audi must be in one of them. When we returned to Willow block, there was a middle-aged man walking into the garage block. I quickly parked the police car and both Steve, the area foot beat officer, and I followed behind on foot. We could hardly do covert surveillance in full uniform, but that's exactly what we were doing. The man turned into the aisle where the newly locked garage and Audi were and when I turned the corner; he was standing in front of *the* garage doors. He looked startled as I grabbed him in a bear hug.

'What the fuck you doing?' he shouted, 'get off me.'

'You are under arrest for…'

'Under arrest? What for trying to get in my garage. Some bastard has put a lock on it. My painting gears in there.'

He was one of the few legitimate workers on Happy Trees who wanted to get his painting equipment out of his garage. Earlier he'd noticed the lock and had gone to buy a hack saw. We spent the next thirty minutes sawing away to reveal the stolen Audi Quattro minus number plates. The scene was preserved for forensic examination and the Audi eventually removed. It had run out of petrol and despite attempts to remove the locking fuel cap; the gang had been unsuccessful and abandoned the car.

Over the next few weeks, search warrants were executed at the homes of all the Craddocks, their associates, Patrick Davidson, their girlfriends, and anyone else in their network. VCR's, microwaves and TV's were recovered and several people arrested, including Colin Craddock and Davidson. But no one named them, and they both remained silent on interview.

Davidson didn't drink. He was young, bright and was arrogant and full of self-confidence. He could also handle himself. With no forensic evidence to link them to the vehicles or the burglaries, they were both released. Several people, though, were convicted of handling stolen goods, but the Audi crew were never caught.

I helped search one of the flats, which was on the ground floor in one of the Happy Trees blocks. The occupant was an attractive, single, young lady called Michelle. She was very polite, nice and would only tell us that her boyfriend's friends had helped to decorate her flat and obtain all the up-to-date accessories to go into it. The flat was immaculate, modern and incongruent with its surroundings. All identifying marks and serial numbers had been removed from all the electrical equipment. Michelle was arrested but wouldn't name names or the identity of her boyfriend. There was no doubt it was Davidson. I saw him a couple of days later, now driving a brand-new Ford XR3i on the estate, smirking at me as he drove past.

Weeks after I found the Audi, had to attend Harry's shop on the estate. I don't think he was called Harry, but that's what the kids had nicknamed him. Harry was complaining that someone hadn't paid for their shopping. He allowed his customers to run up tabs at the shop and when they wouldn't pay up; he called the police to chase up his debt. I refused to be his debt collector and yes it was another complaint against me. He said he also wanted to complain about a transaction for chocolate that he had made. He had bought three boxes of chocolate for a good price, from some wheeler dealers that called in his shop. When he opened the boxes, it was called 'Chocolax, the world's best laxative.' Again, for me, not a criminal matter but more a 'buyer beware' principle.

I was walking back to the police vehicle, which was obviously parked away from the parking bays, when I saw Davidsons' new XR3i parked near to Michelle's ground-floor flat. I walked over and when passing his car, had the fright of my life. A Pit Bull like dog, inside the car, jumped up at the window, incisors showing and eager for a piece of my flesh. At least Davidson had the foresight to leave the window open at the top for the dog. It looked a nasty piece of work.

I returned to the 850cc police mini super machine and began to drive out of the estate. I stopped to look for traffic near to Harry's shop. I had a thought. I turned back, parked outside Harry's and went back inside. I said that I would try my best to help him with the shopping debts and played the sympathy card, but he was now too busy for me. The moment had passed; he had moved on. I asked for a couple of bars of the Chocolax for 'evidence' and left the shop. I walked back to Davidsons Ford XR3i and as I got near it, the black muscular body of the Pit Bull jumped up with such ferocity that the car rocked from side to side. The dark of the dog in stark contrast to the lovely camel coloured leather interior. Most definitely stolen from some poor victim. Barking, gnarling, and aggression was brought to an immediate stop with the first piece of Chocolax. Then another and another and another. The dog was silent bar the gulps as the Chocolax quickly disappeared. The little tail now wagging. In no time at all, both bars had disappeared.

'Who's a good boy then? Good boy, good boy.'

I left the estate and covered a couple of calls and when it was quiet; I returned to Harry's shop and Davidsons XR3i. It was still parked there, and a cursory walk past it didn't even raise a whimper from the occupant who was still inside. I went back to the police car and started writing the numerous reports I was being hounded for.

Thirty minutes or so later, the door to Michelle's flat opened and Davidson came out. He was alone. He saw me and gave me the 'hard look' gaze before smirking as he walked towards his car with that ubiquitous 'bounce' that, without stereotyping, of course, the young criminals of the day had.

'What the fuck, Shell, Shell,' he shouted up at the flat window.

The driver's door opened and a very sorry-looking Pit Bull emerged, continuously sneezing as it did so. It sat down on the footpath, sneezing away and then started to drag itself across the grass verge at the side, as if it was wiping its arse on the grass. It was a funny moment. Davidson looked in the car and covered his nose with his sleeve and arm. The dog now turning in circles, chasing its tail.

'Shell, Shell,' again he shouted, and the first-floor window opened slightly, and a blonde-haired figure appeared.

'Shell, bring a bucket down, will you? Fucking dog's shit in the car.'

147

I started the police car, selected a gear, released the hand brake and drove off slowly, glancing over at Davidson. I waved and pulled away.

For all the dog lovers who will no doubt be horrified that a member of Sandford Police Force would do such a thing to an animal, please don't worry. The dog was fine, a little slimmer, of course and was seen to accompany Davidson in the days after. He did get rid of it sometime later and word on the street was that their relationship was never the same after 'shitgate'.

CHAPTER EIGHTEEN

THE ELEPHANT IN THE ROOM

Bright eyes, burning like fire
Bright eyes, how can you close and fail?

Jimmy McNeil was a likeable rogue. His family hailed from Glasgow, but Jimmy was born, raised, and schooled in Sandford. When I say schooled, he actually attended. When someone organised a school re-union night, Jimmy turned up at the venue, walked in the front door and then climbed out of a toilet window, never to be seen again. Apparently, he was re-enacting the last years of his school life. He worked for the council as a gardener for a while and I saw him with his shears when I attended an abandoned car on Happy Trees estate. He came over to have a look and pre-1977, Jimmy spoke with a dulcet Sandford accent. However, after Kenny Dalgleish scored the winner for Scotland at Wembley in 1977, (remember when the fans sat on and snapped the bar) Jimmy's accent changed overnight to broad Glaswegian.

Back to the stolen and the driver's door was open, the engine still warm and the wiring was hanging from the dashboard. I remember the car radio cassette system with the latest hi-tec C90 cassette deck. I asked Jimmy to keep his eye on the car whilst I went to collect the owner. I have done many foolish things in my life; this was one of them.

When I returned with the owner, the interior of the car had been totally stripped out. It had only taken me about thirty minutes to re-unite the owner with his car and for Jimmy, sorry the thieves, to strip the inside. Cassette system, seats, steering wheel, the lot, all gone. Jimmy had obviously disappeared and when I later caught up with him, he said his boss had called him back to the office when I left to collect the owner. He knew nothing about the car stereo or Ricaro seats. Whether Jimmy had stripped the car, which I doubt, or got a 'seller's fee' for passing on the information, I don't know. Every day was a school day for me. I was still learning.

A few weeks later, I met up with Jimmy once again. This time in very different circumstances. The Kershaw family had a reputation on Happy Trees. They were a 'tough' family who had moved from Northshire. Five brothers and three sisters lived in a three bedroomed flat on Maple block. Not sure where mum and dad were. No one crossed the Kershaw's, because kick one, you know the rest. They were 'hard' bastards, but usually kept themselves to themselves. Sadly, Jimmy had crossed them.

One Sunday afternoon, the brothers visited his flat and beat poor Jimmy to a pulp. Climbing out of his fifth-floor window to escape, Jimmy hung on literally by his fingernails, looking at the 100-foot drop beneath him. With a nod, one of the older brothers, executioner style, swiftly brought his baseball bat down on Jimmy's fingers. Newton's law did the rest and poor Jimmy ended up in a broken heap on the grass verge below.

When I arrived, the paramedics were trying to move him onto the stretcher. He was in a bad way, but was alive. Learning by experience is a wonderful thing and immediately I reflected on the Nora Perch incident and the near hysterical DCI McAvoy.

'Get a written statement, get a written statement, get a written statement.'

Sadly, that mindset of, 'get a quick written statement' is still prevalent in modern day policing. Although he wasn't talking, I accompanied Jimmy to the hospital and luckily there wasn't an ICU admission and no requests for next of kin. Jimmy was going to pull through, albeit with broken bones and severe bruising.

Some hours later, on the hospital ward, two CID officers came asking where Jimmy was. He was sitting beside me in his bed. He was obviously in a lot of pain and had just been wheeled off to the fracture clinic to have limbs plastered. He'd broken all four of them and had a fractured vertebrae and pelvis. The CID officers were as keen as ever to get the written statement as the Kershaw's had been arrested and were in police custody. In those days, pre-PACE (Police & Criminal Evidence Act), detainees could be kept in custody for a long time without any accountability. Now, one can only be held for six hours without some form of intervention. The CID officers stated the written statement was needed as direct evidence of what the Kershaw brothers had done. Only problem was, Jimmy hadn't uttered a word. The hours passed and after several cups of tea, I was instructed to telephone DCI McAvoy at Sandford CID. McAvoy insinuated I should have barged into the operating theatre when they were trying to save Nora and ask for a written statement. It was McAvoy time again, so I made sure I had done everything asked of me.

'Yes, sir, I know, sir, of course I realise how important that statement is Sir. I will not be leaving without the written statement. Trust me, sir, oh you don't trust me, that's the problem, is it?' I replaced the receiver.

McAvoy wanted a CID officer to take the written account when Jimmy was ready to speak, as he had little faith in my efficacy.

The hours passed by and Jimmy was propped up in bed next to me. His legs were connected to pulleys and I can assure you, Jimmy did not have bright eyes. His head was like a beetroot and heavily bandaged. His lips were badly swollen and nose was obviously broken. It was still all picture but no sound. I was asked to work overtime in order to notify CID when Jimmy was talking. He wasn't.

'Jimmy, listen, please. Look at what they have done to you. You don't deserve this.'

Nothing. Not a word.

'I'm not going away, Jimmy and me, and you go back a while. Remember the stolen car and the car seats and stereo?'

Nothing. Not a whisper.

'Jimmy, I'm staying put. I'm going to wait here until you tell me what happened. I'm not going away,' I said.

Nothing.

By now I was feeling tired, and it was around 1am. Jimmy was sleeping, and I was chatting with the nurses in the office. He would probably be discharged in fourteen days or so. They were worried about his liver, as he had the baseball bat tickle him around the midriff a few times. I went back and sat next to him. I couldn't really tell if his eyes were open or closed due to the bruising. All was quiet.

'Got a ciggy,' in a strong Scottish accent came from the bed. I looked at him.

'Got a ciggy?' he asked me again.

At last, he was speaking. Obviously, the nurses wouldn't allow smoking on the ward, so I asked about wheeling the bed outside, but it was a big fat no. At the time, I was a smoker myself, Embassy Regal, the blue ones. Was it worth the risk of letting Jimmy have a cigarette? Morally was it right to coerce Jimmy into making a written statement with the offer of a few drags on a 'ciggy'? Well, that was the plan.

Jimmy, through me, requested a bed pan and when the nurses pulled the curtain around, I asked to stay inside and help Jimmy, if that was alright. They curiously agreed. So, with Jimmy balancing on the cardboard bed pan, broken arms out by his side, he pursed his bruised lips as I held out an Embassy 'ciggy'. He took a couple of big 'drags', inhaling all the smoke and not releasing it. I nipped the end off the cigarette and put it back in the packet for later. With the bed pan cleared, a few wafts of his blanket to rid the smoke, the curtains were pulled back and it was now or never.

'Right, Jimmy, what happened, pal?' I asked in anticipation.

Silence. The bastard, not a word. I waited and waited.

'Jimmy, come on pal, what happened in that flat?'

I woke around 3:00 a.m. and wondered whether I should go or stay. The batteries in the police radio were dead, so I used the phone in the nurse's office to ring the control room. Unfortunately, there were no CID officers available to ask and the night Inspector told me to stay there with Jimmy until the CID told me otherwise. I wasn't going anywhere, fearing another audience with McAvoy.

'Ay you's not gonna fuck off. A need some sleep,' said Jimmy through the cherry coloured puffed out lips.

'Listen Jimmy, I will go when you tell me what happened. We need to put these people away,' I told him.

'Yous ave no fucking idea ave yeah. None whatsoever. I have to live on that estate.'

'Jimmy, everything will be done to protect you. I assure you.'

'Aye, aye am sure. Fuck off, everything will be done to protect you,' he mimicked in a strong scotch accent.

'Alright then, get ur wee note book an al fuckin tell yee what happened.'

The breakthrough had arrived, and I could score some points with McAvoy. I got my pen, my notebook and told Jimmy I was ready. He began,

'I was at home when this big fucking grey thing came into ma front room and give me a good whackin.'

'Grey thing?' I asked.

'Aye, a big, enormous thing. Grey like, with a reet muscular build. Al gee ya a description, note this down, officer. About 10 feet tall, four legs, tail, big fuckin trunk at the front, couple a tusks as well. Big bastard of a thing. Kick the fuck oota me.'

Even I had worked out what Jimmy was describing. Although a little deflated, I decided to join in his wheeze.

'I want you to focus in on his ears Jimmy, tell me what you see?'

'What do a fucking see? What do ya wanna know about his ears for?'

'Well, the African elephant has big ears, whilst the Indian elephant has smaller ears. Just so when we circulate the wanted photographs, we get the right elephant.'

'Oooh a see,' exclaimed Jimmy, 'well a woodna actually know what ears he had cos he was wearing a fucking balaclava. Now fuck off, will ya, and leave me alone.'

CHAPTER NINETEEN.

THE COUNTDOWN

Super Trouper beams are gonna blind me
But I won't feel blue

My original shift supervisors had moved on. The personnel were changing, but life as a patrol officer was becoming the same, tedious routine. I needed a break, or maybe something different to stimulate me. I had walked all the foot beats and driven around all the vehicle beats.

The shift sergeants were replaced by a former Regional Crime Squad (RCS) Detective, who had just been promoted and an old school Sergeant, that really should have been retired through ill health or incompetence. The former, the ex-Crime Squad Detective took an instant dislike to me and became a blocker. Everything I did, I wrote, commented on, he blocked. A contrarian. He made my life very difficult, for no reason. The other supervisor, Sergeant Ron McDonald, (yes, big red shoes, stripy pants, red wig and big red nose) was something else. I would ask people, what is the connection between Sandford Police D Shift and McDonalds? You got it, both run by a clown called Ronald.

It was 6.10 a.m., and I had just left the police station to walk to the town centre foot patrol beat. The first radio call of the day from the control room.

'776 from Sierra One. Can you wait for Sergeant McDonald on the High St? Mr. Christophers is reporting 'a break' at his Fish and Chip shop.'

A 'break' was police jargon for burglary (Break-in). McDonald bumbled along towards me, chatting shit to those who were about at that time. Talk to him on an intellectual level and you lost him, quickly. Talk to him on an inane topic, like bird shit, and you had him for life. He would provide examples of how bird shit had affected his life.

Mr. Christophers worked hard to make his fish and chip shop, The Chippery, a very busy place. It was on my beat. I always gave him the nod as I walked past and call in when on night shift, for a ten-pence wrap, before I took my 'refs'. When the night clubs emptied, everyone headed for the Chippery, some not for food but for the final chance for a fight.

Burglars had smashed the bottom pane of glass on his front door, climbed in and stole pies, drinks and the cash float. They hadn't caused much damage inside. There were a couple of issues here, one obviously being the burglary, but the other being a broken shop door on the High Street. Why hadn't the night shift foot patrol found the smashed window? Before being allowed off duty, the Sergeants would de brief you and the last thing they asked before they let you go home was, 'Have you checked all your property?' If there was an obvious break-in on your patch, and you hadn't found it, like this one at The Chippery, then you were in trouble. Whoever was on night shift and missed the burglary, would be allowed to return home, get into bed, get to sleep, only to be knocked up and summoned back to the police station, in full uniform, and report to the Superintendent. The officer would have to submit a written report as to what time they last checked the property and why they didn't find the break in. There would be no paid overtime and no expenses for this experience. A front door smashed on the High Street that hadn't been found was bad news for the night shift foot patrol. Superintendent Ahern would rub his hands with glee.

Sgt. McDonald bent down to the door frame.

'Wait a minute, wait a minute,' he said.

Mr. Christophers bent down with him, 'what, what?'

McDonald took out a small magnifying glass and held it up to the door frame.

'He's climbed in here. See that fingerprint whorl. I used to be a Crime Scene Examiner,' said McDonald.

Christophers looked at me and raised his eyebrows, inquisitively. McDonald didn't have any powders or examination equipment. Just his naked eye on the door frame.

'Yeah, definite whorl? I haven't got the 16 definitions but I'm up to about nine. I think I bloody know who this burglar is?' said the Sergeant.

Christopher's eyes went from the inquisitive pose to the downright shocked pose. Then they pulled in on the forehead. Then really pulled in and his head nodded to me and then back to McDonald and again back to me. I read the non-verbal communication between us to be something like,

'This man says he can identify the burglar by looking at the door frame with a magnifying glass. Is he some kind of idiot?'

I nodded back in agreement of his non-verbal's. I took what details I needed from Mr. Christophers and explained the *real* crime scene experts would be along soon. Then McDonald and I left Mr. Christophers, but not before he had discussed the caustic effects of ammonia in bird shit on the building opposite.

I had to get away from patrol work. I needed a new challenge, and my mistake was trying to stop the clouds from raining, when probably my best approach in dealing with my new supervisors was to buy an umbrella. One of the Sergeants took umbrage at everything I did, the other had been promoted way beyond his intelligence. The new shift Inspector was a lovely man, but he wasn't a Jim Morley. Life on the shift was no longer enjoyable.

My tipping point came when, lowly Downfield FC, drew the mighty Leeds United in one of the early rounds of the FA Cup. Leeds were 'marching on together' and a bumper crowd was expected at Downfield Park that winter afternoon. The briefing was held at Sandford HQ at 1.30 p.m., which we all thought was late as usual briefings were at 12.30 p.m. or earlier for one of the City or United games. Sergeant McDonald was holding the briefing and the Match Commander was Inspector Lee 'Angry' Fearon. After the briefing, we enquired how we were going to get to Downfield Park. Inspector Fearon wouldn't speak to us, and McDonald instructed us to walk. Somewhere along the two-mile walk, the Control Room asked over the radio,

'Sierra One to Sergeant McDonald receiving. We've got the football club on the telephone, Sarge. They are saying they are concerned as the ground is very busy and there are no police officers there.'

'Sergeant McDonald to Sierra One, tell the Football Club that officers will be there soon,' came the reply

It was now 2.15 p.m., and it was still a thirty-minute walk. It was a 3:00 p.m. kick off. This was very late.

I arrived at the club around 2.45 p.m. and it was hectic. Queues at the turnstiles, singing, shouting, pushing, drinking in the street. The club and players' tunnel door opened.

'Where the bloody hell have you lot been?' said an exasperated club official. 'It's madness in here.'

The atmosphere inside the small stadium was electric. To my left, a sea of white shirts, scarfs singing, chanting, and swaying bodies. Approximately four thousand Leeds fans had occupied 'the home end' of Downfield Park Stadium. A stand that held two thousand, maximum. To my right, a full stand of Downfield FC supporters. The ground was packed. I think the capacity was 10,000 at the time, which looked like it had been surpassed.

'Right, you three come here,' spurted Sergeant McDonald, as two colleagues and I walked down the player's tunnel.

'We've received intelligence that the Leeds United fans are going to cause bother,' he said, spraying us with his spittle. Didn't take Einstein to work that one out, I thought. Now there's that horrible moment when someone else's spittle lands on your lip. I was in that moment. What do you do, wipe it off whilst they watch you or just lick your lips?

'I want the three of you to go over to the far side of the ground and if Leeds wins the toss, stop the Leeds fans from swopping ends.'

This game was pre-Hillsborough and because Downfield FC was only a small club, fences etc. had not been erected. It was common for fans to swop ends at half time. This always resulted in trouble when the two groups of fans met at the halfway point in the ground.

'If they do want to swop ends, I want you three to stop them. That order is from Inspector Fearon. Any questions?' spitted McDonald.

Any questions, any questions! He wanted three of us to stop 4000 Leeds fans from changing ends. Three of us? Now as a child, I had read with interest the story of the 300 Spartans and the pass at Thermopylae. We were 297 officers short and not trained as killers from birth. This was just plain stupid and really, we should have refused but, you couldn't.

Leeds won the toss and decided to kick towards the home fans. This meant both sets of fans started to change ends. The body of white flowed like a river bursting through a dam towards the three of us on the far side of the ground. An area I now call Thermopylae. I recall the look of pure hatred and anger on the Leeds fans' faces as the first brick hit me firmly in the throat. I hit the floor hard with the wind knocked out of me. I couldn't breathe. My two colleagues stood over me, Eric with his truncheon swinging from side to side, whilst Steve was trying to drag me back. The first boot connected, the second, the third, and then everything went fuzzy. Eric had connected with two of the supporters and they lay bleeding on the floor in front of me. I remember the clicking of the cameras and the press being right in the thick of things. Before long, the three Spartans had become six and the St. John's Ambulance teams came in to attend to the wounded. I remember being pulled to my feet by someone and hearing,

'Come on, we've got the bastards on the run; we can have these. Come on, come on lad, let's get em.'

With blood running down my face, pulling me up by my lapels, was a local football fan called Monty. He was a troublemaker and larger-than-life character who supported the football club with a passion. He was excited as he could see the Leeds fans retreating back to the stand. Monty charged through the police line, shouting,

'Come back when you think you're hard enough,' as he gesticulated with arms beckoning to the home fans to join him in his sole attack on the 4000. The home fans chanted,

'Monty, Monty, show us your arse.' Which of course, he duly obliged.

Leeds United marched on to the next round of the cup and there was a post-match investigation into the injuries caused to Leeds fans and the photos of 'police aggression', displayed on the front page of the Sandford Gazette. The findings were that the police operation was well run, well-resourced and well planned by Sergeant McDonald and Inspector Fearon. Inspector Fearon oversaw the investigation and compiled the report. I had a bloody nose, a sore head and throat. My time on patrol was done!

Overall, I enjoyed my time on patrol and provided the best service possible. There were many ups and downs, but such is life. Moving from Littleton down to Sandford rescued me, and I owe a debt of gratitude to Inspector Jim Morley for that. He was later and quite rightly, promoted to a very senior command position within the organisation before he retired. He was a leader.

I was now twenty-three years of age, having started independent patrol duties at eighteen. I learnt a great deal about myself, about life in general, and about the police family. I learnt that I was I, far too young and lacking experience when it came to advising people how to live their lives.

The experience I gained whilst on patrol was immense, but sometimes it was a very bumpy ride. It was a window into life that I had never seen before. A view of life that was to stay with me forever.

CHAPTER TWENTY

VICE

Everybody, all you people gather round
And get your body busy, move it up and groove it down
We're gonna use it up, gonna wear it out

After my yearly assessment I made my intentions clear. I'd had enough and wanted a move either internally or externally. The job was extremely difficult without having to deal with the conflict and confrontation every day on the shift. The supervisors were not the best. My school mates from the estate were off in the spring to work the bars and pick fruit in Europe. It was 1980, and I was working the night shift in Sandford being spat at, punched and verbally abused.

'What are your views on an attachment to the Vice Squad for twelve months?'

I was asked by the new Inspector,

'Can I go now?' was my reply.

Before I could celebrate, I was summoned to see Superintendent Ahern about the move. Remember him, the medallion man who I refused to salute after he had come straight to work from the nightclub. I knocked on his door and had to wait for the traffic light system outside. When the light turned to green, I was allowed to enter. His door was always closed. I waited a couple of minutes until eventually I got green for go. It was so impersonal.

'Mr Ahern, PC Graham Sir, I'm off D relief, you wanted to see me.'

'I know who you are. Pocket book,' he barked.

He then inspected the contents of my pocketbook, front and back. It was up to date and to the minute.

'You're nothing special, are you? You haven't done enough work to warrant a move to the Vice Squad. How many processes have you done in the last month?' he asked.

'Process' or booking people for traffic offences was not my priority and to be honest, I hadn't done many. I had arrested quite a few people for criminal matters and pointed this out, but he wasn't interested. I had to convince him that the work I had done had been quality over quantity and I had been involved in some good arrests. The 'long nosed plier burglars' always came out at times like these. He smirked and handed me my pocketbook and said,

'Close the door on your way out.'

The Vice Squad had several functions. It performed other duties as and when the senior management team decided what they wanted. We were directed by the Deputy of Sandford Police and not Ahern. He was out of the loop. My tutor constable, Ricky, was already a member of the squad and so we were paired up once again. I spent twelve months in the department, and it was just what I needed, a clean break, fresh start and although we still had issues, the supervisors were on a different level to the ones I left behind. I could now grow my hair, grow a beard and it was like being 'under cover'. Well, in a sort of way.

I started my first evening shift with instructions to visit a pub in Brough Ferry that was allegedly serving youngsters and drinking after time. It was difficult to comprehend that I was being paid for drinking alcohol. I was allowed two half pints during the course of the evening. I could claim my expenses back at the end of the month and it was deemed that two half pints would be just under the legal driving limit. Stella Artois hadn't hit the shelves just yet. If I drank more than two halves, then we had to have a dedicated driver to take us home.

The pub in Brough Ferry was the Three Crowns and one I had never been in. I was disorientated as for the four previous years, the level of supervision and discipline had been intrusive, to say the least. Now I was unsupervised and trusted to visit a licensed premises to drink alcohol. There were eight members of the squad and a Sergeant and Inspector. There were two shifts, days and afternoons, and four constables on each shift. One group of four had the Sergeant as their supervisor and the other group the Inspector. Like Albert Crabtree's toilets, it was a breath of fresh air.

Ricky and I, wearing our scruffiest clothes, walked into the pub.

'Yes lads, can I help you?' asked the barman.

'Two halves of bitter, please.'

'Oh,' said the barman, 'You had me confused then. I thought I had done something wrong. You're police, right? You off duty then?'

Well, that was a good start and even our best denials didn't convince the staff. It was a good lesson and so the hair got longer, the beard unkempt and the clothes? Well, even now, the most predominant colour chosen by cops and ex cops to dress in is blue. It was time to dress down, but the police demeanour took a while longer to change. Some say it never leaves you.

It was after having a couple of halves and retiring from duty one night, well early morning, something jumped into my mind. Superintendent Ahern always closed and locked his door. Always. It was 1.00 a.m. and it was open. Very unusual but interesting. He would never leave anything on his desk, which he hadn't. Everything was locked away. Had he set a trap? I wouldn't put it past him. He was still creating havoc with patrol officers, and one of my colleagues on another shift had been disciplined for reading a newspaper in the patrol car. Ahern stated that he had seen the officer, who was in full view of the public, reading a newspaper that he had obviously just purchased. The officer was, in fact, filling out a missing from home report (MFH), which was four of five pages long. He was turning this over when Ahern drove past in his sports car, dressed for a night out on the set of Grease. Ahern didn't back down, and the officer was placed in the disciplinary book for 'Management Advice'. Here I was, Ahern's office door was open, a clean desk and a quiet corridor. I had a plan.

The next morning was hilarious, apparently. I came in for work at 4:00 p.m. and the damage was still evident. I smiled. I heard that someone had unscrewed the door handle mechanism on Ahern's door and tampered with it. Inside the mechanism and connecting the two door handles is a steel bar. So, if someone wanted to be mischievous, they could easily unscrew the door handle, remove the steel bar, and screw it back up again. Pretty similar to the modus operandi (MO) of the 'long nosed plier burglars'. This is exactly what that 'someone' had done. When the door was closed, it was immaterial how many times you pulled down on the handle to open it. The steel bar that operates the locking system was not there. The door would click shut and lock and lock solidly.

After locking himself in his office, Ahern had resorted to banging on the door to attract attention. He also telephoned the mechanics in the garage to assist as well as the janitor. The now large audience scratched their heads trying to work out how the Superintendent had locked himself in his office.

Enter Sergeant McDonald. He knew how to deal with this as he had been in the military. With a four or five pace run, he hit the door square on with his shoulder and the door, the frame and plasterwork went crashing in on Ahern. McDonald fell on top of him, and both rolled around on the floor for a while. I would have given a week's wages for a ring side seat for that one.

In the post-mortem, the missing steel bar was identified as the cause of the Superintendent's demise and the person responsible for this treachery would be charged with criminal damage and put before the courts, Ahern stated in the weekly memo. He was going to find out who had done this and wanted the perpetrator to own up now to save getting into more trouble. As if anyone would own up. As if.

Another little wheeze was to have maggot races across the corridor and under Ahern's door. When his door was locked, there was still a half-inch gap at the bottom. I did a lot of fishing at the time, so would have lots of surplus maggots. Let the maggot races begin! They used to crawl under his door and then nature took its course over a period of a week by turning into a chrysalis before hatching as a lovely blue bottle fly. Many a time I would walk past Aherns office and notice him stood there, newspaper in hand, chasing several of the finest blue bottles around his room.

'Morning Sir.' I said.

'Ah yes, good morning, officer,' swipe, crash, bang, 'missed the bugger. Ah yes, good morning. Bloody flies all over the place.'

It was pure joy.

The early 1980s was a time when heroin was just hitting the streets. In Sandford, we had the odd drug user, but drugs weren't the issue they are today. It was more cannabis and speed, that's amphetamine. After Operation Julie, the country's LSD supply had dried up. Initially, our net was cast to catch pedlars in cannabis, cannabis plants and amphetamine. That was to change and change drastically when the opiates and marching powders arrived.

The first search involved a house on the estate where I spent most of my childhood and youth, Greendyke. I went to Greendyke Primary and Junior Schools before going to Sandford High School, meeting Kevin Hart and beginning this story. Greendyke estate was ok. Of course, it had its problems and wrong ones, but they were in the minority and most people on the estate were hard working and nice.

Just on the periphery of the estate, were a bunch of houses, one being a beehive of activity. Complaint after complaint had been made about the comings and goings at all the hours and the dealing of drugs. The house occupant was Amber Beesley. Amber was a couple of years older than me and went to the same schools.

She was very attractive and had a string of boyfriends. As youngsters, we always looked up to her and most lads on the estate had a

crush on her. Obviously, one of her many boyfriends had led her down to a life of drugs. Such a shame as like many before and after Amber, it was the beginning of the end.

I scored some points with the new Inspector with my knowledge of Amber and the visitors to the house. The main boyfriend who now had Amber under his spell was not from the estate. He was called Mick and again as youngsters, we used to scatter when he walked through our game of footy. Amber's back door was on a flimsy latch and the door burst open with the slightest of pressure. It was early on Saturday morning when we entered with the search warrant. There was no one downstairs when we entered. The house was a dump with bed sheets up at the windows. Amber was in bed and although still attractive, you could see the opiates taking their toll. No one else was in the house.

The sergeant who had 'taken control' of the search was also new in the department. I didn't know too much about him. He was a small, diminutive figure and had used the information I had supplied in the briefing to his own advantage. By that I mean instead of asking me to tell the office what I knew of Amber and the house, he told the group as if *he* knew Amber and then provided the information that I gave him. It was a trend he continued. We called him 'SLT'. Slimy Little T... erm Toad. Will Toad suffice? But please do use your imagination.

Amber came downstairs and was obviously still under the effects of something. She sat quietly amongst pieces of burnt silver foil, burnt spoons, syringe cases and plastic Jiff lemons. We had no idea of the connections. There were also a couple of containers that had once held something and a big container on the mantelpiece. Amber was arrested as she was suspected to be in possession of something. We just didn't know what.

When we got to the police station, we had a look at the items we had recovered and the Sergeant, SLT, gave his expert opinion on the catch. Firstly, he got hold of the Jiff plastic lemon.

'Yeah, this will be lemon juice,' he said confidently and began to squirt some liquid into the palm of his hand before licking it with his tongue. The audience gasped. Even though I was very new to this drugs and vice game, it was glaringly obvious that you don't go tasting stuff like they do on the TV. That was just stupid.

'Let's see what's here,' as SLT sprinkled a white powder into the palm of his hand, licked a finger, and dipped it in before tasting it. One thing I knew, it wasn't kaylie.

'Oh, that's got a citric taste to it, quite bitter as well,' he said.

'Sarge, you're obviously very experienced with drugs. How will you know when you have tasted any drugs?' I asked.

'Take it from me, you know, you just know,' he said reassuringly and winked at me. I wasn't reassured and one thing experience taught me was never to dip my finger in anything and taste it. The final container had a grey powder inside.

'Now you're talking,' said SLT as he gleefully wet his finger and dipped it deep into the powder a second time. At last, I thought, we have some drugs here, but SLT wasn't sure. Again, he dipped in and tasted the powder.

'Not sure on this one, think we could be onto something here.'

With SLT's instant heroin test and tasting kit suggesting we may have recovered drugs, we attempted to interview Amber, who kept calling me sweet. She remembered me from the playground. She hadn't a clue about anything and just wanted to be back at home as soon as possible, probably for her next fix. She denied any involvement in taking or distributing drugs. She was bailed pending the results of the forensic examination of, and in particular, the greyish coloured powder. The following letter arrived before the powder could be sent for analysis. It seemed to explain matters very succinctly and saved the taxpayer some money.

Dear Sir,

We are writing to inform you that we represent our client, Amber Beesley, in the matter of the suspected possession of controlled drugs, contrary to the Drugs Act. We note she has been bailed until the 9th March following the forensic examination of the items seized from her house. We may be able to expedite the matter in hand by requesting the safe return of her late grandmother's ashes that were in the container recovered from the mantelpiece.

Kind regards,

Messrs, JBC Solicitors.

Boom. Poor SLT. His reputation went before him from then on in.

At the weekly briefings, SLT used to continue to steal our information and when the Inspector asked him what he had been doing, which was always first, he gave our information. We had some good officers on the team and soon SLT was being fed bullshit, nonsense and disinformation. It was fun listening to him at briefings whilst trying to dig himself out of the mess we created for him. Sadly, Amber became another statistic when she was found alone, having overdosed on heroin. Mick moved on to find another victim.

Heroin started to flood onto the streets in Sandford, and crime was soon on the rise. One of the biggest heroin dealers in the town was another lad I went to school with, 'Fatty Abdul'. He had teamed up with another bad lad, and between them they were responsible for creating misery for all. At first, we were treading on eggshells about how we policed the influx and sale of heroin. Towards the end of my tenure in the unit, it had become a relentless war. The battles hadn't really started yet, more was to come in the middle and late 80s. The war on drugs hasn't rescinded.

One evening shift, the Inspector asked to come out with me on my enquiries. He wasn't that familiar with the Sandford area so wanted me to give him a tour and explain what these 'young uns', were up to. In particular, he wanted to have a look at where 'Fatty Abdul' lived, as he had received information that at the back of his house, under a sheet, was a car he was proposing to use for drug dealing. I directed him to where Abdul lived, and he asked me if I would go around the back and get the number from Abdul's car.

It was dark by now, so I climbed over a few fences and ended up in Abdul's back yard. I waited a while until it was clear, then climbed back over the fences and got back into the police car. The Inspector asked me if I'd got the number and I slipped the full number plate out of my jacket and handed it to him. His jaw dropped, his mouth opened,

'What's this?' he asked as I handed the number plate over.

'You said go and get his number, so I have,' I replied.

'No, no no. I said, I said, get me the number, like write it down not remove the bloody number plate from the car you idiot.'

I remained poker faced, and looked at him shaking my head,

'No, you said get me the number, which I have done, and you did not say write it down.'

For weeks he told everyone what I had done and seemed to have a good chuckle about it at my expense, or so he thought.

From then on, the pranks continued. One very simple one was wherever I went in the world, I used to send the Inspector a postcard signed from 'Barry & Jen'.

Dear Matt, Jen and I are having a lovely time here in... we heard that Sally was not well and so we wish her all the best. Will keep in touch and off to Wales next we think. Love Barry & Jen.

Sure enough, a couple of weeks later, another post card dropped into the box from Wales. The Inspector sat there racking his brains and repeating, 'Barry and Jen, Barry and Jen, Barry and Jen,' until one day he clicked his fingers, clapped and jumped up.

'Got it, got it, got it. Barry bloody Chambers. Barry Chambers,' as he laughed away to himself. He picked up the phone,

'Hiya Barry, it's Matthew here. How you are doing, I'm heading up the vice squad at Sandford for my troubles. I've been getting the postcards, pal. What do you mean, what postcards? The ones from you and Jen. Jen, your wife, yeah? What do you mean she's called Tracey? What do you mean? I thought she was called Jen?'

And so, it continued. A friend's wife worked with British Airways. She used to post the cards from all over the world. The prank continued for a couple of years until his retirement party, when I presented him with a framed postcard from Barry & Jen. He smiled and muttered, 'you bastard.'

The vice work continued, and I was asked to parade for duty at a police station down in Southshire one evening. It was a top-secret enquiry, and I was to tell no-one. I assembled in the briefing room with other strangers, presumably other vice squad officers from other police stations. The job entailed going into an alleged brothel and asking for services. We were being supplied with a £5 note, the serial number of which had been noted down. We were searched and all our property taken off us, except the note. The Inspector that was searching me asked me to strip down to my underpants. 'What!' I shouted. Yes, I had to do it and everything else off. Shoes, socks, the lot.

Intelligence suggested that a 'hand job' was £5, so the instructions at the briefing were to ask the young lady what services were on offer, get all the prices, then opt for the fiver hand job. When it came to lights, camera, action, I had to make an excuse and leave. Examples of excuses were given as being embarrassed, being faithful to a loved one or you just couldn't go through with it. My experience of the world thus far was sufficient to know that these ladies would just not buy into that. Don't forget that in the early 80s, young ladies who were forced to carry out such acts were seen as criminals and not victims.

Sporting my Barry Sheene racing jacket, a young lady presented herself in front of me, dressed in a long, orange, nylon dressing gown and slippers. She had the frizzy permed hair style of the times and introduced herself as 'Liz'. I think that may have been false. If I didn't want 'Liz', I had to wait until 'Babs' came on at 9:00 p.m. I told the receptionists that Liz was fine. We walked into an upstairs room, basic, apart from a bed and chair. Oh yes, there was a mirror on the ceiling over the bed. Somewhat creative.

'You a cop?' she asked, looking directly at me.

'Nope.'

'You are, I can tell a fucking mile off. What do you do for a job then?'

'Motorcycle mechanic.'

'Let's look at your hands.'

My hands were pretty grimy as I did take my motorcycle to pieces and rebuild it. So, in some ways, I wasn't telling lies, merely playing with the truth.

'Anyway, what do you want? A shag's £10. I'll do a wank and shag for £15. I don't do any oral or you can just have a wank for a fiver.'

I settled for the latter and duly handed over my evidential five-pound note. When it came to dropping the pants and the action, I said I'd changed my mind and now didn't want to bother.

'I fucking told you. You're a cop. Fucking changed your mind, my arse. Fuck off out. When are we being raided?' she shouted.

I walked down the stairs with my tail between my legs. 'Liz' following close behind. It was really embarrassing, but that was the job they wanted me to do. I did it and provided a written statement as to what happened and the description of Liz, the receptionists, and the conversations I had. I was told to report to that same police station at the same time the week after, as they were carrying on the operation with the intention of raiding the brothel on that night. We were reminded of the Official Secrets Act and told not to tell anyone. I was still living at home with my parents at the time and did wonder how the conversation would go down at the dinner table should they ever inquire. They'd have been impressed, I'm sure.

Fast forward a week and press the repeat button. This time it was 'Suzie', a dark-haired local young lady. 'Suzie' also launched into the cop tirade and then mitigated what she was about to do by saying,

'Now I've asked you if you're a cop, if you tell lies, you can't use any evidence against me. Well, that's at least what they say round here.'

The local law advisory service was wrong. She offered the same menu of personal services and requested that if I opted for the hand job; it turned her on when men ejaculated over her bosoms. So, if I wanted to do this, I could. There was no extra charge. I handed over my evidential five-pound note, completed my written statement of events on conclusion and left, returning to Sandford Police Station.

Later that night, the premises were raided, and several people arrested. No doubt 'Suzie' and 'Liz' were, and hopefully they arrested the criminals behind it all. I wasn't really interested as it wasn't on Sandford's patch and for me that was the end of the matter, or so I thought.

I began the afternoon shift the following day, with the Barry & Jen postcard Inspector telling me that I had to return to the brothel meeting room at 6pm for a briefing by the Detective Superintendent for that area, Alfred Young. His disciplinarian reputation went before him. He was highly thought of, but only by those in senior management posts. At 6:00 p.m. I sat in the briefing room and saw some familiar faces from the operation. This was obviously an update and to thank us for our professionalism. Surely?

'This job has cost me my marriage. I am going through a nasty divorce at the moment, so if I have to go through this, then I'll make it my job to make sure you have to go through it as well. I want each and every one of you to hold up your hand if you had sex with those prostitutes,' blasted Young as he entered the room,

'I will bring the girls in here one by one to point you out, if need be, you dirty bastards. You have totally compromised the operation. Even if you had a wank, I want to know, and I want to know now. And which one of you dirty bastards ejaculated on her breasts?'

I sat in silence.

As time went on, the heroin problem grew more serious and the floodgates started to open. We had new members of the department and Ricky and I had been having some good results. I have always treated people with courtesy and respect, whether a victim, witness or suspect. There was a saying, 'always treat your last prisoner as your next informant,' which I did. With my local knowledge, I managed to nurture some of the best informants in the area. The morals and ethics surrounding the police use of criminal informants have been argued since the court of Star Chamber and will continue for a long time after I have departed this world. Use a sprat to catch a mackerel. It is a cost-effective policing tactic in the fight against crime. It does, however, have its challenges.

We recovered a substantial amount of heroin from a Happy Trees resident who had fortified the front door of the flat so much that a forced entry was not an option. Behind the front door was a steel cage, behind that a steel door and so on. If you did get inside, you were locked in. Word on the street was that you would never get through the doors unless you had explosives. We didn't. But the word was that the occupant wasn't the brightest star in the sky because he always let his cat out at 10:00 p.m. each night. He did indeed and at 10:00 p.m. when the unlocking bolts could be heard from the other side of the door, our waiting party was ready.

Recovered from the flat was just short of a kilo of heroin, amphetamine, LSD, and so on. We were also tipped off to look inside the internal wooden doors. Yes, inside the wooden panelled doors. More heroin behind the panelling. Sadly, and once again, inside the flat was the daughter of one of the local councillors and future politicians. Heroin didn't choose its victims.

I was coming towards the end of my tenure with the Vice Squad. I had been photographed on the front page of the Sandford Gazette whilst raiding one of the current billionaire, David Sullivan's, Private Shops.

Sullivan is the current director of West Ham United and successfully appealed a custodial sentence for living off the immoral earnings of prostitutes. His appeal was based on selling soft porn magazines and claiming he made a lot of people happy. Had he dealt in selling illegal cigarettes, he claimed, then that was a different matter.

By the end of my time, I had also had to watch some graphic films and some of you may think that it was a good job, getting paid to watch pornography. Let me assure you that you cannot unsee once you have seen. I wouldn't want anyone else to watch what I did or see what I have seen. There are some sick and depraved people in our society. This was sexual abuse. I had arrested drug dealers, men in toilets, reported licensees for drinking after hours, and selling booze to children and also arrested my fair share of burglars and criminals. Again, it was time to move on.

One of the last raids was again on Happy Trees estate. Quite obviously cats were seen as the Achilles heel for drug dealers, so the dog of the moment was the Pit Bull Terrier. Drug dealers and criminals had started to buy them to protect themselves and their stashes. I had previously attended a house where the Pit Bull dog had savaged a young girl staying at the house. She survived, but it was horrific, and the dog had locked jaws around her throat. The local posse had killed it to release the young girl. It wasn't nice. Davidson also had the 'shitgate' Pit Bull, remember? These dogs were killers.

The drugs industry is best described as an air bed. Stamp down in one corner and another corner pops up higher. Stamp down on that one, and another pops up and so on. Just like the 'wack a mole' game. Exactly the same with drug dealers. Success by law enforcement in one corner of Sandford meant that another dealer in another corner popped up. That corner included Gregory Benson. A truly nasty piece of work. He had already been convicted of drug dealing and hid his drugs on his seat belt. He stapled the brown plastic wraps to his seat belt when it was fully extended. He then let it slip back down into the seat belt holder out of sight. When he wanted to sell 'a bag of brown', he pulled on the seat belt, the packet came up, he ripped it off and allowed the seat belt to drop back down. He would have gone undetected for a lot longer had he been a nice drug dealer, but informants told the cops what he was up to. Use a sprat to catch a great white shark this time.

The raid on Benson's flat was to take place at 5:00 a.m. The door wasn't fortified, but Benson had told his inner circle that his Pit Bull would fend off any officers long enough for him to get to the bathroom. His stash was attached to a cord tied to a bag submerged in the toilet cistern. Once he pulled on that, the drugs would be flushed down the toilet. In the planning phase of the operation, we had to plan for two major issues. The toilet and the dog.

Eggy was a new member of the department. An ex-squaddie he was always good to have behind you. He was a very serious character and I'm not sure what trauma he had been through in his army career. He was briefed to take a fire extinguisher to use on the dog should it attack us. He was to be one of the first through the door with me. Billy and Neil were tasked with removing the waste pipe at the rear and putting a plastic dustbin underneath to capture the toilet flush. It was a second floor flat so not too far up. The rest of us had different tasks. Inspector Matt had moved on and was near retirement. He took his many post cards from Barry & Jen with him. The new Inspector was a good bloke, as was the new Sergeant and the raid on Benson's flat was looking good.

'776 to Neil. You receiving? You good to go?' I asked over the radio.

'Neil to 776, yes yes, ready when you are.'

'Strike, strike, strike.'

Those three words still send shivers down my spine. The door ram hit and smashed the wooden panels, the door bouncing back off the wall. I was one of the first inside and Eggy followed. Stood at the top end of the hallway was a grey and white Pit Bull Terrier with a head the size of a cow. It was snarling and barking as it bounded towards us. Eggy was at my side and came forward with the fire extinguisher. I was thinking, spray it, spray it, for goodness sake, when the dog leapt towards us. Its muscular back legs propelling it some six feet into the air towards our faces. Spray it Eggy! Spray it! I said to myself. I looked across at Eggy, who had a very serious look on his face. It was as if someone had hit the pause button. The dog was mid-air, legs outstretched, jaws open and teeth on display. Step forward Sir Ian Botham. With probably one of the best cover drives I have ever seen, Eggy placed his good foot forward and with the full swing of the arms brought the fire extinguisher through 'full blade' and despatched the dog to the boundary. The blow hit the dog square on the jaw and it cartwheeled backwards, hitting the wall and sliding down before landing with a thump on the floor. We both looked at each other.

'You were supposed to spray it with the fire extinguisher, not hit it with the fucking thing,' I said, as a figure darted across the top of the hallway towards to the bathroom. At the same time, a naked female came running towards me screaming and shouting. I couldn't get past her quick enough and heard the toilet flush. It didn't matter, Billy and Neil had the dustbin ready under the waste pipe.

After all the usual nonsense, fighting and screaming had settled down, people got dressed, got handcuffed and were moved to the front room. I went to the back bedroom window, opened it up and froze at the Delboy situation in front of me. Billy and Neil were in *next doors* gardens with a smashed drainpipe and plastic dustbin underneath. Neil had his thumbs up.

'Nothing flushed yet!' he shouted.

I went back to the hallway and the other members of the team had Benson and the screaming girl in their custody. The new Inspector told me that Benson was asking about his dog and had I seen it.

'No boss, definitely no dog when we came through the door,' interrupted Eggy, 'I didn't see a dog, did you, Jim?' he said, looking at me with piercing eyes.

Eggy took control of the kit bag and there is no doubt in my mind that the dog left in that. He never spoke about the incident again and when I asked him, in his very serious squaddie accent, he told me if I ever asked him again, he would break my legs. It was never spoken about after that.

Found in the toilet cistern was a bag of heroin and the refilled water was sent for analysis, coming back positive for amphetamine sulphate. Benson received 5 years' imprisonment for his second major drugs offence. He never did ask about his dog.

By now, some Detectives in the CID office were getting used to us arresting drug dealers, thieves and handlers of stolen property. Some had even asked if I wanted to go on a six-month attachment as a trainee detective or CID 'aide', as it was called. Both Ricky and I were very interested. It seemed like a natural progression. The events of one of our last night's working together nearly ended that though. Happy Trees estate was extremely good hunting ground, and we now had a network of informants and contacts that would tell us what was going on for their own different reasons. Some to take out the opposition, some to try and make Happy Trees a better place, some to make money. I saw Nora quite regularly, and she was the same joyful and bubbly person that she was, intellectually and academically challenged but harmless and a heart of gold. Fredericks was still inside.

The name 'Spider' was given to me as a young lad on the estate who was receiving all the stolen goods from the heroin addicts, after they had broken into houses and flats. Within ten minutes of a burglary, the property had disappeared, to either 'Spider' or a number of local taxi drivers.

There wasn't a shortage of takers. Spider was easy to trace and when we searched his flat, it was like an Aladdin's cave. Microwaves, VCRs, TVs, car stereos, the lot. He was arrested and was stoned. Due to his condition and the volume of property found, we spoke to the afternoon CID Officer who told us to let him get his 'head down', let him sleep it off in his cell.

The detective said he would request CID staff to pick up the investigation the next day. All done by word of mouth, of course. Both Ricky and I were off duty the next day, so we decided to celebrate on the way home. As a result, I didn't complete my duty diary as I should have done, as my seductive friend, alcohol, beckoned me.

The next morning, I received a very abrupt phone call at home from our very own DCI McAvoy instructing me to get my backside in the police station as soon as possible.

'Don't ask me why, just get down here now. CID Office,' barked McAvoy.

When I walked into the office, several heads turned around and someone said,

'He's here now.'

Three suited and booted senior officers walked towards me and one of them said, 'Follow me.'

We walked along the office corridor until we came to a filing office. 'In here,' one of them said.

They introduced themselves as senior CID Officers from Eastshire Police and had been called in to investigate the serious assault of Stephen Lingard, aka Spider. He was in the intensive care unit at Sandford hospital with a fractured skull, and what did I have to say for myself? I didn't have a clue what they were talking about.

'I see, son, see no evil, hear no evil say no evil is it?' said Detective Chief Superintendent Parish. 'A young man is in intensive care, and you don't know why. Your prisoner is your responsibility. This is down to you, son.'

'I'm sorry I don't know what...'

'Save it, son, save it. We don't want any denials. Tell us the truth of what happened, and we will take it from there. Section 18 wounding is GBH, son, grievous bodily harm, one down from attempted murder. Life imprisonment son, tell the judge you didn't see anything.'

I have heard many times people say there is no smoke without fire, or they have nothing to hide if the police want to do this or that. I desperately felt alone, vulnerable, and scared. I had done nothing wrong. I had no knowledge of what these serious faced senior officers were talking about. Yet I was being threatened with life imprisonment and judges. It was scary for me, and I was a cop!

I gave my account of what happened the previous evening over and over again. I asked if I was under arrest or anything, and all three laughed.

'No, son, you're just helping us with our enquiries and you're not leaving until we get the truth. You assaulted him, didn't you?' said one of the suits.

Ricky was in another interview room, and my account was being compared to his. The interrogators kept coming back in and saying,

'He doesn't say this and doesn't say that.'

Whether the officers were lying to me, I'm not sure, but I stuck to the truth. To hell with what Ricky said.

I needed the toilet, and one of the officers accompanied me. As I was taking a pee, he was chirping away in my ear,

'You battered him, didn't you? The sooner we get to know, the sooner this can all get sorted out. You will only be suspended at this stage.'

After what seemed like hours of sitting alone in a room, going over and over my account time and time again, I was told to go home and speak to no-one. I was told to stay at home until further notice. I felt awful.

It transpired that when the custody staff changed over at 6:00 a.m. that morning, they tried to wake Spider, who was fast asleep in the cell. They couldn't wake him. He was unconscious, and they thought he may still be doped up. It was later confirmed that his skull was fractured. He was taken to Sandford Hospital, where he spent a day in ICU before being transferred to the main ward.

He was then spoken to by Detectives investigating the indecent and claimed that in the middle of the night he was awakened and taken into a room at the police station by two detectives and beaten with a stick. Two detectives on the late 6:00 p.m. to 2:00 a.m. shift were identified as having visited the cells to speak with him, but had denied assaulting him, as they would. This left it all very messy and my only saving grace at this point was Spider said his assailants were not the officers that had arrested him, but two officers in suits and ties.

Two days later, I was told to come back into work. Although the organisation had told me to stay at home, I had to take the two days I had been off as annual leave days and put it all behind me and move on. I had to give up two days of my holiday allowance. It was later revealed that a nurse had found a small purse in Lingard's locker on the hospital ward containing wraps of heroin and cannabis. He claimed the nurse planted it, on behalf of the police, as he would.

Lingard dropped his complaint against the officers and received a suspended sentence at court after pleading guilty to several drug offences and handling stolen goods. I was never interviewed again about it, but one of my 'interrogators' went on to gain notoriety for the mishandling of several high-profile investigations and miscarriages of justice.

I received 'management advice' for not completing my duty diary at the conclusion of my shift. Who or what caused the injuries to Spider? I have no idea. The experience was unpleasant and scary.

CHAPTER TWENTY-ONE

C.I.D.

The tide is high but I'm holding on
I'm gonna be your number one

Every Friday the weekly Divisional orders were published informing everyone on law changes, policy and staff movements.

'On the 4th of January, PC 776 James Graham will commence duties in Sandford CID as an aide to the department for a period of six months.'

This was a big step; it was a feeling of the first day at a new school, as I walked into the CID office. Start time was 9:00 a.m. and detectives would meet in the very large CID office on the third floor for the morning briefing. Looking around me, I felt out of my depth. I could see my old mate and tutor Ricky sat on the far side, but I had been told I was on B desk, covering an area of Sandford I was comfortable with. It included Greendyke estate and thankfully not Happy Trees. Ricky was on A desk and the other two desks, C & D, covered the rest of Sandford. Each desk had a Detective Sergeant in charge and four Detective Constables, plus another trainee detective, who was an aide to the department. i.e., me!

My mentor and tutor whilst on this six-month attachment was Bill Ashton. Bill was young, maybe early thirties, and someone I knew little about. At the end of the six months, I still didn't know a lot about him. The daily briefing or morning prayers, as it was sometimes called, lasted for about thirty minutes. The head of the morning briefing was usually one of the bosses. DCI McAvoy would sometimes burst in mid-meeting and start barking things at the audience and then just walk back out. The boss doing the briefing would usually ignore his outbursts and continue to read messages out of a big white hard backed book, the infamous CID Journal. The office manager or 'day reserve', would leave messages, reports of crime, results, information, and so on in the journal. It was central to the office and investigations were allocated from it. Every crime report, that had been completed by patrol officers was entered into the journal.

'Who covers West Street?' asked the Detective Inspector in charge of that morning's briefing.

'That's B desk, sir,' replied my mentor and CID tutor Bill Ashton.

'Mr. Thomas has reported that an oil painting he had stolen in his burglary last week is in a second-hand store on Rowntree Road. Can I mark you down for that, DC Ashton?'

'You can mark Detective Constable Graham down for that one, sir, please. He will be carrying out the investigation,' replied Ashton.

Detective Constable Graham! I was now a Detective Constable and had my first investigation. After the briefing, Bill Ashton and another detective asked me if I was ready to go. Ashton had volunteered us both to investigate the oil painting and burglary. I was ready and all three of us walked down the stairs, along the corridor on our way to the second-hand store. We walked past Superintendent Ahern's office and I took great delight in seeing him still swatting flies. Remember Ahern, hairy chest, Hawaiian shirt who I didn't salute?

We walked into the garage area and my tutor, Bill Ashton, started up a beige Hillman Avenger and off we drove into Sandford centre. By this time, I was the owner of a suit and more shirts and ties. I looked half respectable. I sat quietly in the back seat of the Hillman whilst the two detectives in the front chatted away to each other.

'Here we go,' said Ashton as we pulled up outside The Emporium second-hand shop on Rowntree Road. I opened the back door and got out of the car. I noticed that there wasn't any movement from the front two. The car was still running. I popped my head back inside the car before closing the door.

'See you back in the office later,' Ashton said, as I watched the car speed away and disappeared into the traffic. That was the first and last time I shared a vehicle with my new mentor and tutor in the whole six-month attachment to the department. I was on my own, day one.

I bumbled my way through the recovery of the oil painting and soon realised my knowledge and experience bank were both empty. I knew the painting was stolen property, but the shopkeeper said he had paid a fair price for it and wouldn't release it. But it was stolen. What do I do? The shopkeeper had taken the seller's name and address, which proved to be false, and so I told the shopkeeper I was seizing the painting. What power allowed me to do that? I had no idea. I walked the mile and a half back to the police station with the painting under my arm, smiling at curious passers-by. I placed the painting in the CID property store whilst I worked out what to do with it. I asked my mentor, DC Ashton, what I should do, and he told me I was a clever lad, and I would work it out. Yes, I was on my own alright.

Over the next few days, I had to meet the hierarchy of the department. They said more or less the same thing: hard work, loyalty, job comes first, and can you drink? Yes, I could and being a serious part of the assessment criteria for being a detective in 1980 was under a heading of 'social interaction' or drinking alcohol!

In those first few months, I found life as a detective extremely difficult. I am a slow burner, a reflector, so need time to work things out in my own way, but I didn't have the time to do that. There was a lot to do, and it came thick and fast. I was very anxious about the unknown, so I made it my job to make it known. At the morning briefing, I would volunteer for some of the investigations and dealt with them mostly on my own, not knowing what I was doing. I was learning the hard way. I did team up with some other members of the office, but never DC Ashton. He left me to sink or swim. What helped was I knew quite a lot of the criminals in Sandford and B desk did cover some of the earlier places I had patrolled and lived.

The Detective Sergeant (DS) overseeing B desk was approachable and was also very good at his job. He was firm and fair. He liked sport as I did. The first Saturday as a Detective Constable, I was due to work a day shift. Unfortunately, this clashed with the quarter final of the Westshire Amateur Football Cup. I was playing for Lostow FC, one of the amateur sides in Sandford, and being the only goalkeeper, I had to play on Saturday. I spoke with the DS and asked him if it would be possible to play? I would work a spilt shift, work until 1pm and then come back at 6:00 p.m. and work until 10:00 p.m.. He told me he didn't see a problem but would clear it with the boss, who was on cover. My luck, it was DCI McAvoy, and the answer was a very big NO. I had joined the CID to work and not go and play football, McAvoy told the Sergeant. I did point out that I had worked over ten hours of overtime in that first week for no pay. The reply was the same. NO. It was a trend that continued throughout my career, give a lot to the 'job' and receive little in return.

Saturday morning, the day of the game arrived, and McAvoy was in the CID office holding court and making sure I was there. He left soon after the morning briefing, saying he would be back at lunch. He was, no doubt to check on me. He stayed around the office until 1:00 p.m. and by now, he too was swatting those 'pesky bloody flies' that had somehow invaded his office. He said he would be back at 5:00 p.m. to make sure we all finished on time.

Around 1:30 p.m. the Detective Sergeant came into the office.

'What time is kick off?' he asked.

'Half-past two. In an hour.'

'Where are you playing?'

'Lostow Park, ten minutes away.'

'What time could you be back in the office?'

'4:30 p.m. to 4:45 p.m.' I didn't tell him it was a cup game and there may be extra time. That was complicating things.

'Get back here before 4:45 p.m. and whatever you do don't break your fucking leg!'

'But you can't, McAvoy says that....'

DS Steele interrupted, 'Get back here before 4:45 p.m., now go!'

I ran down the stairs, drove up to the ground, arriving in good time for kick-off. The game was an excellent example of amateur cup football, end to end, goalmouth action, a clearance off the line and with ten minutes to go, we were losing 1-0. Then step forward Archie Andrews to score two goals in as many minutes, taking us into the final seconds with a 2-1 lead. My mind was now fixed on getting back to the office before 4:45 p.m. and DCI McAvoy. No extra time, please. With seconds to go, the oppositions centre forward volleyed a left foot shot that was destined for the top corner of my goal. I still do not know how I got to it, but I did, diving backwards, arched back, and plucking the ball from the air. The only problem being that I was flying into my own goal and was about to carry the ball over the goal line. With something like a cross between a Fosbury Flop and a slam dunk, mid-air, I took the ball with one hand and lifted it over the bar, where it fell on the back of the net and ran down it to safety. I remember landing twisted in the netting and hearing the applause and cheers from the small crowd. It was probably the best save I ever made. There was no time for the corner and for the first time in their history, Lostow FC, was in the semi-final of the Amateur Cup.

After the game, people were approaching me, wanting to talk about *that* save and shaking my hand. I had to get away. McAvoy was waiting. I quickly got changed in the car, pulling one muddy arm through my shirt sleeve whilst starting the car engine with the other. I arrived at the police station at 4:45 p.m.., went into the toilets, washed my hands and face, and tried to get as much mud off as I could. I dashed into the Detective Sergeant's office, said my thanks to DS Steele, gave a thumbs up and indicated 2-1 with my fingers and walked into the main CID office. DCI McAvoy was sitting at the top desk with the CID journal in front of him and looking directly at me. I felt his eyes follow me as I went to my desk. I sat down and read some reports and when the market square clock chimed 5:00 p.m., I walked over to the journal to sign off next to my name.

'Been busy this afternoon then, Graham?' asked McAvoy.

'Yes Sir, very busy, had a job over Lostow. All sorted now, though.'

'Enjoy your day off tomorrow,' he said as he watched me walk out of the office.

Monday morning came quickly. DS Steele told me that McAvoy had questioned him after I left on Saturday, to see if I had in fact played football. The Sergeant said no, saying that he had seen me on my enquiries. I had done it. I had got away with it. I considered the 10 hours I had worked for no pay, balanced everything out.

During that Monday afternoon, the Sandford Evening Gazette reporter came into the office for the usual catch up on crime reports and witness appeals for the newspaper. We got daily copies of the Gazette, and when the reporter dropped a copy on McAvoy's desk, the back page headline read,

'GRAHAM SAVES THE DAY. LOSTOW REACH FINAL'
An arresting performance by Lostow goalkeeper and local police officer, Jim Graham, saw the second division side.......'

I felt sorry for DS Steele as we both stood in McAvoy's office feeling the full blast of his lungs. I didn't really listen, as I had years of practice of being shouted at. I did, however, hear him say that he was thinking of returning me to my patrol duties, as I would never make a detective as long as I had a hole in my backside. There was no opportunity to speak. The only respite in the five-minute verbal onslaught was when he had to waft away the occasional blue bottle that homed in on his face, kamikaze style. It was funny. As the tirade came to an end, we left his office, and I noticed a large map of the whole of Sandford Police Division on his office wall. On the map were different coloured pins, red, blue, green, yellow and at the side in his own writing was a matrix spelling out what the colours were for, Blue = Burglary Dwelling, Red = Burglary other than in a dwelling, Green = TOMV (Theft of Motor Vehicle) and so on. The pins were scattered all over the map, and obviously, he took great pride in his work. When I say his work, the work of the CID clerk, Sara. She would give McAvoy the daily figures of where crimes had been reported, and then in his mainly quiet day, he used to stick the pins in the map. Interesting, I thought.

My tutor, Bill Ashton, just let me get on with things and after a few weeks, I settled into the routine. News filtered through that DCI Derek Blake was on his way to Sandford and McAvoy was to be the new temporary Detective Superintendent. Word was that Blake was ruthless, didn't suffer fools nor the lame and lazy. He would never put the knife in your back, we were told. He would plant it firmly in your chest whilst smiling and looking in your eyes.

There certainly was a presence when he walked in the main office at 8:55 a.m. for his first Monday morning briefing. Immaculately dressed, crisp white shirt, mauve tie and pocket handkerchief to match, made to measure grey suit and well-groomed wispy greying hair. There was total silence. He sat down and opened the big white CID journal.

'Good morning everyone,' he said in a low, deep, authoritative voice and like a scene from the Apprentice, the audience duly obliged in harmony.

'Good morning, Sir.'

He started to read from the journal, allocating investigations. Then he stopped and looked at the audience.

'When I ask for someone to investigate a crime, I don't want silences or pauses. Do I make myself clear?'

'Yes Sir,' the audience said in unison.

The Detective Sergeants then answered him when he asked for a name.

'Yeah, we'll cover that boss, that's our area,' knowing full well they would allocate the incident to one of the detectives on their respective desks. Most probably the trainee.

Suddenly, the office door burst open and in bounded now Detective Superintendent McAvoy, like the honey monster off the Sugar puffs advert.

'Who has been moving the bloody pins on my map? I've spent a lot of time making sure…'

I smiled.

Blake turned his head around and stared at McAvoy, who matched his gaze. Blake then launched into a verbal assault on McAvoy in front of the whole office and guests.

'Can I just remind you that this is *MY* office and when I want *YOU* to come in, I will invite you? Until that time, can I suggest that you go back to your office and stick your pins in your map. Now please leave us alone, we have work to do.'

McAvoy's face was a picture. The whole floor was truly amazed by what had just happened. McAvoy slowly backed out and closed the door quietly. Blake carried on as if nothing had happened.

'Do you work in this office?' Blake asked a detective on C desk at the far side of the office.

'Yes Sir. On C Desk. DC Mulligan.'

'Who is your Sergeant?'

'Sergeant Townson, sir.'

Townson a big brash ginger haired character chirped up as well.

'What is that you are wearing, son?' asked Blake.

'It's a cardigan Sir.'

'A what? A cardigan?' Blake paused. 'Get yourself home and parade back on this afternoon on the afternoon shift and when you come back, do so looking like a detective and not like a fashion model. Go on, off you go.'

The young man pushed his chair back as the silence in the room was deafening. He put on his coat and then pulled a satchel over his shoulder.

'Ditch the handbag as well, son, will you?' added Blake

'Yes Sir,' as poor DC Mulligan zig zagged his way through the bodies in front of him, desperate to find the exit.

Blake finished the briefing, and there was a clear message. Do not mess with Blake. The audience scattered in silence, and we all listened to the shouting match down the corridor between McAvoy and Blake. It went on all morning. Guess who won? DCI Derek Blake was now in charge of Sandford CID Office, and in charge he was.

There had recently been a feud between two sparring Sandford families. House windows smashed, car tyres slashed, people assaulted, and the latest escalation being 'torching' cars. Colin Walsh, the 'leader' of the Walsh family, had made a comment that the Walsh family ruled Sandford and if the Forrester family wanted to 'have a go', the Walsh's were ready. This saga was read out by a detective on morning briefing when pressed what he was doing about the investigation. Blake listened intently, then cleared his throat and in his deep voice commanded,

'When this meeting is finished, I want you to find the Patrol Inspector and get as many officers as you can. Sergeant Townson, get onto the Tactical Response Unit (TRU) and I want as many officers as you can muster. Sergeant Rogers, ring Eastshire and speak to their TRU and get as many officers as you can and tell them to parade in this office at 3:00 p.m., where I expect your desk to brief them and all the CID staff working today about your investigation. I want each and every member of both families arrested and make it very clear to each and every one of them that *WE* rule the streets of Sandford and not them.'

The plan seemed to work. After a day and night of arrests, the feuding seemed to stop. A couple of charges were brought against family members, but nothing significant. Blake was in charge alright.

Not long after that arrest day, whilst working a Friday afternoon shift, Blake walked into the CID office around 9:30 p.m.. This was extremely unusual. I was alone doing some paperwork. His metal heeled leather brogues clipped clopped along the corridor.

'Get your coat on lad and take me to the roughest pub in Sandford,' he barked.

That was a difficult one as there were lots of rough pubs in Sandford. I decided to pick the Wine Lodge as by this time on a Friday it would be packed with Sandford's finest. As we walked inside, I could see the Walsh family congregated at the far side of the bar. DCI Blake pushed his way to the front and like the scene from 'An American Werewolf in London', where the two visitors entered the Slaughtered Lamb, the place went quiet and heads turned around and peered at us. Who were these two suited and booted men that had just walked in? They were 'the filth', 'Dibble', 'Cops', 'Pigs', 'Old Bill,' and they used every name as we pushed through to the bar. Unflinching, Blake waited, and I told him about the Walsh family who were now staring us out. He asked which one was Colin, the leader, so I pointed him out.

'Three pints of bitter please,' asked Blake when the server approached. The three pints were duly plonked on the bar. Three pints? I was confused, as there was only Blake and myself.

'Do me a favour young man,' Blake asked of the barman, 'would you be so kind as to take this pint over to Colin Walsh over there? He's been helping the CID catch some criminals recently. Will you tell him thanks for the information, from me?'

With that, the young barman carried the pint over to the Walsh corner and entered into a conversation with Colin. The barman pointed over at Blake and Walsh looked up at him.

'For the help you gave the police, the CID Colin. Just to say thanks,' Blake bellowed out and did the thumbs up. Heads turned around, eyebrows raised, people asked, 'what did he just say?' The pint lay untouched on the bar as family members were trying to calm down an infuriated Colin Walsh.

'Did he just say Colin Walsh had helped the cops? Grassing bastard,' were some of the comments from the Wine Lodge clientele.

'Come on, drink up and take me back to the office,' said Blake. 'Walsh's rule Sandford my arse.'

The week after, a rather unusual enquiry landed on my desk. I had been allocated a burglary to investigate that had occurred a couple of weeks before. Sandford pet store had been broken into and some exotic monkeys and parakeets stolen. It was a 'negative line crime', which meant that after all initial enquiries had been carried out, the report of crime would be filed pending any further developments. Here came the further development. A local vet had received a call from someone asking what to give a Marmoset monkey that had diarrhoea. Apparently, the owner had recently bought it and had been feeding it bananas and chocolate with dire effects. It was probably the chocolax from Harry's shop on Happy Trees Estate.

Portclay was a small town on the outskirts of Sandford. It had been struck hard when industry moved away and was situated at the foot of the hills, sufficiently enough for the townsfolk of Portclay to be called 'hillbillys'. There wasn't a lot happening in Portclay. Never had been. It didn't have any traffic lights. It was my birthplace, and I spent a few years there before my parents realised that houses were cheap for a reason. There were around 5,000 inhabitants in Portclay and only three surnames in the phone book. We moved down to Greendyke, nearer to Sandford, where both parents worked. The enquirer at the vets, re the monkey diarrhoea, had said they lived in Portclay. That's if the address wasn't false. It transpired it wasn't.

It was early evening when I called at the address given to the vet, and as I've said before in this book, you cannot unsee what you have seen. I still have a clear vision of an un-caged Marmoset monkey with an upset stomach swinging over the back of the settee, as I quizzed the house occupant as to their ownership of it. You can imagine the stench. Well, the occupant, let's call him Portclay Pete, had tried to be clever. He had to be applauded for effort but clever and Portclay in the same sentence, I'm not so sure.

Pete told me he had purchased the monkey for £50 from a man who placed an advert in the Sandford Gazette. He rang the number in the advert and the man said he would bring the monkey to Pete's house, which he did. Pete paid the money, and the man drove off in his Ford Sierra. Pete didn't have a copy of the newspaper but was confident the advert was in there. Indeed, it was in the newspaper. Why was Portclay Pete so confident? Because Pete had placed it there himself.

These were the days before CCTV, ANPR, mobile phones and dash cameras. So, identifying someone at the Gazette offices may have proved tricky. But Portclay Pete had a tattoo of a spider's web near the thumb on his right hand and the letters PE. His last name was Dawson, so I didn't understand the 'PE'. I visited the Gazette office and the receptionist and now witness said,

'Oh yeah, I remember him clearly. It's not every day you get someone placing an advert for a Marmoset monkey in Sandford, is it. He was like a hillbilly type with a spider web tattoo on his right hand. I bet he was from Portclay.' Gold dust!

The telephone number in the newspaper was for the phone box at the bottom of Pete's road. Both monkey and Pete accompanied me to the police station. The latter was easy to deal with, but the monkey?

A call had been made to the on-call vet and RSPCA etc. and I was awaiting a call back. In the meantime, I took the Marmoset into the CID Office and placed the cage at the bottom of the office. I went to my desk and could see a light on in an office up at the top of the corridor. I could hear talking. It was DCI Blake. I decided to test out his sense of humour as by now, some four weeks since his arrival, we hadn't seen it. Blake was the custodian of the CID Property Store, which was situated on the same floor. The store was opposite Blake's office. Only he had the key. Obviously, it was full of suspected stolen property, including the oil painting that I had recovered on my first day. To get in the store, you had to sign the key out, after Blake had given you permission. I stood outside his office and waited. He invited me in when he saw me and I put the cage on a chair in his full view. The Marmoset was swinging around at the top of the cage. Blake looked at me, looked at the monkey, then he looked back at me. His face turned aggressive as he stared into my eyes.

'Can I have the property store key please, boss?' I asked.

He was silent. Again, he looked at me, back at the monkey, then back at me.

'I've recovered this stolen property from a break-in and want it securing in the store.'

His eyes were now piercing.

'What?' as he turned his head curiously to one side.

I repeated myself and held out my hand for the key, keeping the best poker face I could.

'You can't lock a fucking monkey in the property store, you clown.'

'Why not, I can feed it every day.'

'For how long?'

'Until the trial,' I said.

'What fucking trial?'

'Portclay Pete has been a bit clever and is going Not Guilty so it could be anything up to ten months,' I said.

'Ten months! Ten months! I'm not having a fucking monkey in my store for ten minutes, never mind ten fucking months.'

'But it's evidence, boss.'

'I can't fucking believe I'm having this conversation,' said Blake, as his face started to turn crimson.

At that point, I had taken it far enough and some would say I'd really overstepped the mark. From the corner of my mouth came the faintest of smiles. Blake looked at me quizzically.

'Are you winding me up?' he asked

My smile became bigger and I know I was dancing with the devil. If this backfired?

'I need the key to put other articles I've recovered in the store. The monkey is on the way to the…'

I hadn't finished when he interrupted me,

'Do you think this is funny, son?' he asked.

There was an awful silence broken by a deep belly laugh that lasted a couple of minutes. I joined in, cautiously not to laugh too loud.

'For one minute then, for one minute, you had me, for one minute…' added Blake.

Everyone knew you could not cross DCI Derek Blake. You had to keep on his right side. I thought I had maybe gone a little further than that and built up some kind of bond with him, some sort of rapport between us. Let's be clear about this, I hadn't. He was always the boss with a capital B.

The monkey was returned to the pet store via the vets and the store owners obviously wanted compensation for the bills they had to pay, plus the missing parakeets. Portclay Pete pleaded not guilty but was found guilty of handling stolen goods at Sandford Magistrates Court. When the clerk of the court asked the Magistrate's if they wanted to retire to consider their verdict, they refused, as they had already made up their minds.

Pete was given a fine and told to be a good boy for twelve months. He was ordered to pay £100 in compensation, but he didn't have any money. The taxpayer would have to stump up, again.

196

As he was leaving court, I asked him about the 'PE' tattoo on his hand as it wasn't his initials,

'I wanted PETE but to be honest it hurt that much, I told him to fuck it after the P and the E, I'd had enough.'

I was now coming to the end of my six-month CID attachment, and I hadn't taken my foot off the gas in relation to workload. I had files and files of work. My previous patrol experiences on the estates of Sandford had served me well, and being a local lad, sportsman and now detective, I had a bank of contacts and knowledge of how the drugs networks ran. One 'informant' in particular kept me up to date with all day-to-day occurrences in Sandford. Information as to who had done what was currency and kudos in the CID office.

Stella Jackson was a proud new mum and an Eastshire resident. She lived in the town of Sandcombe, not too far over the border. Both mum and baby waited patiently in line at the local branch of Sandcombe Bank and when they arrived at the front of the queue, Stella placed some cash and cheques for the baby's birth onto the counter. Stella looked up at the server, who never moved.

'Can I pay this into my account, please?' she asked one more time.

Again, no response from the server, who gave a very stern and serious look at Stella and beyond her. Stella turned around to see the two white eyes looking at her. The black ski mask covered the rest of the face. The gunman was holding a sawn-off shotgun across his chest and then gently pushed it on Stella's shoulder and said, 'move.' Stella froze with fright. She clung to her new baby.

'Move,' shouted the gunman, 'MOVE!'

This time Stella stood to one side whilst the masked gunman threatened the cashier with the gun. Money was being handed over, and Stella looked at the door where the baby's pram had been left. There, dressed all in black was another gunman. The baby started to cry and then the alarm started to ring. The gunman with the cashier started to hurry. He grabbed the bag of money and then to Stella's horror took hold of her arm.

'Out, out, out,' he shouted as he frog marched Stella and the baby outside.

'My baby, my baby please no, my baby,' she screamed as the door of a waiting car opened.

She was bundled in the back seat, now sobbing and holding her newborn close to her.

'Please, please don't hurt us,' she pleaded as the car sped away.

After what seemed a lifetime for Stella, the car stopped, the masked man sat next to her leaned across, and opened her door.

'Get out, get out and if you tell the police, we've got your address,' and he held up the cheques and papers that Stella had placed on the counter. Distraught and terrified, Stella stumbled out of the car, and it wasn't long before she attracted the attention of passers-by and told them of her demise.

The first I became aware of Stella's plight was whilst at home watching the local TV news late at night.

'If you saw anything suspicious, then Eastshire police would like to hear from you,' the newsreader said before moving onto sport and who had signed who at City or United. The next morning at work in the CID office, the phone rang,

'That you Jim?' asked the deep voice.

'It is. How can I help you?' I knew who it was as we had previous dealings on Beacon Hill estate.

'This hasn't come from me right, but we don't like what happened yesterday. Your two-gun men at the bank with the woman and baby are Paul and Daz Ingham. The gun and cash are in their next-door's neighbour's chimney in the roof space. They still live on the Esplanade at Sandcombe. You will find the woman's cheques and letters in next doors dustbin. The car they used is on Windermere Road in Sandcombe. Some neighbours boxed it in as it was blocking a driveway. It's still there now. Don't take too long, they're both shit faced after spending some money last night.' The phone went dead.

I knew about the circumstances of the robbery as all the office did, but I didn't know about the specifics, any cheques nor the car's location. This information had never been released. I didn't know what to do, as this was way out of my league and in another police area. I could deal with burglaries, theft of oil paintings and shoplifting but armed robberies and hostage taking, Premier League stuff. Detective Sergeant Steele was on annual leave (AL), and I didn't really know or trust the other DS's in the office. The only other supervisor on duty that day was DCI Derek Blake.

Once again, I stood in the corridor and waited to be invited into his office. No monkey this time. I began telling him what I had just been told on the telephone. The thing that swayed it for him was the cheques and letters that had been taken from the young mum and the threats made by the robbers. Nobody was aware of this. I was told to sit down.

Blake picked up the telephone and asked for the incident room in Eastshire, running the investigation. He asked for the Senior Investigating Officer (SIO) who would have been the rank of Detective Chief Superintendent for an offence of such magnitude. Blake started explaining what I had told him to the SIO over the phone. After a short while, Blake told them about the letters the robbers had hidden, presumably with the victim's details on and the threat not to tell the police. No one should have known this, and then he added the car. Blake then said into the phone,

'No, he can't. If you want the information, you can come here. He's working.' He covered the phone and asked me what my shift was, 'he's on until 6:00 p.m. tonight and will wait in the office for you. Hurry up.'

The call soon ended, and I was to await two senior Detectives from the Eastshire Incident Room. They wanted me to travel down to see them, but Blake refused. Blake asked me if my informant was authorised and registered with Sandford Police, which they were. McAvoy kept the register in the safe in his office. Blake told me to keep the details of my informant to myself as the Incident Room Detectives would want to interview them.

Later that afternoon, they arrived from Eastshire. Blake had gone out, and I sat with the two Detective Inspectors as they debriefed me about the information I had received. I told them everything: the addresses, where the money was, the gun and where the getaway car was parked. By this time, that had been confirmed, and the stolen car recovered for forensic examination. I told them about the letter with the mum's address on it and that it had been hidden in next door's dustbin. The Inspectors asked to interview my 'informant', but I refused, despite the pressure. They left shortly after, saying they would keep me informed of any developments.

I was at home and just on my way to bed that night when the local news came on the television around 10:30 p.m.,

'Since we have come on air, we are being made aware of two arrests in the case of the young mother and baby who were held hostage by the two bank robbers yesterday. Police say they have recovered a large quantity of cash and the gun that was used in the robbery. Two men are helping police with their enquiries. More on that story in the morning.'

It seemed that Eastshire Police had been successful. That was rewarding.

Morning briefing was pretty much the same the next day, the usual burglaries, thefts and odd robbery were allocated for investigation. Blake also read out the Telex telling the police world of the arrest of Paul and Daryl Ingham, the recovery of the gun, cash, car and other items of irrefutable evidence in the case of the young mother and baby being taken hostage. The two men had been charged and were in custody to appear at Court the following morning. I must admit it was a nice feeling and a clear message that the Inghams had overstepped the mark in the eyes of the criminal fraternity.

I carried on my day as normal and watched on TV in the canteen. An Assistant Chief Constable (ACC) give a press conference outside Eastshire Police Headquarters, announcing the arrests and recovery of evidence. Mum and baby were doing fine despite their ordeal.

Around 4:00 p.m., Blake poked his head in the main CID office,

'You got a minute?' he asked as he looked at me.

I followed him into his office and stood waiting for my next instruction.

'Sit down. Who has spoken with you from the Incident Room today?' he asked.

'No one, sir.'

'Well, who have you spoken to since the two Detective Inspectors came to see you from the Incident Room about the armed robbery?'

'No one, sir.'

'From Headquarters?'

'No one, sir.'

'No one has updated you about what's been happening. You know they found the gun, cash and letters and the Inghams are both admitting it.'

'I didn't know, sir, no. I've just seen the news that's all, and what you have told us all on morning briefing.'

He picked up the phone.

'Stay there,' he barked at me.

He punched the numbers into the keyboard.

'Is that the incident room? Put Detective Chief Superintendent Thomas on the line now. Who me? Blake from Sandford. B-L-A-K-E. Detective Chief Inspector Blake.'

There was a short delay before someone came on the line at the other end.

'You got your men, then I see, and you recovered all the cash, the gun, the cars, the letters. You did a great job, well done. May I ask how you got the breakthrough?'

There was a talking from the other end. Blake was listening intently and turning a shade of crimson.

'You are not at liberty to tell me how you got the breakthrough. You are not at fucking liberty to tell me how you got the breakthrough. You cheeky bastard. I'll tell you how you got the fucking breakthrough, shall I?'

For the next five minutes, Blake launched into a scathing attack upon the person to whom he was speaking. Scathing!

'Not once have you rung the lad up to say thanks, not once have you offered his informant any reward, all you have done is grabbed the limelight for yourselves and backslapped each other. You absolute shower of bastards.'

He replaced the phone and looked directly at me.

'What?' he asked.

I shrugged my shoulders and didn't know what to say.

'Well, get out of my office and get some work done.'

I left quickly.

The final week of my attachment to CID came very quickly. It had been hard work. At times, I enjoyed it. At times, I hated it. The day was a conflict, confrontation sandwich with a smattering of sugar here and there. I made lots of mistakes but learnt from them. I got lots of things wrong and some of my peers and supervisors took great delight in pointing these out. I soon realised, as did the leaders amongst them, that I responded to praise, not criticism. I worked harder for people like Blake, but for others? What got rewarded, got repeated. Managers were only task focused, whereas people like Morley, my former patrol Inspector, and Blake were focused on me. Leaders are people persons.

I had an appointment later in the morning to see our very own McAvoy about my six months and final assessment. I arrived early and admired the pins on his map board, which I had left alone for a while due to the volume of my work. McAvoy told me to sit down, and I waited for what I thought would be the usual speech of 'thanks for your hard work…' but before I could speak, I was subjected to a verbal assault for the next ten minutes. I was crestfallen. At one point, I stopped him and asked him if he had got the right person,

'I'm Jim Graham Sir. I think you may have me mixed up with someone else.'

'I know exactly who you are, Graham. You walk around the office as if you own it. You look at me as if I'm a piece of shit on your shoe. Just who do you think you are, son?' he replied.

I was speechless. I had done nothing, well that he knew of, towards him to warrant this abuse. I walked out of his office absolutely destroyed. When I spoke to DS Steele, he told me not to worry as it was standard for everyone. That is what McAvoy did, apparently. His signature.

DS Steele had been very supportive in my six-month attachment. He too, was a keen local sportsman and the one who let me go and play football. He knew when to put an arm around me, when to praise me and when to kick me. He called me in to his office and told me that Detective Chief Superintendent Tommy Baker wanted to see all the CID trainees that morning. Baker was the Head of the whole of CID for Westshire Police. He was a much older, wiser, very experienced detective, who again didn't suffer fools. He was top of the tree.

I was given strict instructions on how to address him, what to say and when and how to say it. The key to Baker's door was cricket.

'Tell him you play cricket, and you should be fine,' added the DS.

I smiled inwardly. As a police cadet, I played for the cricket team and was also a member of Littleton Cricket Club. I waited outside the door for the green traffic light.

'Come in, Brian, sit yourself down. How's the wife and children?' asked Baker.

A couple of issues I needed to raise with him at this point, I thought. I'm not called Brian, I'm not married, and I don't have children. However, I decided to leave it and see how it went.

'Wife and kids are fine, sir, thanks,' I replied.

'Sit yourself down, Brian. So where are you from, young man?'

'Sandford CID, sir.'

'Who has been looking after you son?'

'Bill Ashton, sir.'

I should have qualified this by saying that Bill's method of showing me the ropes was to allow me to get on with it. Sink or swim approach. It is a brutal way of learning but very effective if you can ride the bumps, and there were many. I immersed myself and had to work it all out myself. No regrets about Bill's approach and one I adopted as a supervisor and father, but hopefully with a little more tact, sensitivity, and support.

The conversation was stalling with Baker.

'I have to apologise if I'm a little withdrawn, but I'm nursing a broken finger,' I added.

'Broken finger, lad? How've you done that?'

'Cricket sir, fielding in the slips'

And there we have it. The rest of the conversation was about cricket and mainly Baker, reminiscing about his youthful games. I gave him a good listening to.

'Who's in charge of you?'

'What do you mean, sir?'

'Who's your boss?'

'Mr. Blake, Mr. McAvoy, Mr Rogers. Any one of them, sir.'

Baker burst into laughter and shouted,

'McAvoy, that bloody buffoon,' and continued laughing. He then told me I was being recommended for a full-time post as a detective. I had to wait, however, for a vacancy.

'Well done son, I've heard good reports coming out of Sandford about you.'

He thanked me, told me to give his best wishes to my wife Kathy and the children, and ushered me out of his office before closing the door.

Sat outside and next in was a lad I remembered from my training school days, Brian Jeffries. I nodded and asked him how his wife Kathy and the kids were. They were fine.

CHAPTER TWENTY-TWO

DETECTIVE GRAHAM

Ooh, this old heart of mine,
been broke a thousand times
Each time you break away,
I think you're gone to stay

After languishing on a Maltese Beach for two weeks, I returned to patrol duties on D relief at Sandford. First to have a go at me was Inspector 'Angry' Fearon, who took me to task for daring to write a report in the police station. Superintendent Ahern then asked me into his office, door now fixed and room devoid of flies.

'The CID want you back as soon as possible,' he said as he threw the report down on the table, 'you won't be going whilst I'm in charge and you are being disciplined for dying your hair.'

The Maltese sun had unfortunately bleached my blonde locks, but trying to explain this to Ahern was futile. For the bleached look, I ended up checking stolen vehicles again in the pound and police yard security for a month.

I had been back on patrol for around a month when I had to return some property to the CID Store. My time in the CID was hard work, but as people told me, I wasn't sent there for a holiday. DCI Blake was still the custodian of the property store key, so I duly waited outside his office. He looked up and smiled and asked me how I was doing. I explained that this time I didn't want to put a monkey in the store, just some exhibits regarding a court case. His facial expression never flinched. He told me it wouldn't be too long and I would be back as a permanent detective in the CID. I explained the conversation I'd had with Superintendent Ahern and that whilst he was in charge of the patrol section; I wasn't going anywhere.

'Sit down,' Blake barked and picked up the telephone.

'If you were thinking of ringing him, he's on his leave, sir, so he's not in his office,' I said quietly.

'When's he back?' asked Blake.

'Couple of weeks, I guess, I don't know.'

That Friday, two days later, the weekly divisional orders read as follows;

On the 4th of August PC 776 J. Graham will join Sandford CID on a permanent basis as a substantive Detective.

I am told that Ahern was most displeased when he returned from his holidays and got no joy whatsoever from Blake.

The early months as a substantive Detective I found difficult. I was now allocated investigations that may have been deemed beyond my capabilities when on the trainee attachment. Now, although some investigations were way out of my league, this was my league, and I was struggling. Real serious and complex frauds, solicitors defrauding legal aid, armed robberies, rapes and so on.

At that time, Sandford CID had one female detective whose main job was to deal with any rapes, sexual offences or offences involving children. Betty didn't have children, but she was seen as the best person to look after them. Betty was nice but always complained about not being able to do her job because of all the sexual assaults. She was an alcoholic. The new batch of trainees had also just joined the department and now, as I was a substantive detective, B desk had a new trainee. I tried to be as helpful as possible and teamed up with Ricky, my original tutor constable from Littleton, when I could. I battled on.

The long hours, the shifts, weekend working, and the stress of CID work were all relationship killers. It was drummed into us that 'the job' had to come first. I was twelve when I fell in love and without wanting to rush things, in late 1982, some twelve years later, my childhood sweetheart and I became engaged to be married. On the day of our celebration and evening meal with our parents, a DS rang from the office informing me that a suspect for a fraud I was investigating had been arrested in Reading. McAvoy wanted me to come in to work and travel across the country to go and get him. I explained it was my engagement party that night and I think the reply was something like,

'Well, we all have to make sacrifices if we want to get along in the job, you know.'

The Inspector was being serious and offered me double pay to cancel my engagement party and travel across to Reading. Forty years later, I'm still married, so that will explain what happened that night.

The following spring, ding dong, the bells did chime for our wedding day. My father-in-law hired a Rolls Royce for the day, and when a patrol car started following the wedding car, I thought it was a lovely gesture. It wasn't, as unknown to the new Mrs. Graham and myself, the driver of the Rolls was disqualified from driving and arrested when we got to the reception!

The wedding day was wonderful with family, friends, colleagues new and old, who all came to celebrate with us. We bought a small cottage on Northshire border, near to where my grandparents lived. It was lovely and as we had already been together for a number of years; my wife had become used to the unsociable hours, the weekend and night shifts, and, of course the seductive lure of alcohol.

I was sent up North for my Detectives training course, which I must be honest, was a complete waste of time. We were drilled and drilled to remember definitions of robbery, burglary, theft and every other criminal offence you could think of. We sat at desks in rows, and had to stand and recite definition after definition parrot fashion followed by listening to guest speakers and watching slide shows. No learning whatsoever. We were given areas of the law to research as a project and had to present our findings to our peers towards the end of the course. My presentation was on Section 11 of the Theft Act 1968, which was regarding removing articles from public places. e.g., art galleries and museums, of which there weren't many in Sandford. Sadly, having waited all my career for an investigation to use my Section 11 knowledge, the week after I retired, the Sandford Art Gallery was broken into, and a painting on show by Monet was stolen. I had waited twenty-five years for that moment!

McAvoy was still at his best, although Blake did try to keep him out of the main CID office. McAvoy's office was at the far end of the corridor and the gent's toilet was at the other end. So, when he needed to go, McAvoy would have to walk down the full length of the corridor, looking into the doors of the main office as he passed. I will never forget how he treated me at the end of my six-month trainee attachment and what he said about me.

My desk was situated near the second door in the corridor. Imagine a large office with rooms on either side of a central corridor. The main CID office had four doors that opened onto that corridor and from my desk had a clear view out of door number two. When I heard the clip clop of McAvoy leaving his office, I waited until he passed door number two, as he headed for the gents. When he reached door number four, I dialled his office telephone number from my desk. His phone rang in his office at the far end of the corridor. About turn, clip clop, clip clop as he ran back to his office. Passing door four, door three, my door, door one and then out of sight. Then I replaced the receiver.

'Bastard,' came the shout from the corridor as McAvoy had failed to reach his phone in time.

Clip clop clip clop and off he set again for the toilet. Passing door number two, three, four and then I would dial his number again.

'I bloody knew that would happen,' he yelled as he set off running back to his office.

For a long time, I had some fun. He was up and down that corridor like a yoyo, two and three times before he would finally shout,

'Bollocks, they will have to ring me back.'

He then worked out what was happening. So, instead of walking down the corridor, he would walk through the main CID office, looking and watching for someone using the phone to ring his office. Like a stalking wolf, he would walk by watching you and daring you to ring his phone.

The word guile had been used in my annual assessment many times. I was pleased with that, even though I didn't know what the word meant. I had employed Marjorie, a typist, who worked in the office on the other side of the corridor, into my prank team. Marjorie detested McAvoy. Arrogant, rude and just an oaf were some of the nicer words she would call him. When she saw him enter the CID office though door two, the door nearest me, she would wait twenty seconds or so and then she would dial his number. McAvoy would look around the CID office with prying eyes, but no one would be on the telephone and so he set off running once again, to answer his phone. Clip clop clip clop, jacket swinging as he ran.

'Bloody bastard again,' came the shout from the corridor as the phone rang off before he got to it. Marjorie had replaced the receiver just in time. She was busy typing away and my head was in my writing as McAvoy entered the CID office.

'You lot think I'm stupid, don't you? I know what you're doing. I know it's you. If I find out who it is, I'm telling you they're in for the high jump.'

He turned his back and walked off slowly to a chorus of whispers and sniggers.

That summer, McAvoy went on his holidays and left the office to work in peace. DCI Blake was at the helm, but more and more he too was being pulled away on murders and major incidents as the Senior Investigating Officer. The Detective Inspectors were constantly changing. Some who came were good, others not so. By this time, I was settling into my 'substantive' position in Sandford CID Office.

I remember sat at home early evening when off duty and watching television. The cottage was lovely and married life was good. With long working hours and sports, we hardly saw each other during the week, but we usually celebrated at weekends. I remember early one evening watching Blue Peter, the TV programme. I am still the proud owner of a Blue Peter badge! Those images of John Noakes, Valerie Singleton, the zookeeper and the shitting elephant will stay with me forever. It was just priceless and as a youngster; it became etched deep into the millstone grit. Fast forward a few decades and here I was again watching again. There was controversy, as the Blue Peter Garden had been trashed. The culprits were unknown and children the length and breadth of the country were in tears. Footballers Les Ferdinand and Dennis Wise later denied any responsibility, but presenters and children alike were distraught. The damage didn't look pleasant. But don't despair, John Noakes, was ready with a new idea and a way to create your very own herb garden. He placed a very small sponge in the bottom of a cut off fairy liquid bottle, one he'd obviously prepared earlier, and onto the wet sponge he placed some cress and mustard seeds.

'If you keep watering them within seven to ten days, you should have a lovely crop of cress on your windowsill,' Noakes added.

McAvoy was on holiday; Blake was on a murder enquiry and whilst the cat was away? Next day I 'borrowed' the cleaner's master keys and bought as many cress and mustard seeds as I could find. Would there be enough nutrients in a carpet to support sprouting cress seeds? The answer from my mini trial was, yes.

When McAvoy returned from his holiday, the whole office made sure they were in early. Rumour was something was going to happen, but no one knew what. There was a silence as the clip clop of his shoes started along the corridor and then as usual and to be nosey, he detoured and walked through the CID Office.

'All busy this morning. Good to see the office so busy so early. Hello Marjorie, I've been to Tuscany for a couple of weeks, you know.' No one would engage.

The stage was set, the audience ready and on the edge of their seats. It was time. His keys jangled and rattled until eventually he opened his office door.

'What the bloody hell is this?' came the shout from the corridor.

'Beverley, Beverley, Marjorie come quick. Has anyone seen the cleaner? What on earth has happened here?'

Curiously, I edged my way to the door and peered into the corridor. There was a gaggle of typists and staff stood outside his office with hands covering their wide opened mouths.

'Just come and have a look at this,' was the shout from McAvoy.

I walked to his door and peered in and was proud of the hard work and dedication. Like a Wimbledon tennis court, his office carpet, from wall to wall, was a lush field of cress and mustard. It truly was an amazing sight. The whole office was laughing hysterically.

The post-mortem and enquiry went on for weeks, and I was interviewed regarding the germination and transformation of McAvoy's office into a tennis court. There were numerous suspects all wanting the kudos of 'it being them', but those that knew, knew. I did point out to McAvoy that some staff were admitting it and I would keep him informed. He thanked me.

Shortly after, whilst on a murder enquiry elsewhere in Westshire, McAvoy made a big mess of things. A proper mess. Nothing surprising there, we all thought. He was summoned to Chief Baker's office and immediately relieved of his post at Sandford. The usual office whip round raised enough money to buy him a 50kg bag of potting compound for plants, which someone wrapped up in gift paper and ribbons. His gift was in the corner of the office for all to see and try to guess what it was. He wouldn't be missed.

My first set of night duties was also quite daunting. I was the only detective on duty in Sandford for the whole seven nights. There was a Detective Sergeant based somewhere else within the force who I could contact and also a Detective Inspector on call should the need arise.

211

Early in the week, patrol officers stopped a Ford Sierra, as the driver was the worst for drink. He was duly arrested, and the Sierra impounded and taken to the police yard, where the poor constable on punishment duty had to secure it. The drunken passengers were sent on their way, but they headed for the police station. They all climbed over the security wall and barbed wire fence and then tried to steal the Sierra from the police station. The guarding officer saw them, and the struggle ensued. The men made good their escape, but without the Sierra. Why were they so keen to get to the car? Once the boot was opened, the answer was clear. AK-47's, up and over shotguns, Enfield's, SLR's the lot. The drunk driver was now in deep trouble and wanted to do a deal.

I called the Detective Inspector who called in to Sandford Police Station to see me. He was very old school and on the cusp of retirement. It had now been established that the guns in the Sierra were part of a deal between criminal gangs, and one of Sandford's Mr. Bigs was behind it. Remember the Walsh family having the feud? Well, this was the head of the other family, Bobby Forrester. It transpired that Bobby had just met the four occupants of the car at a local Sandford pub and the cash was handed over for the firearms. The landlady of the pub was knocked up in the early hours and confirmed that Bobby had indeed met four lads in the pub that night, but she didn't want to get involved. Who would?

It was go and get Bobby Forrester time. Bobby was a very handy lad and lived with various girlfriends all over Sandford. You could never tie him down. I knew of at least one girlfriend and when the Inspector said that his idea was that we should go and get Bobby, my eyebrows raised to the back of my ears.

The Detective Inspector shouted, 'Grab this,' as he threw me a double-barrelled shotgun from the back of the car. 'Let's go and get Forrester.'

I have never been so frightened in all my life. Not from Bobby, but from the gun between my legs. As the Inspector knocked on the front door of Bobby's girlfriend's house, AK47 down by his side, I waited at the back door for Bobby to come rushing through. I was holding the shotgun with memories of Fez diving for cover at the training school. What the hell was I doing? I was at the back of a terraced house at 4:00 a.m. in the morning with a shotgun waiting for Bobby to come dashing out of the back door. Absolutely stupid idea. What would I have done if he had come running out? The good news was that Bobby wasn't at that particular girl's house that night, but the Inspector told me to look on the positive side. We had saved a lot of time and costs by not calling out the Firearms Response Team.

I was to meet Bobby Forrester again and again, but this time on the sports field. He played amateur football, and there was always a nod of recognition between us. He could be found in the bars and pubs at weekend doing his wheeler dealer tricks and always with another young lady on his arm. A local clothing retailer got cleaned out one weekend and although not responsible for the burglary, intelligence suggested that Bobby was shifting the gear. When police were later called to a fight at Littleton Workingmens Club, remember the recorded darts match that time, the rear rooms of the club looked like a gent's outfitters. My mate and former landlord Phil had moved on, and the new occupant had some explaining to do. Half the stolen clothing was in the back of the club. It was decision time for him. Keep quiet and take the rap or name names and maybe keep your licence and livelihood. He chose the latter and so this time, not armed with AK47's or shotguns, I went with three of four other 'tough detectives' to the girlfriends. Bobby was there. He was no trouble at all, but was disappointed that he wouldn't be able to play his beloved game of football that afternoon. As a keen sportsman, I knew how he felt, so against all advice and criticism, Bobby and I did a deal. He was released from custody and bailed to re-appear at the police station five hours later at 6:00 p.m. I was asked why, and the simple answer was so Bobby could go and play football. Colleagues said he wouldn't come back and answer his bail. He did and played football and scored a couple of goals. He pleaded guilty to handling stolen goods and received a suspended sentence.

For the rest of my time at Sandford, I got on very well with Bobby Forrester.

CHAPTER TWENTY-THREE

COURT

Uptown girl
She's been living in her uptown world

My first court encounter was at Sandford Magistrate's Court. It was for the first 'process' or ticket I ever issued. Parking on a double yellow line on Littleton High Street was an offence, or so I thought. Local businessman and a well-liked local car dealer disagreed. So did the Magistrates. The older generation of cop would have just had a word or walked past, but don't forget young constables like me were being ruled with the likes of Himmler. If we didn't hit our quota, down the non-existent league tables, we would go.

The Detective Sergeant Reggie Arbuthnot 'I'm a cricketer' experience will stay with me forever. That was my first real crown court experience. The Northshire Police Detective Sergeant delaying an interview with a suspect whilst he played cricket. Shockingly unprofessional, but glass houses and all that. The Force got back ten times what I ever took out.

Whilst on patrol duties, the main court of use was the local Magistrates, 'the wild west'. It was crazy then and I believe it is unrecognisable now. Most courts are now closed and refurbished as apartments. Due to austerity and under resourcing, the judicial system at the moment is broken.

When I moved into the Vice Unit and then the CID Office, the investigations became more serious and complex, which ultimately meant a visit to the crown court. I loved the pure theatre of crown court and still do. Watching a good barrister forensically tear apart someone's argument, strip by strip, is a joy to watch. So long as it's not your argument.

I have mentioned one of the families in the chapters before, the Kershaw's from Happy Trees estate. They knocked poor Jimmy McNeil senseless before he blamed his injuries on an elephant. Two or three of the brothers had been arrested on another matter over a weekend and I had been due to finish my last night shift at 6:00 a.m. that Monday morning. Well, the excitement of two days off was brushed aside when I was told to stay on duty and cover the courts as they were short staffed. No negotiation, court duty immediately after a week of night shifts.

I got the chance to shower and have a coffee before parading in the custody office at 7:30 a.m. to begin the task of waking the overnight arrests and transferring them to the court section. There was a corridor and tunnel that led to the courts. Anyone that had been refused bail over the weekend had to be fed, washed and moved over to the court cells before 9:30 a.m. From the court cells, when called, the defendant was escorted up the steps into the courtroom. If they were lucky and got bail, they didn't come back down the steps, they went out of the front door and around to the police station to collect their belongings.

The Kershaw brothers had been on the prison bus and had appeared for committal proceedings. This was where the prosecutors wanted the case to be committed to the crown court for trial. This could have been due to the more serious nature of the charges or that the Magistrates didn't have sufficient powers. Magistrates can only send people to prison for a maximum of six months. The testimony and evidence had to be read out before the Magistrates to ensure there was a *prima facia* case to answer. If the Magistrates thought there was sufficient evidence, the case was 'committed' to the crown court. It was laborious as the prosecutor had to read page after page after page.

It was nearing 11:00 a.m., as I looked at my Casio watch. I had been awake now for about 22 hours. I was sitting next to the three Kershaw brothers in the dock whilst the evidence was read and read and read. I fought hard, I really did, but my lead burdened eyelids could hold out no longer. I put my head back against the pine wall covering in court three and just rested my eyes for a second. I was floating in that wonderful halfway house, immersed in total relaxation. I could still hear the prosecutor reading the evidence and just floated along with it.

'Hey dickhead,' said the voice in my dream as my body drifted towards nirvana.

'Hey, hey, yeah you, hey.'

It was a wonderful warm feeling brought to a very abrupt end. That realisation that the noises, the voices, were not a dream.

'Hey,' said the voice as my shoulder was grasped and shaken, 'hey, they want you.'

My mouth was wide open as I opened my eyes and quickly resumed position in my chair, I lifted my head forward slowly. I looked to one of the Kershaws looking at me, face to face and pointing towards the bench.

'Officer, officer,' said the chair of the bench, 'may I remind you that although justice may be blind, it certainly isn't deaf. Would you refrain from snoring, please?'

With the Kershaws laughing, I wiped my chin, coughed and resumed listening to written statement after written statement. At 12:30 p.m., it was done. All over. The Kershaws went back to their cells, and I went to the Doffers Arms for some local anaesthetic. I was in bed for 6:00 p.m. and slept well for 14 hours.

Crown court to me was an act. I have earlier covered the pomp, the ceremony and don't forget the class issues as well. As in any walk of life, there were some outstanding people involved, some good ones and the rest. There was, and still is, a misconception within the police ranks that defence solicitors and barristers are there to frustrate justice.

'How can you be pleased getting criminals off with their crimes? How do you sleep at night?' are questions that get posed to them.

An easy retort to any police officer would be to list the hundreds and hundreds of names of those innocent men and women involved in miscarriages of justice.

'Yes but, there is no smoke without fire,' they say. From my personal 'Spider' experience, let me assure you, there is.

I liked the older, Harry Potter style, crown courts, with the old mahogany carvings and creaky floorboards. All but a few have been closed now in these austere times, which is a shame as history had died with them. Many a Judge has interrupted a trial to tell people to stop walking on the creaky parts of the floor or, 'who has got a squeaky shoe?' A crown court trial was once described to me as a game of two sides, where the spectators don't really have a clue what is happening. The role of the witness, i.e., me, was to assist the jury in understanding the evidence I gave. The role of the defence barrister is to question and scrutinise that evidence, so the jury can be absolutely sure of guilt or ascertain if there is any doubt. The Judge is the referee who, well most of the time, knows the rules. Don't forget our criminal judicial system is an adversarial one. Two sides pitched against each other, and it is whoever wins on the day.

I always used to go inside the courtroom and get a feel for it on the morning of the trial. I would always try to seek out the prosecutor, but as the volume of cases increased, their work became more demanding. I found it better to find the respective court and sit outside with the name of the defendant on a folder that the clerks or barristers could clearly see. Eventually, someone would find you. Or in some cases they could choose not to.

I arrived at Sandford Crown Court for one appearance, sadly the worst for wear, after yet another boisterous, liquid send off for a colleague the previous evening. There was always a licence to celebrate. Staff may have only moved offices, but any excuse for a drink. That morning, I was in a state of self-induced suffering and pain. I was unshaven and must admit, wasn't the finest example of Sandford CID that morning. I sat outside court with my folder and rested my head in the recess, and drifted off into a deep sleep. I must have slid down a little, as I was now taking up most of the seat. I became the focus of ridicule as barristers clip clopped their way up and down the marble floor past, discussing plea deals and the like.

'Morrison?'

I awoke to a wig and gown crouched down beside me and nodded. It was still difficult to speak.

'Yes,' I muttered as I grasped the file from the bench.

'I have spoken with the prosecuting barrister and what they are saying is that your fingerprints are inverted in the bathroom. That means they are upside down under the windowsill. Do you follow?'

'My fingerprints?' I replied.

'So that would indicate that the point of entry was the bathroom, and they suggest that you must have pulled yourself inside the building at that point. What do you have to say to that?'

'I'm the officer in the case, not the defendant, counsel.'

'Oh dear, I do apologise. You do look like a defendant, I might add.

Lesson learnt.

At my next crown court appearance, I was trying my best to explain how I had applied the law according to what a colleague had said in the office one day. He told me the law had changed and foolishly, I listened. Mick had just been on his advanced CID course and so he knew his stuff. It turns out he didn't and when I had to explain to counsel what I had done; the Judge interrupted and asked me to explain my actions.

'Well, Your Honour, what it is, a Detective from our office has just been on his CID Course and he says that Section 3 no longer applies and that it is in order to go straight to Section 4. Section 3 is no longer applicable in these types of criminal cases,' I said.

The Judge looked at me as he replaced his pen in its holder. He looked over the top of his glasses at me with laser beam eyes.

'This Detective. Is he a friend of yours, officer?' he asked.

'He is your Honour, yes. DC Mick Salt, Sandford CID,' I replied.

'Well, would you give Detective Salt my compliments, but could I remind you officer, if that is permissible, that it is *my* job to advise this court, in fact *my* court, on the law of this land. It certainly is not yours or Detective Salt's. Would you be so kind as to just give your evidence officer and leave the rest to me?'

Giggles erupted in the jury. Point made. Tail between my legs, but at least this time the Judge was nice.

Some Judges were real characters playing to their audiences and played they did. As the jury cleared at the end of this particular day, His Honour Judge Jessop looked at the now emptying courtroom and asked the prosecuting counsel a question regarding one of the police officers that had just given evidence. A conversation between them ensued and just before rising, the Judge turned to the barrister and said,

'It is a bad day in my court counsel when the defendants tell more convincing lies than the police. We shall adjourn until 10:30 in the forenoon.'

Mouths opened. 'Did he just say that?'

Any officer that says they are not nervous before giving evidence has either not given evidence before or is telling lies. However nice and rosy you make it; the experience is not pleasant. I truly admire and respect victims of crime and witnesses, who have already been subjected to an horrendous ordeal, to have to go through it all again. But this time under pressure and under cross-examination.

I was sitting outside Crown Court number two, looking at the tiled floor, when the next witness was called into the trial of two men, charged with an armed robbery in Littleton. Mrs. Brown was down visiting her sister and as she left the house that day to go shopping, she saw a man running out of the local Co-op wearing a ski mask and holding what she thought was a shotgun. He jumped on the back of a motorcycle, whose rider then sped off down the street and turned right at the roundabout in a haze of smoke. I interviewed Mrs. Brown and took a written witness statement from her at the time, detailing her account of the events that morning. The written statement is an indication to the Crown, the CPS, (Crown Prosecution Service) what the witness is likely to say when they get to court. This is where truth is established, in the 'arena'. Sometimes witnesses give accounts in their written statements, which differs from their oral evidence in the arena. This usually creates an interesting cross-examination.

Ten months later and here we were at crown court. Mrs. Brown entered the court, shepherded by the court usher, with her black gown trailing behind. I sat outside inspecting the tiled floor as Mrs. Brown gave her evidence. The silence was suddenly broken by both court doors bursting open and banging the corridor walls as they were pushed back with so much force. Mrs. Brown stood in the doorway in tears. She held her bag to her chest as she sobbed and then looked directly at me.

'I'm terribly sorry, love, but I think I've dropped you right in it in there,' she spluttered, as she scurried away down the corridor.

At that moment, and catching the two doors on the rebound, the court usher came outside and enquired,

'Do we have a Detective Graham here, please? The Judge would like to see you now.'

I turned to my partner at the time who had worked on the case with me. He laughed and said, 'Good luck,' as I headed for the courtroom door. It was the walk of death, all eyes on me walking into the old courtroom, down the creaking floorboards with my squeaky shoes. My misdemeanour, which was eloquently pointed out to the court, is that I had inadvertently led the witness when I interviewed her and obtained her account. As she was visiting her sister and the area, she was unaware of street names and her written account should have reflected this. Unfortunately, I had helped her by telling her the street names. When asked about 'Brick Lane' under cross examination, Mrs. Brown quite rightly pointed out she didn't know the names of any of the streets or roads and that

I had been more than in helpful assisting her make her statement.

'Officer, on behalf of the witness, may we thank you for the assistance you provided her when she gave her written account. She could not have done it without you.' A good point and well-made followed with,

'Your honour, you must be as confused as we are as to the content of the witness's account. Is this her account or that of the police officers?'

The defence made an application to have the evidence withdrawn, and the case discontinued but as the evidence of street names was not wholly probative; the Judge allowed the evidence to stand and the robbers were convicted, not before I received another lashing of the tongue from the Judge. The interviewing of victims and witnesses has changed over the years and interviews are certainly not like they used to be. The Achieving Best Evidence Guidelines (ABE 2022) cover all aspects of witness interviewing and, not leading them, as I inadvertently did with Mrs. Brown.

At the time, Kevin Keegan was the captain of the English national football team. He was a 'Player of the Year', a Golden Boot winner and the face on every newspaper, poster, sticker book and post card. Sometimes, of course, for all the wrong reasons, like the airport luggage belt incident. Generally, Kevin Keegan was a household name in Britain in the 1980s.

86-year-old Annie Birchall was at home watching the World Cup finals. Despite her age, she did enjoy her football. Another victim of a 'bogus official' burglary, Annie had let the thief into her home to check the water pressure. Her purse, pension book and her cash savings had all gone. With more mature members of the community, identification of the offenders is usually an issue, but this time it was different. Annie knew her man.

'He just favoured Kevin Keegan, love,' she said as I asked for a description, 'to a tee, his hair, his size, and his good looks. I nearly asked him why he was working for the water board when he was playing in the World Cup. To me, love, Kevin Keegan has just robbed me,' she answered.

Mick Salt and I looked at each other as the words left her mouth and simultaneously, we said, 'Besty. Stuart Roger Best was a Kevin Keegan look alike. He was a 'bogus official' burglar who preyed on the elderly. This was right up his street.

Stuart was arrested, and a small amount of evidence was recovered from his car. Another witness had seen him leaving Annie's home, and they too had described him as a Kevin Keegan look alike. When an identity parade was held, Best had shaved all his hair off, which had the desired effect. No one picked him out.

As counsel pointed out, in the opening speech on the day of his trial at Crown Court, the case would be decided on identification.

'Your honour, the case before you this morning rests upon the identification of this defendant at the scene by witnesses and his likeness to Kevin Keegan.'

At this point, the judge peered over his glasses,

'Kevin who?' Mr Elias.

'Kevin Keegan, Your Honour.'

'Should I know him, this Kevin Keegan?' asked the Judge.

'He's a footballer, Your Honour,' replied Elias.

'A footballer, well I'm at a loss, Mr. Elias. I don't think I know him.'

To remind you, Kevin Keegan was big news at the time, England footballer, shell suits and frizzy perms were his fashion. Kevin and the England football team were playing in the World Cup finals. Keegan was on TV every day.

The Judge looked bemused.

'What type of football, Mr. Elias? Rugby or Association?'

'I do believe Association Football, Your Honour,' replied Elias.

I leaned across to Mick Salt and said, 'The writing is on the wall here, Salty!'

We lost the case, no fault of anyone really, and Besty went on to terrorise the elderly again and again.

When defendants had been helpful during police investigations, they sometimes request the officers put in a 'good word' for them when they appear at court. Over the years, this method of assistance has been professionalised and somewhat sanitised, so no one will ever know who did, or who said what. At one time a good example of how you found out who the snitch was, was to look at the sentencing of the defendants. Three defendants get ten years in prison whilst the fourth gets a suspended sentence. Not difficult to work out, is it?

Asghar Ali Shah was an opportunist, a thief, burglar, robber, and did whatever it took to provide for his drink and drug addiction. He had stolen £500 from a shop, having been disturbed in the back room. He made good his escape, but from the witness's description; it was Asghar. The money was never recovered, and he denied the offence. He was, however, extremely helpful in assisting the police in other areas. When he was found guilty by the jury at his trial, there was a slight adjournment whilst the court found the pre-sentencing reports. The defence counsel approached me and asked if I would be willing to inform the court before Asghar was sentenced as to how helpful he had been on these other matters. I naively agreed.

I was in the witness box and halfway through giving the character reference for Asghar when the Judge interrupted. He looked directly at the defence counsel.

'Mr. Dreyfus, may I ask what on earth you are doing here?' asked the Judge.

'I am merely bringing information to the court's attention as to the character of this defendant,' Dreyfus replied.

'Mr. Dreyfus, I do not require any further information about this defendant, as I have a list here in front of me that paints a very good picture of him. Robbery, burglary, theft, robbery, theft and burglary'

As the conversation carried on between them, I stood anxiously in the witness box. There was a lull in the conversation and then the Judge's head turned very slowly in my direction. I'm sure I could hear it creaking.

'Officer, who gave you permission to give evidence on behalf of this criminal?' he asked me. His eyes now narrowing as he scowled.

'Permission Your Honour? I don't understand,' and I genuinely didn't. My understanding was brought up to speed extremely quickly as the Judge exploded into a tirade.

'You have the audacity to come into *my* court, uninvited, without having the professional courtesy to inform me, this court, or even your own counsel to speak on behalf of an utter urchin, a thief, a vagabond... and you stand there and say you don't understand. How dare you. Who is your senior supervising officer?' the Judge snapped.

'Det. Superintendent Blake, sir,' I said in a trembling voice.

'Can he come to this court now?' asked the Judge.

'I'm unsure Your Honour,' I said as that same feeling of being caught by mum when twelve-years old with a packet of Embassy No 6 cigarettes in my pocket.

'Well officer, I am going to find out and, in any case, and I want you to make him aware of what you have just done on behalf of this criminal.'

'All rise,' said the usher as the Judge made his way through the doorway.

Oh dear! I was shaking and speechless. I could hear my heart whooshing in my chest. I had only just started my investigative career and here I was being taken to task by a Judge, and now being reported to Blake. I knew he would kick me out of the CID.

I was told to wait at the back of the court as the Judge wanted to see the prosecuting counsel in his chambers. That wait seemed forever. I sat down and stared at the tiled floor once again. Oh, dear!

I then saw the highly polished black Loake brogues in front of me and looked up to see the gown and the wig,

'The Judge would like to see you now,' said the prosecuting barrister, who from that point never spoke a word as we walked through back doors, up steps, along corridors and finally stopped outside a tall, old, oak door.

'Wait here,' I was told.

I waited for about five minutes when a smartly dressed usher walked towards me with a silver tray containing a silver coffee set and a small plate of biscuits.

'Are you waiting to see the Judge? I shall tell him you are here,' said the usher as he walked through the door. I noticed there was only one cup and saucer on the tray. I saw the Judge. He was sat behind a desk in an old-fashioned, but plush office. He was now minus the wig.

The wait seemed to be forever.

'You may go in,' said the usher.

I walked in slowly and held my breath as I approached his desk. The Judge began pouring his coffee. I stopped before the desk and he looked up at me,

'Will you ever do that again?' He smiled.

Before I could answer, the Judge continued, 'Now off you go.' I didn't wait. Did I tell Blake? What do you think?

Having learned my lesson, a similar incident took place a short while later. A court case involving a young man called Piggott, determined that it was now mandatory for police to inform the court, if the defendant had assisted them. That assistance or good word is contained in what is now called a 'Legal Text'. No, not a message on a mobile phone, but a detailed written report about the information or assistance supplied and the outcome. i.e., did the police act on the information and what was the result. The report must go through all the channels and is authorised at a high level. The 'text' is given to the Judge, backstage in their chambers before the defendant's court case. No one will know of the text or its content, except those that need to know. Dependent on the outcome, the Judge may consider some form of leniency, but no one will ever know. Even if the information is poor, the police still have to provide the report or text. The Sandford Police policy was brand new at that time, and no one in the office had provided a 'text' for anyone. As a result of my previous advice from Judges, I followed the policy it to the letter.

DCI Blake had moved on to the Serious and Organised Crime Department and the new Detective Chief Inspector enquired about my crown court appearance that morning. He asked if he could come along so he too could familiarise himself with this new 'text' procedure.

We arrived at crown court, and I explained to the Clerk the reason why I was early. Everything was kept secret, so a duty of care to the defendant was upheld. If word got out that the defendant was a 'snitch' or 'grass' and something happened, then the finger of blame would point to the police. We were directed into the back corridors again and the flashbacks of my reprimand came rushing back.

'Miss Ross will see you now officer,' said the usher and beckoned me towards another huge carved wooden door. 'Only one I'm afraid,' she said as she put her arm across the door to stop the DCI. He kindly offered to wait in the corridor.

I walked into the regal office to see Queen Elizabeth I at her desk. Pale, white face, ruby red lips, short dark hair and smoking a cigarette in a long black holder.

'I believe you have an envelope for me, officer,' as she held out her hand. I duly obliged and passed the brown envelope over the table and not under it. She opened the sealed envelope with a small cutlass style letter opener and began to read the contents of the 'text', the report. I was never invited to sit.

'You want me to show this man some leniency, then do you?' she inquired, never raising her head.

'That is a matter for you, Ma'am,' I answered.

She took a long draw on her cigarette and has she exhaled said,

'I am fully aware of that officer, thank you for reminding me. But what I cannot overlook, officer, is that this man has been an *absolute twat.*'

She looked at me. There was a long pause, and I considered my reply.

'Indeed Ma'am,' I replied. I honestly didn't know what else to say.

'Thank you, officer,' she said as she put the 'text' back into the brown envelope and winked at me.

With that, I walked out of her chambers, walked down the corridor and met with the new DCI who, immediately, asked what she had said.

'She says he's a twat'.

Whether the defendant got any leniency, we will never know.

Judge Jessup was probably the best character. It was his Court, and he loved it. He was funny, kind, compassionate and brutal, all at the same time. He played to the public gallery.

'I am going to adjourn for lunch now and I want you all to come back at 2:15 this afternoon. You two scoundrels,' indicating to the two car thieves in the dock, 'you will stay with me as guests in my restaurant during lunch hour. Are those your family at the back of the court?' inquired the Judge.

'Err yeah,' replied one of the two defendants as their families waved from the back of the court.

'Are you their family?' Jessop bellowed to the back of the court as the posse of women and children stood and nodded their head.

'I am going to adjourn for lunch now and your two family members in the dock, the defendants, are staying with me for lunch. I want you to come back at 2:15 p.m. when I will be sentencing them. Do you understand?'

Again, nods of approval from the family and public gallery.

'Would you be so kind and go into Sandford on your lunch, members of the family, and buy these two scoundrels some toothpaste, toothbrushes and some shaving equipment, please. They will need them where they are going. Is that okay?'

Faces in the public gallery were now shocked and stunned as the last sentence started to sink in.

'Take them down.'

'All rise.'

At 2:15 p.m. when court resumed, Jessop sentenced the two to suspended prison sentences, and they were released to the custody of their families, who now possessed carrier bags of soap, shampoo and shaving equipment. The two defendants remained at liberty only for a short while, as they were both arrested shortly after for stealing more cars.

Detective Constable Tony Smythe and I had to wait behind to see Judge Jessup, for him to sign a Fail to Appear (FTA) warrant, enabling us to arrest a defendant who hadn't turned up at court that morning. We knew where the defendant was, so armed with that warrant, we could go immediately from the court to get him. As the court was cleared, the clerk asked Judge Jessop if he wouldn't mind waiting so that we could swear out the warrant and he could sign it there and then. The clerk was talking to the Judge as he beckoned us towards him. The Judge peered over his bench.

'So, it's Detective Graham and Detective Smith then. Well, go ahead gentlemen, one of you tell me what's happening with this warrant,' said Jessup.

As I was about to speak, Tony interrupted me, which I thought at the time was a bad idea, knowing Jessup's reputation

'Your Honour, can I just correct you there please, its Detective Constable Smythe, not Smith,' said Tony, bravely!

The Judge looked over his glasses,

'Shit, Shyte, Smith, Smythe, it's all the fucking same in my court son, now tell me about your warrant.'

CHAPTER TWENTY-FOUR

LOYALTY

I believe the children are our future
Teach them well and let them lead the way
Show them all the beauty they possess inside

Late one night I was at home in bed when I heard my neighbour shouting for help. They had disturbed burglars who had run off down the lane. I gave chase and caught one, but in the tussle my knee had an argument with a car wing mirror resulting in a hospital attendance. The previous CID supervisors were long gone, McAvoy was stacking tables and chairs somewhere, Blake was the Head of some squad and the Detective Inspectors had changed again and again. I now needed an operation on my knee, which meant being out of the action for a while.

The operation went well, and I was at home convalescing when a colleague rang me. He told me that he had been present at a meeting and the new CID management were now seeking to replace me, as I was going to be out of action for a while. The specialist's report had arrived, and my supervisors wanted me to offload me, to be returned to uniform duties. It was very unsettling, to say the least. In my time in the CID, my loyalty wasn't in question, and I delivered beyond what was asked. I now realised that stood for nothing.

Just before my admission to hospital, I had the pleasure of dealing with another of Happy Trees' finest. He was a lovely young man, very polite but a prolific burglar. I got to know him as he passed through the different care homes and the judicial system. I remember his parents continually reporting him missing and the police, including me, catching him, and taking him back home. It was what we all thought was the best for him until his father was sentenced to twelve years' imprisonment for sexually abusing all his children.

Oliver Peart was clever and had brought himself up on the streets, or should I say, the back streets, of Sandford. Whilst interviewing him at the police station one day, he admitted a string of burglaries and wanted to go back to prison. *He saw life as prison and prison as life.* On one of his later appearances at Crown Court, I happened to see him outside the courtroom. He said he'd just been released after receiving a nine-month custodial sentence, but as he had served that period of time on remand waiting for his case, he was free to go. He was anxious as he had no money, nowhere to live, and nowhere to go. I gave him a lift back to Happy Trees, which I shouldn't have done, but I knew it wouldn't be long before Olly would be back in custody for more crimes.

An initiative in the criminal judicial system at that time was the prison 'write off' system. This was where a convicted prisoner, who wanted to clear their slate, could confess to all their crimes and have them 'written off' against the sentence they were serving. It was therefore in their interest to admit everything once they got to prison and not before. There was a degree of proportionality involved in that you couldn't admit stealing apples from the orchard and get sentenced to a term of imprisonment, only then to admit a murder and have the murder 'written off.' There had to be a balance. It was also a political move as a crime 'written off' to a prisoner appeared to the public that the police were detecting most crimes. Sandford CID appointed a 'write off' detective whose main job it was to research patterns of crime, analyse intelligence reports and visit prisoners to get them to confess and allow them to have all their crimes 'written-off'. That meant no gate arrests for the prisoners. It was too good to be true and the 'write off' detective soon became two, such was the demand. The detection rate started to look impressive. If there were only league tables.

Quite simply, the process was abused. For example, months after a burglary was reported, forensic or fingerprint evidence eventually may identify the real perpetrator. Investigators would then discover that a serving prisoner had already confessed to that particular burglary to 'clean the slate'. They hadn't committed the crime, as the fingerprints didn't belong to them, but for whatever reason, they had confessed to it. The reason for admitting things they hadn't done were varied. It may have been an extra packet of ciggies from the officer. This undermined the prosecution of the real offender, whose fingerprints had been recovered. I can hear the defence barrister now asking the very relevant question, 'how can my client be guilty if someone else admitted to committing this crime?' Fair point.

Oliver Peart, by this time, was now back in custody on remand to await his next trial. He just couldn't stop his criminality. Prison was no deterrent for Olly. That meant he appeared before Sandford Magistrate's Court every Wednesday to hear that he was being remanded in custody again until his ultimate appearance at the crown court. Every Wednesday for weeks, the prison service would have to escort him and others from prison to the courts to be told to bring him back again the week after. For Olly, it was a day out. With the advance in technology, thankfully this process on the whole has ceased. Oliver was charged with around ten burglaries, either on or around Happy Trees Estate. Had he committed them? Yes, without doubt. He usually sold the TVs, video recorders, microwaves, jewellery and the like within minutes of committing the burglary. His rewards? Enough money to get kebabs, a few cans and some ciggies. He would commit two or maybe three burglaries every single day. He didn't do drugs. I asked Olly just how many burglaries he had committed in total. He couldn't really tell me but wanted to be produced from prison either a day earlier than his court hearing or a day later and spend that time at Sandford Police Station. He said he would take me out, around the Sandford area, and point out all the burglaries he had committed. The new CID management were reluctant for this to happen as there were more pressing things to do, but eventually, they gave me one day with Olly.

'This one I kicked the front door in and oh yeah, I made myself some eggs and chips. That one over there by the black door. They'd left the key under the mat, oh and that red door one, I climbed the drainpipe on that and got some cash… oh and that one…' and so it went on. His memory was exceptional.

We walked across one of the landings that linked two blocks on Happy Trees and Olly had a pair of handcuffs on, concealed under a coat. In big letters sprayed on a staircase wall was,

'Mr Graham is a twat'. Olly laughed and pointed it out.

'That's you, you know. Mr Graham. That's respect,' he said.

'What is?' I asked.

'They've called you Mr. Graham. That shows they respect you. If they didn't, it would just have been Graham is a twat.' I laughed at the logic.

As we returned to the police station for lunch, in that morning session, Oliver Peart had admitted nearly thirty burglaries. Obviously, I now had to research each and every crime, and in view of the system being abused, I made sure that each victim was visited, and all the reports tallied with what Olly had said. On the whole he was being truthful, and this was borne out by some crimes, not even being reported to the police. The new management team at Sandford was now sitting up and listening. Before Olly went back to HMP Kirkton Park the following day, he had admitted over 50 burglaries. In the week before his next appearance, I visited the victims and researched each crime and so it went on. Before his eventual appearance at Sandford Crown Court for sentence, he had admitted over 350 burglaries in and around Sandford.

An argument then ensued as to the correct means of disposal for the offences that he had admitted, in that, should the court be made aware of them before he was sentenced? The simple answer was, yes. However, he was already charged with a dozen or so burglaries and wanted another fifteen taken into consideration before sentence.

If we were to add another 350 crimes to his 'taken into consideration' list, then his sentence would have been doubled or trebled. Olly didn't like this. It was the only way forward.

The months passed and eventually, at his Crown Court appearance, Olly refused to have the 350 offences taken into consideration, probably due to the legal advice he had received. There may have been sufficient evidence to charge him with some of the crimes, but as the prosecutor quite rightly pointed out, why? It was not in the public interest to charge him with anymore.

The judge sentenced Olly to three years' imprisonment and, having spent eight months on remand, his term would have been around two years and four months. Halve that for good behaviour and he was looking at being released on licence in just over twelve months' time.

'See you then, Mr. Graham, give us a lift back, eh,' he said laughingly as he hopped and skipped down the steps.

Two weeks later, I received a letter from his solicitor saying that he was now at HMP Frankland and was concerned about the 350 offences he had admitted. Could he now admit those offences whilst serving his sentence and have his 'slate cleaned' so to speak? I got the green light from management and the prosecution team. A month or two later, I travelled up North to Durham, with the completed list of 350 Sandford burglaries that Olly at one time wanted to admit. I entered the prison at 11:07 a.m. that morning and I walked back out through the gates at 11:36 a.m.. I was inside the prison twenty-nine minutes whilst Olly signed the forms, saying that he was responsible for the burglaries. He didn't want me to stay any longer or 'chat shit' with him as the other prisoners would think he was a grass and he would be targeted.

'See you when I get out, Mr. Graham eh,' he laughed jokingly.

The detection rate for burglaries in Sandford rose to its highest ever peak. We were always told that there were no league tables showing how individuals, departments or police divisions were preforming but Sandford had just moved up from near the relegation zone and was now competing for a place in Europe.

All thanks to Oliver Peart.

Let's get back to my admission to hospital and the operation on my knee. The management, behind my back, wanted to replace me. Still under the effects of the anaesthetic, my dreams were wild and weird. Stood at my bedside was the new Detective Chief Superintendent for Sandford and he was waving papers and shouting in a slurred voice, and everything was happening in slow motion. The effects of drugs! Except it wasn't. It wasn't a dream; it wasn't hallucinations it was real. He was standing there shouting and as I started to focus; he was holding a newspaper.

'Police Force offices raided in corruption scam,' read the headline. It wasn't Sandford but somewhere else and an internal investigation had revealed that the prison write off system was being abused and crime figures manipulated. Sandford's place in Europe next season could be under threat here, I thought.

'No, *you* are under investigation,' was the sobering message coming from the Superintendent's lips. The internal investigation had thrown up some questions about Olly Peart's 350 crimes, and it looked like I was about to take the hit. Fingers were pointed, voices were raised as the Superintendent pointed out in no uncertain terms what was going to happen to me, and incidentally him, if I had messed up. I wasn't being off loaded; I was being thrown under the bus.

Now out of hospital and at home convalescing from the knee operation, I was visited numerous times by very worried members of the Sandford management team. It appeared the Sandford 'write off' allegation was very serious. Never mind a European slot, this was relegation. I was being advised; it not only could cost me my job but also my liberty. I was also advised to obtain the services of a Police Federation representative or solicitor for the interview I was soon to have with the Senior Investigating Officer on the Professional Standards Investigation Team. I didn't take up the offer, but was confident that I had not intentionally misled or deceived anyone with the Olly Peart offences.

The day arrived for my 'corruption' interview. I travelled to headquarters and waited outside the Professional Standards Office.

A Detective Superintendent, who I had never seen before, came out and invited me to the interview room.

'I see you're not represented. This is very serious,' he said.

I wanted to say, 'well spotted Einstein,' but I guess that wouldn't have helped my predicament.

'That's correct, sir, I'm not represented as I have done nothing wrong.'

A Detective Chief Inspector joined us in the interview room, and the interview began. Tape recorded interviews were a few years away, so it was me against them. The Detective Superintendent cautioned me and asked if I was responsible for submitting the form and now exhibit he produced. It was indeed the form that Olly Peart and I had signed when he admitted the offences of burglary.

'Is this your signature officer?' he asked as he pointed to my squiggles.

'It is, sir, yes,' I replied.

'Now I want you to think very carefully before you answer this question, very carefully. Did you interview Oliver Peart in Frankland Prison where he admitted committing 350 offences of burglary?'

'I did, sir, yes.'

'He admitted 350 burglaries when you visited him?'

'He did, sir, yes.'

'You expect us to believe that in twenty-nine minutes, Oliver Peart remembered then recited 350 burglaries which you wrote down on this form and you both signed? In twenty-nine minutes?'

'No, I don't expect you to believe that,' I exclaimed.

They both leaned back and smiled. A small point, I thought, but the form was typed. All 350 offences had been typed onto the form. Did they think I had a portable typewriter in the visiting area? The Chief Inspector leaned forward and placed a copy of the signing in register at HMP Frankland.

'You entered at 11:07 a.m. and left at 11:36 a.m.?'

'That's correct and as you can see, the report is typed. This was prepared well before that visit. The visit was purely for Peart to sign the form. Nothing else,' I said.

'When did you prepare the form?' asked the Superintendent.

'In the weeks whilst Peart was in custody on remand. He took me out on the Happy Trees estate and pointed the offences out to me. This took weeks, not twenty-nine minutes,' I answered.

'These offences should have been put before the court and not 'written off' to him in prison,' said the Superintendent.

'I agree,' I added, 'but you will have to take that up with the Principal Prosecutor at Sandford. They said it wasn't in the public interest to charge when he denied them at court.'

I was feeling confident now and I could see my punch had landed.

'We have checked Peart's PIN phone and prison letters and he did not correspond with you nor invite you to visit him in jail. This was all pre-planned before his court appearance as you went to see him uninvited. This was perverting the course of justice officer,' said the DCI. 'You withheld these crimes so Peart wouldn't be punished for them'.

'This letter is from Oliver Peart's solicitor.' I then produced the letter which explained about Peart wishing to see me.

'So, his solicitor requested you visit?'

My thoughts overtook me, 'Well that's what the letter says Einstein,' which I then formulated into the following phrase as I didn't want to appear flippant,

'Yes, sir, I visited him because his solicitor asked me to.'

The Superintendent then leaned forward, and I could see he was becoming frustrated. He had left his most impactive question until the end. Here it came, and I was ready.

'On the 1st of September, Oliver Peart was sentenced to nine months' imprisonment at Sandford Crown Court. Your records show that on the 7th of September, seven days later, he was committing a burglary on Happy Trees estate.

He couldn't have been. He was in prison when you say he was committing a burglary, you fool. You have manipulated these reports. He was in prison; he couldn't have committed the crimes.'
I sat in silence and looked at both interrogators.

'Please allow me to explain,' I said, 'on the 1st of September, Peart was sentenced to nine months' imprisonment at the Crown Court but left the court with me. I gave him a lift back to Sandford, which maybe I shouldn't have done, and I accept that. He had already served his time in custody on remand whilst waiting for his case to come to court. I think you will find he made egg and chips whilst inside that particular flat on Happy trees when he burgled it on the 7th of September. He was released from custody on the 1st of September.'
Bosh! My two interrogators looked dumfounded.

'Egg and chips?' asked the Superintendent.

'Yes, I visited the victim, and she said the burglar had actually cooked chips and fried an egg before leaving with her TV. Oliver Peart admitted to making his dinner during that burglary. I didn't even know about burglary or the egg and chips until he told us.'

The celebratory drink lasted well into the night as the management team relaxed and Sandford remained third in the crime league table. I was now back at work and aware that the physician's report about my knee had arrived. I was told that I was to return to uniform duties forthwith, as the CID could not accommodate me due to my injury and proposed absence. I was to go back on the public enquiry desk with Tommy 'the bomb'. My transfer day was announced, and I questioned why I was being moved, as I was now fully recovered. They said it was because of the physician's report. I asked to see the report, but no one could find it. It had gone missing. The Superintendent asked me to obtain a copy from the Specialist. I refused. That word 'guile' again. I stayed in the department.
Loyalty only seemed to work one way.'

CHAPTER TWENTY-FIVE

AN UTTER SCOUNDREL

You spin me right round, baby
right round like a record, baby
Right round round round

I had been seconded to many murders and serious incidents growing in experience, knowledge, and confidence. A new wave of management style was being introduced after the Yorkshire Ripper review and the publication of the Byford report. The old school response of making a decision and sticking to it, whatever, was now on the wane. The criticism in the reviews of policing was scathing. The shift in direction was to make all police officers 'thinkers' rather than just 'do-ers'.

Crockett and Tubbs, dressed immaculately in white linen suits, stood back-to-back, guns in position, with the Miami skyline as a backdrop. The series Miami Vice had hit the screens and my new partner Andy and I mimicked our American colleagues during our next early morning 'turn out'. We were up early, before dawn, on Happy Trees estate to locate and hopefully arrest one of its finest inhabitants. Sandford had recently been plagued by more 'bogus official' type burglaries, where predominantly older people were being conned on their doorsteps and allowing criminals to enter their homes. Some offenders used violence at times, but this latest spree comprised of either sneak in burglaries, or the offender saying they were from the water board, electric board, or simply asking for a drink of water. The older victims would say the offender was a charming young man, really nice and 'you would never have thought it,' approach.

Norman Hardaker was a full time bogus official burglar. That was his day job, and he was a very good one at that. The day before our Miami Vice type operation, Norman was sat on the canal bank at the top of the estate, as we drove past on a totally unconnected matter. Norman was only young, dark hair, slim, tall and another victim of a broken family and adverse child experiences (ACE). He was always in the betting shop and was probably waiting for it to open when we saw him. He was a very good thief and an excellent 'con man'. I noticed he was sporting a broken arm as he threw stones into the canal. He didn't see us.

Two days before seeing Norman, the elderly victim was at home watching Crimewatch UK when her doorbell rang. She couldn't answer it as her ninety-four-year-old body couldn't move in time. So, with her frame by her side, she sat and continued to watch the TV to see what our national criminals had been up to. A face appeared at her rear window, followed by a knock. The face began to shout,

'Open the door love, come on, open the door.' Unable to move, terrified, she sat in silence. The man then produced a tool of some sort and began to scratch away at the putty between window and wall. She could only watch. After a few minutes, the man completely removed her living room window frame and climbed in. She was petrified as he burst out laughing,

'Ha ha, look at that, you're watching Crimewatch and all that. I'm not going to hurt you love, just tell me where all your money is, and I'll leave you alone.'

He searched the house and stole her money whilst she sat in silence throughout. He came downstairs and sat down next to the victim and drank a glass of water. He then said farewell and jumped out of the hole in the wall that once was her window. In a second, he was gone.

Barry 'Bazzer' Wilkinson, the local window cleaner, was collecting his money that Thursday night and took a shortcut along the canal bank. A figure came through some bushes at the bottom of a garden. The young man nodded to Barry, who in turn told him to be careful, especially with that broken arm.

When I arrived to see the elderly victim, she was disorientated and terribly upset, as you can imagine. She was adamant that she would recognise the offender again, which was great news. That information was written also in the initial crime report completed by the responding police officer. The crime was discovered when the carers came to put Alice to bed. Police officers and crime scene examiners had already been before I visited the morning after.

I knocked on the door and waited a long time before I heard the latches being undone.

'Hello, I'm from the police. I'm here about your burglary.'
The lady put her hand to her ear.

'I'm from the Police. I'm here about the burglary,' I shouted.

'You're friends of Lisa?'

'No, I'm from the Police. I'm a detective from the CID. I'm here to investigate your burglary. Police,' I shouted.

'You're the Police?'

'Yes, I'm from the police, from the CID.'

'Oh good, that's handy, I'm waiting for the police,' she said, looking over my shoulder.

With that, I took my warrant card and photographic I.D. from my pocket and held it up to show the victim before I went any further. She looked at the photograph and squinted her eyes. Again, I shouted,

'I am from the CID. Look at the identification card.'

'Yes, that's him, the bugger. I would recognise him anywhere. Took all my money, you know.'

It was sad and unfortunately, time gradually takes away what we now take for granted. Any identification of the offender by the poor victim was going to be troublesome.

'He was a lovely, nice boy, really. He didn't harm me, just took my handbag and money. He had his arm in plaster. He's a builder, you know, and a beam fell on him. He'd been in hospital all day, but he's going to fix my window tomorrow. Nice boy really.'

The coincidental elements of crime are when the victim, location, and offender all meet. We had them all. Along one stretch of Sandford Canal there had been thirty-five sneak in or bogus official type burglaries. Some of the victims had disturbed and chased the thief who, unknown to them, was upstairs in their house, whilst they watched television downstairs. All descriptions were bland, 'white male, 6ft tall with dark hair'. It was going to be Norman. It had to be. The pieces of the jigsaw just needed putting together.

So back to Crockett and Tubbs, not the Miami Vice pairing, but Andy and I, embarking on our next mission at 5:00 a.m. on a cold, dark, winter's morning. We were now climbing the staircases of Happy Trees estate, heading for the top floor. The stench of urine was overpowering. We went from doorway to doorway, covering each other, as we mocked our Miami counterparts. I held my hands out in front of me as though holding a revolver. I nodded to Andy to make the dash to the next walkway.

'Go, I'll cover you,' I said in an American accent, as Andy walked backwards down the walkway, arms outstretched with his imaginary pistol in front of him. He walked past the graffiti and my tag, 'Mr. Graham is a twat', as I covered him, arms outstretched.

'Go, go go,' I shouted as Andy scurried around the corner aiming his imaginary pistol.

There was an almighty crash. White liquid trickled past my feet and I heard shouting. I jumped around the corner, arms outstretched, shouting,

'Freeze motherfucker,' to which the prostrate milkman shouted back,

'Don't shoot, don't shoot,' with Andy stood over him, hands still together holding his imaginary weapon. Oh dear!

We dusted the milkman down who went on his way, nervously looking over his shoulder as he did so. We arrived at Larch block and the last known address (lka) of Norman Hardaker. We stood either side of the door, backs to the wall and imaginary guns drawn. I placed my hand on the door handle and surprisingly, the door was open. It was still dark, and the element of surprise was now clearly on our side. We tip toed down the hallway and the choice was left or right. I chose wrong. Very wrong. Pitter-patter pitter-patter as the largest doberman, ears now pulled backwards and snarling, headed my way. Pitter patter. Teeth now showing and with saliva dribbling, I thought it may be wise to drop my imaginary 'revolver' and lower my hands. I gritted my teeth and held my breath as the dog approached. Andy stood behind me and the slightest of whispers left his mouth,

'Oh shit.'

The moist black nose sniffed and sniffed again and firmly presented itself in my groin. I walked backwards and felt my back against the wall. I stayed motionless as the doberman pushed deeper and deeper, side to side, and then sneezed. My groin was released and now it was Andy's turn, as the dog enjoyed a good few pushes and pokes in his groin. Pitter patter pitter patter, down the hallway and through the open door and onto the landing outside. The dog then looked both ways before tip toeing away into the early morning.

Norman was fast asleep in bed and, unfortunately, was still in possession of some jewellery from a burglary the previous evening. The occupants of the house didn't even know he'd been inside. He had opened the back-kitchen door and sneaked in whilst the family watched TV downstairs. He removed the jewellery from a bedroom and tip-toed out. If only they had a doberman.

He lifted up from the mattress like the corpse on the mortuary slab, still fully clothed. No duck down quilts on Happy Trees.

'You're under arrest Norman and we want to search your flat,' I said.

'Don't mess it the place up lads, arrested what for?' he said, rubbing his eyes.

When we arrived at the Police Station, Norman was found suitable accommodation. In the CID office all the telephones were continually ringing out. It was only 5:30 a.m., but someone was in demand. I picked up the phone,

'This is the Force Control Room, have you got an armed operation on-going over there on Happy Trees estate?'

The next to go was the police radio,

'Sierra One to Night Crime Patrol receiving, Night Crime Patrol are you receiving?' (NCP).
Night Crime Patrol was usually the one detective on night duty.

'Night Crime Patrol, go ahead,' came the response over the radio.

'We are getting calls that an armed police operation is ongoing on Happy Trees estate. Two detectives with guns and a doberman. Any knowledge Night Crime Patrol?' said the radio operator.

'No negative, certainly not me', replied the night detective.

That afternoon, the late edition of the Sandford Gazette showed local milkman Ernie Whitworth with his hands in the air, 'stick em up' style, as he re-lived his ordeal at the hands of the two-armed police officers. Sandford Police issued a statement denying any armed officers were on duty that day. Ernie was, 'not mistaken', he said, 'pair of em had big silver revolvers.'

Hardaker admitted over 90 offences of burglary, including the Crimewatch one. When interviewed about that burglary, where he removed the whole window, he laughed,

'Yeah, pissed myself at that one. She was sitting there watching TV. I tried to force the widow but the whole bloody frame came out it was that old. I climbed in and she was watching Crimewatch UK,', he began laughing out loud, 'I think she thought I was her grandson, I'm not sure.'

Hardaker was kept in custody to appear at Crown Court, charged with five burglaries and 91 other offences of burglary to be taken into consideration when sentenced. At his appearance at Crown Court, Judge Jessop called him an 'utter scoundrel'. His defence counsel, Mr. Bromley, put forward that Hardaker was from a broken home and had, unfortunately, become addicted to gambling. He resorted to these criminal acts to feed his habit.

'Your Honour,' said Bromley, 'it is inevitable that the defendant faces a custodial sentence and all that I ask is that you consider that when sentencing him, that you sentence him in months, rather than years.'

With that counsel became seated and Judge Jessop paused, looked up and then ripped into the 'utter scoundrel'. At the end of his tirade and by way of sentencing Hardaker, the Judge bellowed in his deep gruff voice,

'I have listened carefully to what your counsel, Mr. Bromley, has said and take note of your current domestic situation. I also share his view that any custodial sentence I give you will be in months, rather than years.'

What I thought! This man had preyed on the old and vulnerable and Jessop was going to give him months in prison. I kept quiet as Jessop continued,

'You will go to prison for 90 months. Take him down.'
The doberman went onto a new life elsewhere.

CHAPTER TWENTY-SIX

FRED FLINSTONE

Never gonna give you up
Never gonna let you down
Never gonna run around and desert you

The Graham's were now a full family unit as Rick Astley hit the top spot. Our daughter Louise was born in the summer of 1986 and her brother, Andrew, some 15 months later. Life in the Graham household was extremely busy. Long shifts, two babies, a promotion exam and life had taken on a whole new meaning.

Another Detective Superintendent had arrived. He was a nice man; he listened and created a great atmosphere in the office. He liked a laugh as did some of the other management team. One day the Superintendent sat me down in his office.

'The world doesn't end at the Sandford boundary, Jim,' he said, 'there is a big wide world out there if you push through those doors at the end of the corridor. There is no doubt you are now a big fish in Sandford CID. But Sandford CID is a very small pond.'

I think he also used that word 'guile' again in my annual appraisal. I had a lot of time for the new boss. He was a people person. A different leader.

I was now receiving information from all quarters about crime, drugs, stolen property and the volume of work and complexity of it was increasing. The same families were running wild and the

Craddock family was still involved in criminality. This time a burglary at a local jewellers. They stole a 3.5-ton flat back lorry and welded a steel girder onto the back. As late-night revellers enjoyed their curries in the Tandoori Spot, the lorry reversed into position and whacked into the jewellery shop front window with such force, the front of the shop totally collapsed, taking the front of the Tandoori Spot with it. The jeweller's owner, who had heard of an impending attack, slept on the premises to thwart the burglary but was now entombed deep in the rubble. Four masked men went into the jewellers and helped themselves to the contents of the smashed display cabinets. They sped off in a stolen car, leaving behind a scene of total devastation.

Next morning, I received a telephone call to say that the Craddocks and a new kid on the block, 'Beaky', were responsible and the rings were now in possession of a handler called Mr. Flintstone. After the crime scene examiners had finished, they said the attackers, it seemed, were wearing socks over their footwear. Two of the Craddock brothers had just been convicted of a number of burglaries where safes were targeted. They were convicted from forensic examination of footwear impressions at the scene matching their trainers. Lessons learnt. Socks over the top of their trainer's next time.

I was now standing in Craddock's front room, holding the search warrant and there was indeed a new face looking at me. He was on the settee in between the brothers. How was I going to find out if this was 'Beaky'?

'What's your name?' I asked him, thinking this may be our suspect. Before he could answer,

'Tell em fuck all, Beaky,' came the reply from one of the Craddock brothers. Job done. Don't tell them Pike! Beaky was duly arrested and although he didn't exactly know where Flintstone lived, he pointed out a street and the rest was down to us. Never before or since have I ever commenced house to house enquiries looking for Mr. Flintstone. I had no idea what or who we were looking for except a man in bare feet, leopard skin suit, white tie and wavy black hair and carrying a wooden club shouting Wilma. It didn't work like that and although we got some very weird looks and answers from the first few houses. House number five threw up something quite interesting.

'We are from the CID at Sandford and we are making enquiries into a bur...'. Before I could finish, the tall bespectacled man at the door said,

'Sandford CID eh, Yabba Dabba Do.'

My colleague and I looked at each other.

'Yes, a burglary at Simpsons Jewellers where...' again he interrupted.

'Simpson's Jewellers eh, Yabba Dabba Do.'

'You Fred Flintstone?'

'Yeah'

'You're under arrest. Where are the rings?'

Recovered from his attic were a large number of rings and necklaces, but not the full amount. The Craddock family remained tight-lipped and were eventually cleared at crown court. The evidence against them was flimsy, Beaky was sentenced to 12 months imprisonment for his part and Mr. Flintstone to six months. Yabba dabba do!

Growing up in Sandford, I had met one or two bullies when I was younger. The local gangs on the estates had to be avoided at all costs. I was robbed, beaten and punched and unfortunately only later, and after a few beatings, I realised that I had a good turn of speed. If they didn't get me in those first 10 metres, I was away.

Craig Jervis was a hunter. It really was the animal kingdom on the estates. Jervis was always on the prowl, and he picked on the weak and vulnerable. He was a horrible young man. No one dare go anywhere near him. He was hard, and he looked hard.

Broken nose, missing teeth and just scruffy. He would tax all the school kids of their dinner money as they walked to school. That is, of course, when he attended school. One morning when getting ready, when my mum
was warming up the lard to put on my hair and quiff, a figure came into our back garden. Mum shot to the door and through the gap, I saw Jervis running away and onto the large playing field at the back of our house.

'The little bugger! He's taken the bird nuts. Why on earth would he do that?' Mum wanted to take it further, but even then, I knew it was unwise to let Jervis know where we lived. He eventually found out and the nuts would go missing week after week. The nuts weren't for human consumption, and it was hard to work out why he would deprive the blue tits of their protein.

The next incident involving Jervis was a couple of weeks later. He was sitting on our garden wall as I came out to walk to school. Mum asked to me put some small jars of salmon paste in the dustbin as they were well out of date. Jervis was straight in the bin to get them. As we walked up to school, he devoured the contents of the jars. I can see him now with his finger inside the jar, extracting the last bit of paste and sucking his finger. I didn't connect the dots at the time. It took me years and a phone call to Sandford CID to realise what was happening.

Jervis continued his reign of terror through the years, causing havoc for the people of Sandford. Robbery, burglary, theft, TWOC (Taking a vehicle without consent), GBH, ABH and a list of other convictions and prison time behind his name. I never dealt with him as a suspect, but most of the office had.

It was 4:30 p.m. and Friday, when *that* phone call from social services came. It was the same time, the same day every week. The agency was so predictable. The caller would always say that any further contact with social services over the issue would have to be with the on-call duty social worker, as they were now finishing for the weekend.

'Hello, my name is Crabtree and I'm with the Social Services department. Can I just inform you of an allegation of physical and sexual abuse?' said the caller, 'and I'm off duty now for the weekend so any further...' You know the rest.

Craig Jervis was a lot older and now living on one of the nearby estates. I went to see him the next morning and the hard-looking man with the broken nose opened the door. His scars were still evident and his teeth were still missing. His flat wasn't too bad, and he told me his sister called round and tidied it up at times. He had just come out of Armley jail in Leeds and had now picked up the courage to speak to the police. His sister and younger brother wanted to speak to me as well. Here he was, the hardest bully, thug and bastard that walked the streets of Sandford, plucking up the courage to speak to the Police. It didn't sound right.

The next three hours were heart breaking, gut wrenching and sickening. Recollections of starvation, physical beatings, whippings, and being tied up in locked rooms. Accounts of rape, serious sexual abuse, degradation and psychological trauma that would never heal. Jervis broke down and cried like a baby and all I could do and sit and watch. It was a funny feeling looking at this man in tears, having interviewed so many of his victims. The bird nuts, the salmon paste, and the robberies all clicked into place. Now I understood and even though I hated him for what he had done to me and all those other victims, I felt sorry for the real Craig and that sobbing child that was still inside him wanting to be loved.

All three siblings gave similar accounts of abuse, neglect, and total abandonment. Mr. Jervis senior was duly arrested and complained about his arrest. I interviewed him about the allegations. His solicitor was present. Jervis Snr. was a well-built man. It was apparent he liked his food and beer, which is probably where all the family money went. He had jet black hair which was greased up and brushed back over his head. He wore black-rimmed glasses and was now in his early fifties. His suit was smart, and his appearance was incongruent with the squalor in which Craig and family had lived. The interview started,

'Mr. Jervis, I have spoken to Craig, your son, and I want you to tell me about how you used to tie him up and hang him all night on the back of the door,' I asked.

'Is this going to take long, as I have a snooker match in an hour?' came the reply.

'Tell me what happened on bonfire night when you beat him with your belt buckle and then raped him.'

'I'm bored with this, officer. Is it going to take long?'

'What about the continual sexual abuse, the lack of food and general neglect of Craig and all your children?'

'Officer, I've got important things to do. I'm the snooker club secretary and I must open up the club soon. Now if you don't mind.'

He didn't answer any further questions about the allegations, which was his right. I looked at him eye to eye as the interview concluded. Inside, I was raging. I fought to maintain my composure and Jervis stared straight back at me. You cannot unsee what you have seen, you cannot un-hear what you have heard. I wanted to put this man away for the rest of his life. The tension in the room was palpable and too uncomfortable for the solicitor.

'Shall we go to the charge office gentlemen?' he asked.

As Mr. Jervis senior was leaving the room, his solicitor pulled me to one side,

'If you charge him, you better get a move on, as he is in the advanced stages of cancer. I can't see him appearing at any future court hearing.'

Jervis Senior died shortly after and before his Crown Court trial. Craig and family never did get their day of justice. I remember going home feeling down and looking forward to my meeting with my good old friend, alcohol. I played with the children that night thinking how lucky I really was, then saw Craig Jervis at the hands of the monster. It was a sickening thought and alcohol sufficiently dulled the pain. Tomorrow was another day.

CHAPTER TWENTY-SEVEN

SANDRA
The road is long
With a many a winding turn
He ain't heavy, he's my brother

Sandford had a gunman on the loose. The smaller Building Societies were his preferred choice and brazenly he would walk in, produce a revolver and tell the cashier to fill up the carrier bag. The description of the offender was white, dark curly hair, tall, medium build and several of the victims had noticed, despite their ordeal, that he had a 'cut here' tattoo on the side of his neck. Searches of all the intelligence databases revealed there were half a dozen Sandfordians fitting that description, but 'cut here' was emblazoned on only two of them. Carl Froggatt was about 10 years of age when I started my first day in the police at Littleton. He lived there and with his older brother Steven and both terrorised the local estate. Now it was Carl's turn again to terrorise. He was circulated as a 'wanted person' on the police systems and being armed, he was described as 'extremely dangerous'. He hadn't discharged the weapon, but I for one didn't want to stand before him and suggest it wasn't loaded. I had been allocated six of the robberies to investigate and the others he had committed were scattered in other areas of Westshire.

Some weeks before the spate of robberies, I had been making enquiries on Beacon Hill estate into recent burglaries and was speaking with the occupants of a ground-floor flat that had been burgled.

'Don't go in the bathroom, the geese are in there,' said Sandra, the occupier of the flat.

Sandra was young with long blonde hair and was attractive. She didn't go unnoticed by the local suspects who all frequented her flat in the hope of producing more of the human race. It was a doss house, really, and it was anyone's guess who had stolen the contents of the meter. If at all they had been stolen. I listened to the conversation amongst the occupants of Sandra's lounge. It was stimulating. They were discussing that cigarette ash or an aspirin in the bottom of a cider bottle will get you pissed quicker. Or alternatively, drink it through a straw. It wasn't a Mensa meeting for sure, but they were reporting being burgled. Or at least Sandra was. It wouldn't be long before we would see her on the estate pushing the pram. And yes, the geese were in the bathroom.

Fast forward two weeks and another armed robbery, this time on Beacon Hill at the off licence. Armed man, tall, scruffy, last seen running towards Sandford centre. Had a tattoo on his neck. Dotted lines. It was Carl Froggatt. A group of young undesirables had gathered outside the off licence, and after concentrating on winning the spitting competition, they all declared that they had seen 'fuck all'. One of them I recognised from Sandra's flat and he kind of acknowledged me with a nod, after gobbing the biggest pile of phlegm on the bookmaker's window.

'She kicked us all out, didn't she,' he told me. 'The new boys in there now shagging her. He's called Carl.'

It was now around 10:00 p.m. on Sunday. I should have finished a long time ago. Things started to move at the police station and my instructions from supervision were to drive past Sandra's flat to see if there were any signs of life. There wasn't. Another Detective in the office had a contact who lived across the street from Sandra, who when telephoned, confirmed that a lad called Carl was indeed associated with Sandra. He had gone into the flat around 9:00 p.m.. The robbery was 8:30 p.m.. He was in there with a gun. I was told to 'stand down' and to parade back in the CID office for a firearm briefing at 4:00 a.m.. I went home but couldn't sleep because of the impending operation and the joys of a teething baby.

I arrived at the office a little late and apologised. I was still cross eyed as I sneaked in the back of the room, I saw one of the new Detective Inspectors holding court at the front of the office. DI Whittaker had arrived from another area after his recent promotion. I noticed sat around the office a dozen or so officers in blue overalls, some with bob hats others with storm trooper boots on. It was the 'elite' Firearms Team. There were another half a dozen detectives and the same number of uniform staff in the room who sat and listened intently to DI Whittaker. I was still very groggy due to a lack of sleep. Sometimes even Calpol didn't work.

'As you enter the front door, the staircase is in front of you here,' pointed Whittaker, as he sketched out a plan on the board. 'To the right is the living room, straight on is the kitchen and upstairs are the bedrooms. Tango 1 are to be deployed here, Tango 2 here,' and so he went on.

Observations by plain clothes staff had confirmed that no one had entered or left 187 Whiteholt Crescent since observations commenced at 10pm the previous Sunday night. Carl Froggatt was still in the flat and he was armed.

'Okay people, that's it, let's go and get him. Any questions?' asked Whittaker.

'Any questions?' I said, 'yeah, there is no upstairs in the flat. It's a ground-floor flat, the electric is off and there are geese in the bathroom.'

Boom! Silence. Like a scene from the Exorcist, heads swivelled around to seek out the voice emitting the words. A rather large and aggressive officer in a blue boiler suit shouted at me,

'There's no upstairs? How the fuck do you know?'

'I was in the flat two weeks ago; Sandra Montgomery lives there. She had a burglary and there are geese in the…'

'Get him and let's go,' barked the muscular giant. The Firearms team started picking up their equipment. They'd heard enough. I was whisked off and placed in the front of what I presume was an armed response carrier.

The lights came on and inside sat the gun crew from upstairs. I had to draw and fully explain the layout of the flat and I used the words 'I think' at one point.

'You think. No time for that pal. You have to be 100% right here pal, this is life or death,' said the leader. He was right and my eyes were now uncrossed, and I was more focused as the crew behind me prepared their weapons, helmets, face masks and shields. There was a nervous tension like I had never felt before. The odd fart and belch rang out.

'Turn left here, straight on up to that white house, then right. That's the Crescent,' I told the driver.

We stopped a distance away and the rather large leader was indeed the Tactical Firearms Unit boss.

'Now take us to the address,' he commanded.

I remember it being cold and looking up at the stars as I walked up Whiteholt Crescent, leading a group of ten or so boiler suited and booted firearms officers. They shuffled in pairs, not a word spoken but now lots of nervous belching. This was real.

'That's the door,' I pointed and then froze. Do you know that feeling when doubt hits your mind? Is it the right address? Is this number 187?

'Wait a minute,' I said. Doubt hit me full on. The muscular leader was now purple in the face. He was fuming. I looked again and again at the door. Was this the flat I was in two weeks ago?

'Yeah, that's the door 100%,' I said.

'Go, go, go,' the leader whispered.

The group split up into pairs: two here, two there, four at the front, two at the back. Silence, stillness, quiet.

Boom. Bang, flash, bang, flash, smoke, screams, shouts and more shouts. It lasted a couple of minutes. Someone shouted for the police van to come to the front of the house and when it arrived, four officers, each with either an arm or leg, ran across the garden of 187 with a naked Froggatt wriggling, screaming and shouting. The geese soon followed in a state of shock, wondering what the hell had just happened.

'Open the doors, open the fucking doors,' they screamed as the rear doors opened outwards. With a swing, Froggatt was despatched with sufficient force to move the van forward three feet when he hit the inside. He crumpled to the floor. Boss leader, the muscular one said to me, 'Get in,' and the doors closed behind me. Froggatt was handcuffed behind his back. He was staring at me. He was only wearing white boxers. The lights were on in the back of the van as we both sat looking at each other. He had a large bruise on his forehead and circular marks, where the barrels of the guns had been placed on his body. I helped him up to sit on the bench. We set off for Sandford Police Station and he just stared at me. As we neared the police station, he said,

'Will you get me a ciggy?'

'When I can,' I replied.

'Will you look after Sandra, mate? She has some films that have to go back to Blockbusters, and I've re-wired her electric,' he said, as the van pulled to a stop.

I thought these were the least of his worries.

The van doors opened, and the boiler suited greeting party whisked him away to his cell without stopping. He was deemed too dangerous to take his personal details at this point, a thought that didn't cross anyone's mind when I was asked to sit in the back of the van with him. I went to the debrief in the CID Office and it was back slapping all round and Detective Inspector Whittaker, who gave the misinformation about 187 Whiteholt Crescent, was now to head up the investigation.

Later that morning, I went back to the address, spoke with Sandra, and took the Blockbuster videos back. The electric meters had been illegally re wired and after chatting with Sandra, she decided she was going to move back to Brough Ferry and live with her sister. The ants had already started crawling back to the flat, now they knew Froggatt was in custody. They could at least look after the geese until the council came to board up.

Back at the Police Station, Froggatt had managed to get one hand out of his handcuffs and had wrapped his blanket around his arm and was using the bent handcuff like Captain Hook.

'The first person that comes in here, I'll rip their fucking head off.'

I haven't written this book to be from a conceited point of view, but some of the people employed by Sandford Police just didn't have that 'common sense' approach. There were shirkers, drinkers, lazy, lame and criminals amongst my peers. The police force represented reality and life. The police are the public and the public are the police. Some would aggravate situations; some would calm it down. Some couldn't speak to people; others could chat shit all day. For some, it was a black or white issue, no grey. But for me, common sense and humour were my sword and shield. Sometimes I got it wrong, but overall, my weapons saw me through. Oh, and the 3Ps as well from day one of this book.

Froggatt was holding the whole of the Custody Unit at bay with his weapon. How on earth he had forced a handcuff off his wrist when it was behind his back and then bent it into a sharp weapon. I will never know. We were now waiting for the riot squad to kit up with shields, helmets, batons. Froggatt was ready and waiting.

'Can I just go down to the cell block and see him? I need to tell him something.' Mouths opened as I finished speaking. The top brass were now involved, and this was turning into a full-scale Cat A critical incident. Full Command and Control. I could hear Froggatt shouting and screaming, as could the whole building. Command and Control weren't for letting me go and speak to him until I told them that at some stage, I would have to interview him about the armed robberies.

As I approached the cell, I opened up the small hatch where years ago, I placed my hands when opening suspected bomb packages with Tommy. As soon as the hatch came down, the face appeared and Froggatt started spitting at me.

'I've taken your films back and Sandra is going to live with her sister for a while. She says she loves you.'

The spitting, screaming, shouting stopped.

'Did she say she was going to wait for me?' he asked.

'She did, Carl and I will try to arrange a visit at some stage.'

'You got that ciggy?' he asked.

'Yep. But you know what I'm going to ask for, though.'

I didn't have a handcuff key with me and when I returned to the main custody office, a team of six officers were ready with helmets, batons, shields, and riot gear. I got a hand cuff key and asked them to just give me a minute as they peered at me through misted visors.

'Where are you going with that key?' the custody officer asked.

'To get the handcuffs off Froggatt.' The riot squad tried to follow me.

I returned to Carl's cell and passed the key through the hatch. I could hear the comments behind me. The handcuffs came out within a couple of minutes, one bent as though it was plasticine. Froggatt leaned his head through the hatch, I placed the cigarette in between his lips and lit it. His face disappeared, the smoke bellowed out, and there was silence.

'When can she visit me?' came the voice through the hatch.

'In the fullness of time Carl, but we have a few issues to clear up before then.'

'I know,' he muttered.

'There is the electric meter at Sandra's and also the milk from next door's step. Six pints in all I think.'

'You fuckin what,' came the voice from the other side. The head was back at the hatch.

'Then there's some other milk from doorsteps down Whiteholt Crescent.'

'I'm a fucking bank robber me, what you on about milk off doorsteps? I've done armed fucking robberies, not nicked milk off doorsteps; you dick.'

With that, he started laughing and laughing and laughing.

'Nicking milk off doorsteps, fuck off. Ha ha ha. Can I have a brew mate?'

Over the next two weeks, Carl admitted everything, except the location of the gun. He said he'd thrown it in the canal somewhere but couldn't remember where. I didn't believe him. Despite this, I got on well with him, which maybe down to the rapport we built on our first meeting. When he was brought to the Magistrates' Court each week from prison, he was treated as a 'Category A' prisoner. There were lights, guns, helmets, riot shields and always a weekly assault. He rose to the occasion every time. The powers that be, McAvoy in his new job, wanted it that way, with all the guns and lights blaring for his escort. They wouldn't listen. Carl loved it and he stepped up to the plate each week when he had his audience. All this for me? He would fight and assault someone different each week, a police officer, a prison officer, it didn't matter. If you've put this show on for me, I won't let you down, was his attitude. He was, however, on the inside a gentle giant not withstanding that he had terrorised over a dozen victims at gunpoint and stolen just short of £50,000. He had spent most of it on drugs, booze and his Blockbuster account with Sandra.

On the day of his crown court appearance, he pleaded guilty to all the charges, the armed robberies, the assaults on police and prison staff, and, of course, diverting Sandra's electric. He was sentenced to 15 years imprisonment and when the antecedents officer gave evidence about Carl's past; the Judge asked the officer to pass on to the Chief Constable of Westshire Police his thanks and gratitude for all the hard work the staff had contributed in making Sandford a safer place. In particular, he wanted the officer in the case, Detective Constable James Graham (that would be me of course) to be 'commended' for his outstanding police work and skill in dealing with such a violent individual. He asked if I was in court, then asked me to stand where he personally thanked me. It was an extremely rewarding moment.

Carl wrote to me when in prison and asked me to visit, which I did. I took him some tobacco, and he chatted about Sandford, and of course, Sandra. I had a lump in my throat as he asked me to visit her and tell her that he loved her. His eyes started filling with tears as he said she shouldn't wait as he couldn't deal with the thought of her when inside.

'When you're inside, Mr. Graham, you can only think about what's happening inside. I loved that girl, but please tell her to forget me. She has a life in front of her. I don't.'

Sandra hadn't been slow in moving on and had two children by this time. I didn't tell him. I saw his release from prison on divisional orders about eight years later and officers were warned to be extremely vigilant and not to approach him. I didn't hear much about him after that but, one day, when off duty, I saw a tall thin heroin user on a street corner waiting for the drug dealer's car. It was Carl, over six feet tall and now about six stone in weight. Not long after that, I saw his name in the obituary column in the local newspaper. He was thirty-five-years-old when he died from a heroin overdose.

The commendation from the Judge, never came. Well, not for me, it didn't. Before I left Sandford and moved on to pastures new, and in order to add the commendation to my CV, I tracked down the antecedent's officer and asked about the report he submitted after Froggatt's case. He told me had had sent a copy of the Judge's report at the time to the Chief Superintendent at Sandford so I could be commended. I never received it, so he kindly sent me another copy. It arrived a few days later and the Judges words were written in the report as he had spoken to them that day in court and the antecedent's officer had submitted his report with the final line reading;

'*That the officer in the case, DC James Graham, be commended for outstanding police work in bringing Froggatt to justice.*'

That report had been forwarded through different departments until it eventually reached Sandford CID. I found the original report buried deep in the administration office. The original report never made it down to my level but had stopped at a certain Detective Inspector's desk. It had been duly returned with all the congratulatory comments in the margins. It now read;

'That the officer in the case, DI Whittaker, be commended for outstanding police work in bringing Froggatt to justice.'

My name had been overwritten and DI Whittaker had duly received his commendation. I sat and stared at the report. The hard work, the dedication, the long hours, the family sacrifices, and the loyalty. DI Whittaker had changed the report.

CHAPTER TWENTY-EIGHT

THE BEGINNING

Been around the world and I, I, I
I can't find my baby.

We are back to where we started and the fact that big Davey Peters had been more successful than Sandford CID in recovering his stolen property and identifying the burglars. The old man Ronnie had been kind enough to offer the suspects a safe haven where they could hide under the radar. What they didn't know was the relationship I had with Ronnie and his family. Three people were now under arrest, Davey had recovered his TV set, but the video recorder had been sold to the local Fagin, Isaac Warren. During his arrest, Warren had broken free and now, with the blade of a carving knife protruding through my hand, I was trying to stay alive. There was no doubt Warren was intent on killing me. With blood running down my hands and sweat stinging my eyes, I looked into Warren's face. His hand was above his head, bringing the carving knife down towards me time and time again. He switched hands, then back again. I held the blade at one point as the metal ripped through my palms. John, my colleague, was behind him, trying to pull him down. It seemed to last forever. Our eyes met again and with all the might I could muster, I leaned backwards. I was back on the football field; I could see the ball swinging in from the right and I rose to head it and bang!

With as much thrust as I could, I smashed my forehead into Warren's face. It hurt. I heard and felt the crunch, and his grip on me loosened. We fell to the floor. The knife went up into the air and fell somewhere behind a kitchen cupboard. There was blood everywhere. I didn't feel any pain; I didn't feel anything. John turned Warren over and handcuffed him as I searched for the knife. I was exhausted and collapsed against the wall, my hand numb and bleeding. My thumb nail hanging off.

'Look at his face, look at him,' came the shout.

I don't know who it was shouting, as everything was blurry. I looked across at Warren and he was purple, he was comatose, not breathing. I couldn't find a pulse. With quick chest compressions, John started mouth to mouth resuscitation. In what seemed to be a lifetime, Warren responded with a deep groan. Angry faces were now looking at us. I couldn't find the knife. I was disorientated, confused.

'Just who the fuck do you think you are?' said the face as it bent down towards me. I could see the clenched fists. This ordeal wasn't over yet. I could see the tattoos and the white vest, bracing myself for the blows. My hand was bleeding heavily. I felt sick.

'Can you hear me? Hello, can you hear me?'

The face had changed, it was softer and smiling. I could see the glasses frame.

'Can you hear me? What's your name?'

'It's Jim.'

'Ok Jim, I'm just going to put something on your hand. It may sting a little. You'll be alright love,' said the young paramedic.

I looked across at Warren, he was wearing an oxygen mask. John was in the doorway on the police radio. I could see he had the knife.

We followed the ambulance to King's Cross Hospital. My brain was very foggy. Warren was being treated in the next cubicle as more uniformed officers came into the A&E department.

John came and told me that Warren was fine and that they were admitting him, under arrest, for a night on the ward for observations. I was going to be treated and sent home. My hands and arms were cleaned, my thumb was stitched, but sadly, my nail was a victim.

I was dropped off at home at 4:00 a.m. and was still in a state of shock. I explained what had happened to my wife. We both lay there until dawn. I recall it being my wife's birthday on the Sunday and as always; I had left things until the last minute. As I lay there in that halfway house between sleep and awake, the phone rang. It was DS Townson from the CID Office. It was 8:00 a.m..

'Isaac Walton has been released from hospital and he's in custody here at Sandford Police Station. What time are you coming in to deal with him?'

I couldn't speak. I had no energy. It was my day off in any case, but surely anyone with a modicum of intelligence would be able to see that I was not in a good place nor the best person to interview anyone, especially after they had tried to kill me. I put the phone down. I rang back later and said I couldn't stomach coming back to work. I hadn't slept. I said I would return to work the day after, Sunday, which was of course my wife's birthday.

I went back into work on the Sunday and in total that weekend, John Suthers and I arrested eleven suspects over Davey's burglary, the stolen property and other burglaries on the estate. We never recovered Davey's video recorder, but did find lots of other stolen items and many others responsible for the recent crime. As with everything else when there was a 'job on', unfortunately, the birthday had to wait. I went home on birthday night to a house in darkness, hands still bandaged and sore and now mentally unwell.

The next morning, Monday, word had got around the station about the Warren incident on Friday night. I walked into the office with my hands still in bandages. Colleagues wished me well and then Detective Inspector Whittaker invited me into his office. Eight of those arrested were appearing at Sandford Magistrate's Court in an hour and Kenny Bamford, plus one other had to be taken to Sandford Crown Court. It seemed I had to be in four different places at once and still had a host of paperwork to do before court at 10am.

'Your investigation reports haven't been submitted since last week,' is what I thought I heard him say. Investigation reports were the weekly update submitted to supervisors as to the status of your investigations.

'Are you listening to me? Where are your progress reports?'

The noise was coming out of Whittaker's mouth in slow motion. I was really finding it difficult to understand the situation. I tried to explain about the weekend, the stabbing, the eleven suspects, my wife's birthday and I could feel myself becoming emotional. I started to cry.

'If you can't stand the heat lad, get out of the kitchen,' said Whittaker as he brushed by me and went into the corridor.

'I say Mr. Colclough, sir, (Detective Superintendent) if you can't stand the heat, Graham here, look at him. He says he can't cope.' Colclough just looked at me and walked on.

I walked back to my desk too busy to really think what had just happened. I needed to be in four places at once and complete paperwork and phones ringing. I could no longer focus. I managed to get through the day and then the week, but now life was different. Warren made a complaint, and I received discipline papers for 'the attempted murder of Isaac Warren'. I was suffering from something. Anxiety, stress, or maybe PTSD, who knows? To declare such a thing in those days was a weakness and it would ensure your exit from the CID and possibly the Force.

I kept the secret to myself, but those at home knew there was a problem. From Doctor's visit to doctor's visit, from a bottle of whisky to bottle of vodka, I tried to battle away against the fog. My work was deteriorating. I couldn't cope anymore. I was literally hanging on. I couldn't focus, couldn't relax and became too dependent on my good old friend alcohol. The colour had gone from my life. Everything was now just grey.

Weeks went by with no improvement and Isaac Warren and others were due to appear at Sandford Crown Court. He was pleading not guilty to assault occasioning grievous bodily harm on me. (GBH or Section 18 of the Offences Against the Person Act)

He was also charged with other offences, including handling the stolen video recorders, lawn mowers and the like. I prepared myself for the case.

The phone rang in the office. It was Davey Peters, who was obviously a witness. He wanted a lift to the court. I agreed and early the next morning I called at Davey's house, picked him and some more witnesses up, and then headed for Sandford Crown Court. Outside the court, Warren approached me and held out a hand. He apologised and had been told to expect a prison sentence of up to 5 years. I shook his hand, but wasn't quite functioning correctly.

Warren pleaded guilty to all the charges; the court was quiet. The Judge spoke,

'Mr Warren, I give you credit for your plea of guilty in what is a very serious matter before me. I have listened carefully to what your counsel has said and agree that the assault on the officer was not a personal assault on him, but an assault to resist arrest. The offence, however, carries a life sentence for a reason, and I cannot see any other sentence that I can pass but imprisonment. For the GBH charge on the police officer, Detective Graham, you will go to prison for one day, for the assault occasioning actual bodily harm on the officer, you will go to prison for one day, for handling stolen goods you will go to prison for one day. Those sentences will run concurrently. I am informed you served 14 days on remand whilst waiting for trial, so you are free to go.'

The court was quiet. There was movement next to me. The pressure cooker was about to explode. If Davey was in possession of his trusted baseball bat 'Walter' that morning, I'm sure he would have used it on the Judge. He jumped to his feet,

'You what, you what? A day in prison, a fucking day. You call that justice.'

Shouts of 'silence in court' echoed loudly as ushers and police officers rushed our way. Davey was manoeuvred out of the court, and I sat and pondered for a while as Warren was reunited with his family.

I listened to Davey rant and rave in the corridor with barristers hastily avoiding him. Davey was furious. Eventually, he calmed down, and we shook hands and went our separate ways. I walked across the square outside crown court and saw, heading towards me, PC Tina Rowntree. We had been in the same recruit class years before when I fired the gun at Fez's head. Tina was in full uniform, smart, and had a beaming smile. She was with two other older people.

'I've just been to a reception at the Town Hall to collect my commendation from the Chief Constable. This is my mum and dad.' I greeted both of them.

'That's brilliant Tina, I'm in a state of shock, to be honest,' I said.

'Yeah, my commendation was for rescuing a sheep from the canal,' she said.

I forced a smile. I had been to hell and back, been stabbed and was suffering with whatever this fog was. My paperwork was late, I had been chastised, ridiculed, and told to get out of the kitchen if I couldn't stand the heat. I had neglected my family to get the 'job done' and here was Tina, who had been commended by the Chief Constable for rescuing a sheep. Something inside me snapped that morning.

That night I stayed up late with my seductive and sedative friend Jack Daniels until the bottle was empty. I drank to forget. I lay awake hoping for sleep to come and take me to a better place. It never did. My mind started the cycle of worry, of anxiety, and engulfed me. I am going to end up in hospital with the people of Happy Trees estate, I thought. If I lose my job, who will pay the mortgage? I will lose the house. I will end up on Happy Trees estate.

The following morning, I went into the office and during the morning briefing, I could hardly make sense of the words as I tried to hang on. Colleagues were asking me if I was okay. Petrol, set on fire, matches, victim and hospital.

'That investigation has been allocated to DC Graham, Sir,' said the voice.

A poor young woman had been subjected to the most horrific experience as her abusive partner emptied a can of petrol over her and taunted her with a box of matches. He had actually thrown two matches, but the petrol failed to ignite. I tried to function but couldn't. I know that the victim didn't get the service she was right to expect and entitled to. I did arrest her partner; he did go to court, but things weren't right with me. I got there in the end, but I should and could have done a lot better for her. I knew I couldn't continue. I became extremely emotional. I was burnt out.

The doctor praised me for recognising and admitting I had a problem, and I did have one. He advised me to go off work with 'stress', a word that was unheard of at the time. That would have ended my police career. With my confidence shattered, I struggled to get out of bed in the morning, to answer the phone or see who was knocking at the door. My cheques were returned from the bank as the signature was undistinguishable. Beta blockers, temazepam, uppers, downers, alcohol, a day job, a speeding mind and a dark fog on a daily basis. My challenge was bigger than any fight or stabbing with Isaac Warren, bigger than any arrest of Carl Froggatt. I needed time or a break to heal from this, whatever it was. Time, I didn't have.

I returned to work after the Christmas festivities that year, but I was broken. Then I saw this on Divisional Orders;

'On the 14th of January, DC 776 J. Graham will be transferred to the Regional Organised Crime Unit (ROCU) in Northshire until further notice'.

ABOUT THE AUTHOR

James Graham is a husband, father, grandfather, and former police officer. He served in one of the country's largest municipal police forces from 1974 until his retirement in 2006. Spending the initial years of his career in uniform, he moved into a detective role in 1980. He transferred to the Regional Crime & Drugs Unit in 1989 and involved himself in international drug trafficking investigations, sometimes in undercover roles. He was promoted to Sergeant in 1991 performing uniform and patrol duties before returning to CID to continue his career as a detective.

In the mid 90s, James was invited to give presentations at the police crime faculty and his career moved into learning and development. He gained a BA (Hons) and Post Graduate Certificate in Education at university. (Sandford obviously) He taught at the crime faculty for five years before returning to investigating serious crime in a covert police unit, dealing with drug trafficking, murder and terrorism. One of his last assignments was investigating a notorious crime family, involved in terrorist activities, in Northern Ireland.

After leaving the police, James formed his own training company, teaching national and international law enforcement agencies investigation and interviewing techniques and of course, highlighting the way it used to be done. James has a keen interest in reading, sport, walking and enjoys trekking in the Himalayas.

Printed in Great Britain
by Amazon

31407378R00155